ROOKHURST HALL

The discovery of two old photographs, one of a large house, the other of three teenage girls in Edwardian dress, puzzles twenty-year-old Lucy Armitage and sends her off on a quest with antique dealer Ben Manton to find their origins. Because although she is sure it can have nothing to do with her, one of the girls in the photograph is uncannily like Lucy herself...

ROOKHURST HALL

Elizabeth Jeffrey

Severn House Large Print
London & New York

This first large print edition published 2010
in Great Britain and the USA by
SEVERN HOUSE PUBLISHERS LTD of
9-15 High Street, Sutton, Surrey, SM1 1DF.
First world regular print edition published 2008 by
Severn House Publishers Ltd., London and New York.

British Library Cataloguing in Publication Data

Jeffrey, Elizabeth.
  Rookhurst Hall.
  1. Antique dealers--Fiction. 2. Genealogy--Fiction.
  3. Love stories. 4. Large type books.
  I. Title
  823.9'14-dc22

  ISBN-13: 978-0-7278-7869-4

Severn House Publishers support The Forest Stewardship Council
[FSC], the leading international forest certification organisation. All
our titles that are printed on Greenpeace-approved FSC-certified
paper carry the FSC logo.

 **Mixed Sources**
Product group from well-managed
forests and other controlled sources
FSC www.fsc.org Cert no. SA-COC-1565
© 1996 Forest Stewardship Council

Printed and bound in Great Britain by the
MPG Books Group, Bodmin, Cornwall.

One

Lucy Armitage wheeled her bicycle round to the yard at the back of Rosewood Antiques and propped it against the wall under the steps up to her flat. She was halfway up to the flat, which was situated over the top of the antique shop, when she heard a voice from below.

'Have you got a minute, Lucy, my dear? I've got something here I want to show you.'

She looked down and saw Alec Manton standing at the door of his workshop, a long low brick building, converted from stables and outhouses, which took up the whole of one side of the yard. A stocky grey-haired man in his late fifties who specialized in the repair and restoration of old furniture, Alec was the owner of the antique shop.

Puzzled, she went back down the steps and across the yard and followed him into the workshop, where the aroma of wood shavings, Scotch glue and French polish mingled with the dusty smell of old furniture. Behind the long work bench a consul table, several Chippendale chairs, a chest of drawers and a French

5

escritoire, all needing some degree of repair, were waiting for his expert attention.

'I wondered if you might know these people,' he said, dusting an old, faded sepia photograph on the drill apron he always wore at work and handing it to her.

She stared at it for several seconds without speaking. Then she looked up at him as he stood by his work bench, watching her and quietly cleaning his hands on a piece of rag.

'No, I don't know them, Mr Manton,' she said, without much interest. 'Who are they?'

Alec nodded towards a small antique oak bureau standing beside the bench.

'I thought you'd know who they were because the picture was in your bureau, there.' He gave an apologetic smile. 'I'm sorry you've had to wait such a long time for me to repair it for you but as you know I'm busy getting things ready for the antique dealers' fair in London.'

'That's all right, Mr Manton. I told you I wasn't in any hurry for it,' she said absently, her eyes still on the photograph.

'Well, all I can say is, thank you for being so patient. After all, it's six months since you moved in and it's been sitting in my workshop all that time waiting for me to repair it.'

'Gosh, is it as long as that?' She looked up in surprise. 'Yes, I suppose it must be.'

It was true; she had been living in Laxhall St Mary's almost exactly six months. She had moved into the flat just after Christmas, when her mother had set sail for Australia with her new husband, and it was now June.

She turned back to the photograph and tapped it. 'But I've no idea who these people are and I don't understand how you could have found their photograph in my bureau. I was quite sure I'd emptied it completely before you fetched it down here to repair.' Her smile widened. 'I even checked all the secret drawers.'

'Oh, you reckon you found them all, then.' He nodded sagely.

'Oh, yes. Heaven knows, I spent enough hours searching for them when I was a child. I used to pretend the bureau was my office and I used to keep old envelopes and odd bits of paper in all the little cubbyholes and drawers. I felt very efficient.' She gave a rueful shrug. 'I expect that's why I became a shorthand typist and ended up working in a solicitor's office.' She tapped the photograph again. 'So where exactly did you find this, Mr Manton?'

He grinned delightedly. 'In one of the secret drawers. Obviously one you'd missed. Look.' He went over to the bureau and pulled out the two wooden stays, letting down the fall on to them. Now there was revealed a writing desk with space for a blotter, behind which was an array of small cupboards and drawers, all delicately carved and fretted. He pulled out one of the drawers, put his hand in the space and pressed a spring. Immediately one of the two columns either side of the little door in the centre sprang out, revealing a narrow space just large enough to hold two or three letters or a

7

few precious photographs.

'Ah, that's clever. No, I hadn't found that one,' Lucy breathed, her eyes widening.

'There was another photograph with it, too. Look, do you recognize this house?'

It was a red-brick Georgian house, with two long windows either side of a large front door with steps leading up to it and an ornate fanlight. Three smaller windows were placed symmetrically above and there were three small attic windows set into the roof. Set back from the main façade and half concealed by trees the house widened into two smaller wings. In front of the house a gravelled carriageway swept round a circular lawn, formally set with flower beds, in the centre of which a stone fountain played.

She shook her head. 'No. I know I've never seen this house. I'm sure I would have remembered if I had! It's a lovely old house.' She turned back to the other picture and looked at it for a long time. It was clearly a studio portrait. Three girls, carefully posed, two of whom were obviously twins of about seventeen or eighteen, and another sister some two years younger. The youngest sat with her elbow resting on the wooden arm-rest of her chair and the other two were standing; one behind the chair with her hand on her sister's shoulder and the other slightly to the right with her hand resting on the back of the chair. The older girls were dressed in the dark ankle-length skirts and pale, highnecked blouses beloved of the Edwardian era

8

and wore their hair swept up in the style of the day. The young one wore her hair in ringlets with a large bow at the side and a dark-coloured dress with a pin-tucked bodice. Peeping out from under the dress was the border of a white petticoat, lavishly embroidered with broderie anglaise. Her legs, what could be seen of them between the hem of the dress and her little boots, were encased in black stockings. A potted fern stood to one side to balance the picture.

She shook her head again. 'No, I've never seen this house and I don't know these people, either,' she said definitely.

Alec looked at her in surprise. 'Are you quite sure, Lucy?'

'Yes, of course I'm sure,' she said with a laugh. 'I've no idea who they could be.' She gave a shrug. 'I suppose both these pictures must have been tucked away in the secret drawer years ago and forgotten. By the look of the clothes they're wearing it must have happened long before my mother bought the bureau.'

'Your mother bought it! You mean it hasn't been in your family for generations?' He still sounded surprised.

'Good heavens, no. Why? What difference does it make?'

'Look at the photograph of those girls again. Can't you see a likeness in any of them, Lucy?'

'A likeness?' She gave a shrug. 'Well, yes, they're obviously three sisters.'

'I didn't mean that.' He took her by the shoulders and walked her over to a large gilt mirror hanging on the wall waiting for repairs to the frame. 'Now look. Can't you see, Lucy? One of the twins, the one standing with her hand on the back of the chair. She's exactly like you. It could be you, in fact.'

Lucy put her head on one side, frowning. 'Do you think so? Well, yes, I suppose she is, a bit. She's got quite a long face and her mouth is a bit wide, like mine. I wonder if her eyes are brown, too.' She stared at her own image a moment longer, seeing an attractive girl with regular features, a wide, smiling mouth and short fair hair curling round her ears. She gave a little shudder and turned away quickly. 'Oh, that's a bit spooky, isn't it?' She looked at the photograph again. 'No, on second thoughts she's not really like me at all. Her hair's long and swept up in a kind of bun. Anyway, hers is quite dark and mine's fair.'

'Well, it could just be coincidence,' Alec said lightly, seeing that Lucy was a little unnerved.

'Couldn't be anything else, could it?' Lucy laid the two photographs on the bench.

'As you say, the hair's certainly much darker,' Alec said, glancing at Lucy's blonde bob. He picked up the photograph of the girls. 'Tell you what. My Martha's invited you to supper on Saturday so we'll show this to her and see what she thinks.' He held it at arm's length and put his head on one side. 'It's just that it struck me ... but it's not always easy to tell from these old

10

sepia photos, and my eyes aren't what they were.' Both these statements were less than the truth. The photograph was in fact exceptionally clear for its age and Alec's eyes were as sharp as ever; they needed to be for the delicate work he did. But his words had the desired effect and reassured Lucy.

'You didn't find anything else in here?' Lucy said, running her hand over the smooth wood of the bureau. 'Is it finished? It looks really lovely.'

'Yes, it's finished and no, there was nothing else. I'll get Ben to help me carry it up to your flat when he comes back. He shouldn't be late tonight.' Ben was Alec's son. Like his father very knowledgeable about antiques, he did all the buying, attending sales and purchasing from private houses. Alec was much happier in his workshop, where he worked miracles restoring the furniture to its former glory.

Lucy left him and went upstairs to her flat. Rosewood Antiques was a high-class antique shop, covering the first two floors of a large Georgian house overlooking the square in Laxhall St Mary's, a small market town in Suffolk. The house itself made a perfect setting for the furniture and china Alec and his son dealt in, with large rooms, high ceilings and ornate plasterwork typical of the period. The top floor had been converted into a comfortable flat, with a large living room, a smaller bed-room, and a minute bathroom with an Ascot water heater over the bath. The kitchen was quite modern, light and very well appointed. There was a smaller version of the bathroom water heater over the sink, and a stainless steel draining board. Next to this stood the electric cooker with an enamel splashback and the small fridge provided by Lucy's mother. On the opposite wall stood a tall kitchen cabinet with drawers and cupboards and next to this a red formica-topped table and two plastic-covered chairs. There wasn't room for much else but it was quite adequate for Lucy's needs.

The living room was much larger; an elegant room, light and airy, with walls of duck-egg blue. Two long windows, draped with brocade curtains in a deeper shade of the same colour, overlooked the busy little square, where a market was held twice weekly and where the children from nearby houses congregated to play on summer evenings.

Yet Lucy's brand new G-Plan Scandinavian furniture, with its clean, uncluttered lines, which she had chosen and her mother had willingly paid for, fitted surprisingly well in the old house, although the television set standing in the corner looked a bit out of its depth. However, the old oak bureau had looked very much at home, standing between the two windows. Shortly it would do so again now that Alec had finished restoring it.

Lucy knew that her mother had been surprised that the oak bureau had been the only thing she wanted from her old home on the outskirts of Norwich. Margaret had told her she could take whatever she liked when she left. Lucy was realistic enough to know this was not from any sense of generosity on Margaret's part, but rather because it meant there wouldn't be so much to dispose of when the house was sold. But Lucy had wanted to start a new life uncluttered by constant reminders of the past. A past that had not been altogether happy. Not that her childhood had been deprived. Far from it. Everything she could possibly want, and much that she didn't, had been lavished on her by her mother. Home from school, where she was a weekly boarder, there were always new clothes and the latest records by Alma Cogan, Tommy Steele, Cliff Richard, or the up and coming Elvis Presley waiting to be played on her up-to-the-minute record player in her room. Anything she asked for – which was not much – and even more that she didn't, Margaret would buy her. Except, that is, the one thing that money couldn't buy: love. Although she was never treated unkindly, from quite an early age Lucy had sensed that her mother had never really wanted her; that she regarded her as nothing more than an encumbrance, a nuisance that cramped her lifestyle. Lucy didn't remember her father; to her he was just a photograph of a handsome young man in pilot officer's uniform, his cap tilted rakishly over dark, slickly Brylcreemed hair and a lopsided smile. In a corner of the photograph was written in a flamboyant, sloping hand, *To my darling Margaret. Yours till hell freezes. Roddy.* No mention of his daughter. But of course there wouldn't be; he'd never known her. He was shot down in flames in the Battle of Britain just a couple of months before she was born.

Yet in spite of her mother's indifference, somewhere in the back of her mind Lucy had warm memories of her early childhood, of being cuddled and loved. It was more a feeling of warmth and safety than an actual memory and, try as she might, she could never get any clear, tangible picture. Just this warm, safe feeling. But it was not something she could ask her mother about; Margaret had no patience with what she called childish fancies. Perhaps that was just what it was, a childish fancy or, more likely, a dream born of a desperate wish to be loved and wanted.

Now Margaret was gone; after a whirlwind courtship she had married Harold Brewster, a rich merchant banker – Margaret would never consider marrying anyone without money – who had then whisked her off to live in Australia. Both she and her new husband had made half-hearted, insincere attempts to per- suade Lucy to go with them but Lucy, having just celebrated her twentieth birthday, had asserted her independence by declining their offer – and with a good deal more sincerity than it had been extended. Lucy doubted that she would ever see either of them again.

This didn't trouble her at all; she was far too busy enjoying her new, bachelor-girl life in the quiet Suffolk market town well away from the city of Norwich where she had been brought up.

Lucy had finished eating her supper and was just washing up when she saw Ben Manton coming up the steps with a drawer from her bureau under each arm. His father was following with the third one.

'It means we'll have a little less weight to carry when we bring up the carcass,' Ben said with a smile as he came through the door. He was a tall, slim man of about twenty-five, with well-cut brown hair over a square-jawed, rather craggy face. Although it was the end of a working day he still looked smart in a dark grey suit with a blue shirt and tie. He wasn't a bit like his stocky, rather shaggy-looking father and Lucy had formed the impression early on that he was a bit of a smooth operator. She realized this was a little unfair since she really didn't know him well enough to make a judgement.

The two men went back and fetched the rest of the bureau. It was not easy, manoeuvring it up the narrow stone steps to the flat, but it was obvious that they were quite used to handling furniture and they soon had it back where it belonged, between the windows.

'Looks good there, Lucy,' Alec said, wiping his hands on the working apron he was still wearing.

Ben examined the interior. 'Nice bureau,' he said. 'I'd be happy to buy it from you if we could agree a price.'

'You might have said that before we carried it

up those steps,' his father remarked. 'I'm not keen on lugging it all the way down again.'

'You won't have to, Mr Manton,' Lucy said quickly. 'It's not going anywhere. It's not for sale.'

'Pity. I'd give you a good price for it.' Ben turned to his father. 'It would look good on the stand at the fair.'

'It looks good where it is. And that's where it's staying.' Lucy was becoming annoyed at Ben's persistence.

He followed his father out of the door. 'Well, if you change your mind...' he called over his shoulder as he went down the steps.

'I shan't,' she called back and shut the door. She decided that she didn't like Ben Manton very much.

The following day Lucy took the photograph of the three girls into work with her. She was secretary to Bernard Foster, a partner in the local firm of solicitors, Payne and Foster, whose premises were across the square and down a side street, a short cycle ride from her flat. She loved her job because it was not a large firm and she found the work interesting.

'Do you think one of the girls in this photograph looks at all like me?' She handed the photograph to Janice, secretary to the senior partner, with whom she shared an office barely big enough to contain two desks, let alone shelves of box files and cupboards crammed with bundles of documents tied with pink tape.

Janice studied it, then looked up at Lucy with

a shrug. 'Could be. The one sitting down's a bit like you, I suppose.'

'Not one of the twins standing behind the chair?' Lucy persisted.

Janice shrugged again. 'Maybe. She's a lot darker than you, though. But don't ask me, I'm not very good at recognizing people. And everybody looks alike to me in these old photographs. Why?'

'No reason. Just that it was found in a secret drawer in my bureau.'

'Oh, how exciting! Are they related to you, then?'

'No. I don't know anything about them. That's what's so odd.'

'Let me see.' Bernard Foster, Lucy's boss, had just come in with some typing for her. 'Hm.' He looked at the photograph thoughtfully. 'Three pretty girls, but not one of them half as pretty as you, Lucy.' He put his head on one side and studied her admiringly. 'But yes, there's a definite likeness, the same tip-tilted nose...' He put his hand under her chin and turned her face to the light.

'My nose is not tip-tilted.' Lucy pushed his hand away and took the photograph from him. 'It doesn't matter. It's not important,' she said quickly. She put it in a drawer and picked up the sheaf of papers he had brought in. 'I'd better get on with these forms if you want them by tonight.'

'I think you'll find it's all pretty straight for-ward stuff,' he said, still hovering by her chair.

17

'Yes, it looks like it.' She leafed through them then turned away and wound paper into her typewriter.

'Do you want me to explain anything?'

'No, I can see perfectly well what I've got to do, thank you, Mr Foster.'

'All right, then.' He cleared his throat. 'I'll be in my office if you have any problems. Don't hesitate...'

'I won't.' She modified her comment. 'I won't have any problems.'

'Good.' A moment later she heaved a sigh of relief as the door closed behind him.

Janice leaned over from her desk. 'He fancies you, you know,' she said with a grin.

'Fancies himself, more like. Thinks he's Clark Gable, with that silly little moustache,' Lucy replied shortly, without looking up.

'Well, he is quite good looking, isn't he?' Janice persisted.

'If you like that sort of thing. Me, I prefer Richard Chamberlain. Give me Doctor Kildare any day.' She gave a dreamy sigh. 'Anyway,' she said briskly, 'he's married.'

'Who? Richard Chamberlain?'

'No, stupid. Bernard Foster.'

Janice put her elbows on her desk and steepled her fingers. 'To tell you the truth I don't think that worries him too much,' she said in a confidential voice, glancing towards the door to make sure she wasn't overheard. 'From what I hear on the grapevine our Bernard is not all that happily married. Apparently, his wife is always ill, or rather, always imagining she's got something or other wrong with her. He spends a fortune on doctors and private treatments.'

'Then either he must be very fond of her or he needs to pay her more attention,' Lucy answered, scowling as she tried to decipher his writing but determined not to go and ask him. 'You could...'

Lucy lifted her head. 'Oh, for goodness sake, Janice, I've just told you he's not my type. He's too much of a lady-killer for my liking. Anyway, he's much too old for me, and added to that he's already got a wife,' she said firmly. 'I'm not in the market for breaking up marriages.'

Janice sighed and began to leaf through the papers on her desk. 'Pity. You'd make a lovely couple.'

'Oh, shut up.' Irritably, Lucy threw a book at her and went back to her typing. In truth she was beginning to find Bernard Foster's attentions not a little annoying. After leaving school at sixteen and spending two years at secretarial college learning shorthand and typing, she had been at work quite long enough to learn how to deal with office Lotharios and to laugh off mild flirtations. But Bernard Foster was her boss; she couldn't laugh off his attentions as if he were the office boy and he seemed quite immune to the cold shoulder treatment. It was becoming quite a problem, one that wasn't helped by the fact that Janice seemed to find it all so amusing.

Two

On Saturday Lucy went down to the market. The square was full of stalls, all covered with rainbow-bright awnings. Ever since early morning the stall holders had been vying with one another as to who could shout their wares the loudest to the crowds that jostled their way through. First came the housewives, often using prams or pushchairs as battering rams as they searched for the freshest fruit and vegetables and the choicest cuts of meat. Later in the day came the groups of Teddy boys in their long drape jackets, drainpipe trousers and thick, crepe-soled 'brothel-creeper' shoes and their slicked-back DA hairstyles, far more interested in eyeing up the giggling 'talent' – girls in jazzy circular skirts over frilly petticoats, their waists nipped-in by wide plastic belts, than in anything the stalls had to offer. After a quick look round the market they usually congregated in the milk bar on the corner, to drink milk shakes through straws and jig around to the latest Lonnie Donegan songs playing on the juke box.

Lucy enjoyed the atmosphere of the market; she usually bought her fruit and vegetables there and she liked browsing among the stalls that sold everything from plastic handbags to pot scourers. She smiled to herself as she noticed that one entrepreneurial stall holder had even stocked up on washboards – no longer so much an aid to laundry as an essential percussion instrument for aspiring skiffle groups. Clutching her shoulder bag to her side she eventually managed to elbow her way through the crowds to the flower stall where she bought two big bunches of carnations for Mr Manton's wife, Martha.

A plump, homely woman, Martha Manton was an extremely good cook; Lucy always looked forward to supper with her and her husband. The evening was still warm after a day of sunshine, so she put on her favourite flowered dirndl skirt, fully gathered and with a nipped-in waist, and with it a crisp white blouse with cap sleeves. Finally, she brushed her hair till it shone and applied a trace of make-up – not too much; she had a feeling Mrs Manton would think an excess of eyeliner and lipstick 'fast'. A red handbag and matching wedge-heeled sandals completed her outfit.

As she made her way across the square she could hear the strains of the Everly Brothers singing 'Cathy's Clown' from an open window. She hummed it to herself as she walked, wondering idly if Ben would be at supper with them tonight. He had his own flat at the other end of the town so he didn't often join them, and Lucy was not sorry about this. She didn't feel altogether comfortable in his presence and she hadn't really forgiven him for trying to buy her bureau, though to be fair he hadn't tried very hard. But she had sometimes caught sight of him dealing with customers that came to the shop and thought his manner rather too slick, although she had to admit he was not bad looking in a suave, over-polished way.

However, despite their very different appearances, father and son appeared to have a good working relationship. Alec was a craftsman and was happiest in his workshop, although he always attended to customers in the shop if Ben wasn't around. And Ben often wasn't around because he liked to be out and about. He was obviously the dealer in the family. He attended all the sales and did all the 'call-outs' to private houses. Alec often chuckled that Ben was a consummate antique dealer in that he could buy from people who didn't want to sell and sell to people who didn't want to buy. He said it as a joke, but Lucy rather suspected it was true and she wasn't sure she approved.

In fact, although Ben was always quite pleasant when she saw him, somehow Lucy didn't trust him. But that meant little because there were very few people that she did trust, her upbringing had seen to that.

However, Alec and Martha Manton were among those few and in their company Lucy felt totally at ease. Tonight Martha had made a steak and kidney pie for supper, followed by a light-as-air lemon soufflé. After helping Martha put the flowers she had brought into two cut-glass vases Lucy did full justice to both.

'If you keep feeding me like this, Mrs Manton, I'll get as fat as butter,' she laughed as she helped Martha clear the table after the meal, following her through to a kitchen warmed even in summer by the Rayburn stove that was never allowed to go out.

'Not you. You're as thin as a rake,' Martha replied, setting a tray with tea things. 'You look as if you could do with a bit of fattening up.'

'Then I'd have to buy all new clothes.' Lucy gave an exaggerated sigh.

'Well, as long as you don't go in for those "shift" things all the young girls seem to be wearing these days,' Martha said, venting her disapproval by swirling hot water round the teapot to warm it. 'They've got no shape nor make about them, to my mind. They're not at all flattering.'

'Oh, you don't need to worry about that, Mrs Manton. I may not be very fat but I don't have the matchstick legs for tight skirts.' She laughed as she spoke.

'I'm very glad to hear it,' Martha said, joining her.

They were still laughing as they took the tea tray into the lounge, a large, comfortable room with deep, chintz-covered armchairs and settees. A tall grandfather clock stood in one corner and a corner cupboard decked with delicate china in another. In contrast, there was a very modern three-bar electric fire in the hearth.

'What's so funny?' Alec asked from the depths of his favourite armchair.

Lucy kicked off her sandals and curled up in a corner of one of the settees, feeling quite at home with her friends. 'I was just telling Mrs Manton that if she feeds me like this none of my clothes will fit.'

'Oh, aye, she's not a bad cook when she puts her mind to it,' Alec grinned as he tamped down tobacco in his pipe, pleased at the compliment to his wife.

'I've had plenty of practice, feeding you all these years,' Martha retorted, handing him his tea. 'You've got an appetite like a small horse.'

It was clear, from the look that passed between them, that behind the banter there was a wealth of long-standing love.

She cocked her ear. 'Ah, that's Ben's key in the lock. I'll fetch another cup. He'll be sure to want some tea.'

'And you can show him the photographs, Lucy,' Alec said. 'You did bring them, didn't you?'

'What photographs?' Martha demanded, turning back halfway to the kitchen. 'Have you brought pictures of your mum's wedding?'

'Good gracious, no,' Lucy laughed. 'I'm not even sure any were taken and if there were I'm not likely to see them.'

'Oh, that's a shame. Well, what are these pictures, then?'

Alec waved her away. 'We'll tell you later. Go and fetch a cup for Ben or he won't stay long enough to drink it.'

Martha scuttled off to the kitchen as Ben came in from the hall. Lucy noticed that he wasn't his usual suave, smartly-suited self tonight but looked hot and tired and slightly dishevelled in a short-sleeved check shirt and grey trousers. His brown hair flopped untidily over his forehead and he needed a shave.

'You'd better sit down. Your mother's gone to fetch a cup for you,' Alec said by way of greeting.

Ben frowned and brushed his hair back impatiently. 'I can't stay long. I've got some stuff in the car to unload at the shop.'

'I know. That's what you always say. But you can spare the time to drink a cup of tea. It'll please your mother,' Alec persisted.

'All right. Ten minutes. I must say I can do with a cup. It's been a long, hot old day.' Ben flopped down in an armchair with a brief smile of recognition towards Lucy. 'Mum been feeding you up on her famous steak and kidney pie?' he asked.

'Yes, it was delicious,' Lucy replied.

'You should have been here, then you'd have had some,' Alec growled.

'Fat chance! I've been at that sale over at Halesworth all day. I've only just got back,' Ben said with a yawn.

Alec paused in the act of lighting his pipe. 'Ah, yes. You said that was where you were going. Did you do any good?'

'Yes, not bad at all. Got one or two nice

pieces.'

'Need a hand with them?'

'No, I can manage, thanks.'

'What did you buy?'

'Oh, a Pembroke pedestal table, a set of Victorian spoon back chairs in very good nick – you won't have much to do on them, at all – some treen...' Ben turned to Lucy. 'That's what we call odd bits of china, glass, small ornaments, things like that.' He turned back to his father 'Oh, and a rather nice walnut davenport. There'll be quite a bit of work on that, though. It's got—'

Martha came back from the kitchen. 'That's enough shop talk, you two,' she said firmly as she poured Ben's tea. 'Now, what's all this about a photograph, Lucy?'

Lucy took the photograph of the three girls from her handbag and handed it to her.

'Oh, I've always liked those Edwardian fashions,' Martha said as she took it. Then, looking from the picture to Lucy and back again, 'Good gracious, that girl standing behind the chair looks exactly like you, Lucy. Who is she? Your grandma?'

'I've no idea who any of them are,' Lucy answered uncomfortably. 'It's just an old photograph Mr Manton found in my bureau.'

'Well, that girl is very like you, don't you think so, Ben?' She handed him the photograph, pointing to the girl in question. 'Perhaps it's your grandmother.'

He studied it for several minutes. 'Could be, I

26

suppose, from the clothes they're wearing,' he said. 'I'd guess this picture must have been taken in the early nineteen hundreds, round about the time of the First World War, so that would make it about right.'

'No, it wouldn't. Whoever she is, whoever they are, they've got nothing at all to do with me,' Lucy said firmly. 'Mr Manton found it in a secret drawer in my bureau when he had it in his workshop to repair. It must have been there for years and years. It's no more than an odd coincidence that one of the girls looks a bit like me.' She shuddered. 'I find it all a bit creepy, to tell you the truth.'

'I don't see it as creepy at all,' Ben said, looking at her with raised eyebrows. 'After all, if the bureau has been in your family for generations...'

'But that's just the point. It *hasn't*,' Lucy insisted. 'My mother bought it from a second-hand shop.' She grinned. 'Well, Mummy said it was a second-hand shop. It could have been your antique shop for all I know.' She went on, 'It wasn't really to her taste at all, she liked everything modern and up-to-date. She told me she only bought it because her mother saw it and liked it. Obviously, that would have been when they were still speaking to each other; they had some sort of quarrel and fell out while I was still small. I don't know what it was all about and I don't remember my grandmother at all. And all I know about the bureau is that it used to stand in a corner of one of the bed-

27

rooms. Mummy was always saying she was going to sell it but she never got round to it. I used to play offices in it.' She pulled out the other photograph. 'This was with it, too. And before you ask, no, I've never seen this house, either,' she said.

Martha took it, shook her head and handed it on to Ben. 'No, it's nowhere I know,' she said.

Ben studied it for several minutes, frowning. 'Oh, I've got an idea I do. In fact, I'm sure I've been there,' he said slowly, rubbing his stubbly chin. He stood up and took it over to the light to study it more carefully. Then he came and sat down again, nodding. 'Yes. I remember now. I've been to look at furniture at this house. I remember that fountain in the middle of the lawn.'

'Well, I'm absolutely positive that house has nothing whatever to do with my family,' Lucy said. 'I know my family history well enough to know that they could never have lived in a house like *that*. Not in a million years.'

'How can you be so sure, Lucy?' Martha asked.

'Oh, I'm sure, right enough,' Lucy said, a trace of bitterness in her voice. 'I should be, the number of times my mother drummed it into me. She never tired of telling me that I should think myself lucky to be so well provided for because she had been brought up living in a cellar, with hardly any furniture, just a bed and a table and chair. I daresay she exaggerated a bit, but probably not much. From what she told

28

me her father had died, I think before she was even born, and there was no family to support her and her mother and nowhere they could get help – I guess it was round about the time of the depression. So her mother had to take in washing and scrub floors to earn enough money to pay the rent. It seems they used to go round the market at the end of the day and pick up the vegetables that were left so that Alice, that's my grandmother, could make soup. I've heard all that so many times I could recite it off by heart. Just as I've heard Mummy say over and over again how she swore she would never allow herself to sink that low.'

Lucy looked round at the three faces rapt with attention and gave a ghost of a smile as she went on, 'She didn't either. She was married when she was about twenty to a young air force pilot whose family was apparently pretty well-heeled.'

'Perhaps his family owned this house,' Ben suggested.

She shook her head. 'Not if it's local and you think you've been there. My father came from Yorkshire, as I understand it. Mummy met him soon after he joined the RAF at the beginning of the war. Unfortunately, he was killed in the Battle of Britain so I don't remember him. And Mummy never had anything to do with his family, although whether it was from her choice or theirs I never found out.' Her mouth twisted wryly. 'However, what I do know is that there was never any shortage of money in our house, even though Mummy had very expensive tastes. I think Daddy must have left her quite well off and she had a number of rich men friends over the years, although as far as I know there was never anything serious. Until recently, that is, when she married her merchant banker and he whisked her off to live in Australia.' Lucy spread her hands and gave a shrug. 'Well, there you are. That's my family history, for what it's worth. If nothing else, it proves that neither of these photographs can possibly have anything to do with me.'

'What about Alice, your grandmother?' Martha asked. 'What happened to her?'

Lucy shrugged again. 'I've no idea. I imagine she must have died years ago. I only know there was some kind of quarrel between her and my mother, but I was never told what it was about, I guess I would have been too young at the time to understand, anyway. I don't remember her at all.'

Ben tapped the photograph he was still holding. 'If I get a call to this house I'll let you know,' he said casually. 'You could come with me, if you like.'

Lucy looked doubtful.

'Are you likely to get a call?' Martha asked.

He shrugged. 'You never know. But it came back to me while Lucy was talking and I remembered. I've been there two or three times, as a matter of fact. It's always the same. The old lady, Lady Bucknell, calls me because she's got something to sell, but when I get there I find

30

she's changed her mind and doesn't want to sell after all. Mind you, I did manage to wheedle a picture out of her once, but not a lot else.' He sighed. 'I shall be hearing from her again, though, I've no doubt. She's quite autocratic, I get summoned rather than requested to visit.'

'Where does she live?' Martha asked.

'It's a place called Rookhurst Hall, just outside the village of the same name. I guess they were once lords of the manor.'

'Is it far away?'

'Twenty miles or so. Just south of Framlingham.'

'Is she rich?' Martha was nothing if not persistent.

'Oh, leave the boy alone, Martha,' Alec growled good-naturedly from a haze of pipe smoke. 'Stop asking daft questions.'

His wife bridled. 'They're not daft questions. They're perfectly reasonable.'

'Well, it's difficult to tell, anyway,' Ben answered. 'She lives in this big house and she's surrounded by things that are worth a lot of money.' He spread his hands. 'But if she can't bear to part with them and has no money in the bank ... or on the other hand, maybe she's got so much money she has no need to sell anything but just wants to know what things are worth ... I really don't know.' He turned to Lucy. 'If you'd like to come with me next time I go you can see what you make of her.' He grinned, a surprisingly boyish grin. 'I can always introduce you as my assistant. As I remember, she

31

was quite a sprightly old bird.'

'I think you should go with Ben, Lucy,' Martha said, her eyes shining. 'After all, you never know.'

'You never know what?' Alec asked caustically.

'Well, just ... you never know.'

Ben burst out laughing. 'You'd better come with me when I go, Lucy. If nothing else you can act as Mum's spy. She's afraid I might be missing something.'

'I'm interested. That's all,' Martha said, offended.

He drained the last of his tea and got up, dropping a kiss on his mother's head as he passed. 'I've got to go now, Mum, and get the van unloaded. But we'll keep you posted over Lady Bucknell, won't we, Lucy?' he said to her with a wink.

Three

Lucy didn't expect anything to come of Ben's offer, so she was not disappointed when several weeks went by and she heard nothing. She sometimes saw him loading and unloading furniture in the yard outside his father's workshop when she was in her kitchen or bedroom and she began to wonder if she had misjudged him, whether the smooth, suave figure he presented to customers was not at all like the real Ben. Nevertheless, she was not anxious to spend a whole afternoon visiting some dotty old lady with him; for one thing, she had never been very good with dotty old ladies, and for another, she couldn't imagine what in the world she and Ben would find to talk about in the car.

But seeing the mysterious photographs and then telling the Mantons what little she knew about her childhood had set Lucy wondering about the equally mysterious grandmother her mother had fallen out with all those years ago. She couldn't help feeling curious as to what she was like, especially since Alice was probably the only relative she had left now that her own mother was on the other side of the world. In any case, Lucy herself had no quarrel with her grandmother. It wouldn't do any harm to look her up, if indeed she was still alive.

With some misgivings – as she well remembered, her mother had always seemed to go tight-lipped and cross at even the briefest mention of Alice – she added a postscript to her weekly letter, saying that she had found a couple of old photographs in her bureau and wondered if they might possibly belong to Granny. (Well, she told herself as she wrote the words, it was possible, even though not very likely.) If so, it might be nice to return them. Had her mother any idea where Alice lived?

She posted the letter without much hope of a response to her question, and thought no more about it.

Four weeks later, she was dashing down the steps from her flat with her sandals in one hand and a piece of toast in the other, late for work as usual, just as Ben Manton was unlocking the back door to the shop.

'Looks as if you're a bit late,' he said with a grin as, the toast stuck in her mouth, she bent down to fasten the buckle on her shoe.

'Mm. Overslept,' she mumbled through the toast. She straightened up and removed it from her mouth. 'Again! I'm always doing it.'

'Don't you hear Dad opening up the workshop?' he asked in surprise. 'He's always there before eight every morning and he puts his radio on as soon as he gets there because he likes to listen to the news.'

'No. I don't hear a thing. I must sleep like the dead.'

He grinned. 'You'll have to get yourself an alarm clock.'

'I've got one. I don't hear that, either,' she wailed. She glanced at her watch. 'I must fly. I'll be getting the sack.'

'Hang on a minute before you dash off,' he said. 'Will you be free on Saturday afternoon?'

'Why do you ask?' she said warily.

'No sinister reason,' he said with a laugh. 'It's just that I've been summoned to see Lady Bucknell at Rookhurst Hall. Remember? The house in your photograph?' She nodded cautiously and he went on, 'I offered to take you next time I went there, and I'll be going on

34

Saturday, so...' he spread his hands, 'would you like to come with me? That's all.'

She hesitated, then answered slowly, 'Yes, I think I could manage that.'

'You don't sound very sure.'

'It's just that ... Yes, I am. Quite sure,' she said, her voice becoming firmer. 'I would very much like to come.'

'Good. I'll pick you up at two o'clock on Saturday, then.' He put his head on one side. 'Unless you change your mind, that is.'

'No. I won't change my mind. I really would like to come.' She gave him a quick smile. 'Thank you for asking me.'

'My pleasure.'

She mentioned the proposed trip to Janice during their afternoon break, as they drank tea and ate the doughnuts it had been her turn to buy from the nearby baker's.

'Oh, how exciting. You might be about to discover some long-lost relative,' Janice said, her mouth full.

'Don't be silly. I'm only going out of curiosity,' Lucy said crossly.

'Are you going to take the photograph with you?'

'I'll put it in my handbag but I don't know whether I'll show it to anyone.' She shrugged. 'I might not get the opportunity because I'm supposed to be going as Ben's assistant.' She made a face. 'Not that I know the first thing about antiques, but I must confess I'm curious to see what the house is like inside. The outside looks quite grand in the picture.' She licked the sugar off her fingers before taking out the photograph and handing it to Janice.

'Oh, my word, it certainly does,' Janice agreed, handing it back. 'Just think, it could be—'

'Don't start speculating. It's only a picture. But it will be strange to actually see it, well, not in the flesh, but in proper bricks and mortar.' She stared at it. 'I don't quite know what to wear. What does one wear as an antique dealer's assistant going to a posh place like this, for goodness sake?'

Janice hunched her shoulders. 'I've no idea. Something smartish, I suppose. Not trousers.'

'Thanks. That's a great help, I must say, since I'm going to visit an old lady who would probably be scandalized at the sight of a woman in trousers,' Lucy said with a sigh.

In the event, after much deliberation she chose a pale blue linen skirt that reached to just below the knee and a blouse in blue and white striped cotton with three-quarter length sleeves and a white Peter Pan collar. With navy sandals and handbag she felt suitably businesslike yet summery at the same time.

From the approving look he gave her as he held open the door of his green Hillman Minx for her, Ben clearly felt she'd struck the right note, too. This helped a little towards calming the butterflies in her stomach, and she was glad to see that he was wearing light-coloured trousers and an open-necked shirt with the sleeves rolled up, rather than his business suit.

'I thought I'd bring my car today,' he said as he pulled away from the kerb. 'It's more comfortable than the van and if Lady B. runs true to form she won't be selling anything that I'll be needing the extra space for.'

'You certainly wouldn't get a very big piece of furniture in this car,' Lucy said with a laugh.

'You've got plenty of room, though, haven't you?' he asked. He glanced across at her. 'Good grief, you're clutching your handbag as if your life depended on it. Does my driving make you nervous?'

'No, your driving's fine. It's not that.'

'What then?' Another quick glance at her.

'I don't know. I suppose I'm a bit apprehensive about meeting Lady Bucknell.'

'You needn't be. As long as you can cope with tea in thin porcelain cups and tiny cucumber sandwiches you'll be all right. And you don't have to say anything. Remember, you're my assistant.'

'But I don't know anything about antiques. What if she asks me something?'

'She won't. To tell you the truth, she doesn't know much about them, either. All she knows is that she's got stuff that's been in her family for generations and that some of it might be worth a bit.'

He drove on in silence for a while. Then he said, 'I hope you've brought those photographs.'

'Yes, I have. But it occurred to me that I could

just as easily have given them to you to bring.'

'Got cold feet?'

'A bit.'

'What? Do you think you're going to find a long-lost relative?'

'Of course not. Nothing like that.'

'What, then?'

She shrugged. 'I honestly don't know.'

'Well, then. Just relax and enjoy the scenery. Not that there's a lot to look at. Although, come to think of it, John Constable found plenty to paint. He liked the wide East Anglian skies of course, and there are some very pretty thatched houses with pink or terracotta washed walls. They're quite a feature of this part of the country. And look, there's a little church with a round tower; you'll only see that in Suffolk and Norfolk. Ah, now you can see Framlingham Castle, or what's left of it, over on the horizon. That means it won't be too long before we're there.'

Ten minutes later, after driving through the village of Rookhurst with its narrow roads and single shop, and past a brand-new housing estate that was still in process of being built, they came to a quaint hexagonal-shaped lodge. Next to it hung large, rusting wrought-iron gates that had been left open for so long that they were half obscured by long grass and ivy. Here they turned into a long tree-lined drive, overgrown at the sides and with weeds growing through the gravel. At the house, the drive swept round a circular lawn with flower beds, also overgrown, and a fountain in the middle.

'Gosh! It's exactly like the photograph,' Lucy breathed, leaning forward, her eyes widening in surprise.

Ben stopped the car outside the imposing front door and pulled on the handbrake. 'Except that there was probably an army of gardeners to look after the place when that photograph was taken,' he remarked. 'It all looks a bit unkempt and neglected now, don't you think?'

She nodded. 'And it doesn't look as if the fountain works any more. I can see a big crack in the bowl, so it wouldn't hold much water.'

'Obviously the frost has got into it.' He got out of the car and went to open the door for Lucy. 'Pity. She should have sold it to me. I offered her a good price for it a couple of years ago. It wouldn't be worth as much now, of course.'

He waited as she got out and straightened her skirt. 'OK? Ready?' He gave her an encouraging smile and went up the steps and rang the doorbell.

A woman of around sixty, clearly the house-keeper, answered the door. She had springy grey hair and was wearing heavy black-rimmed spectacles that kept sliding down her nose and had to be constantly pushed back. In spite of the heat of the day she had on a thick, shapeless cardigan over her pink nylon overall. Lucy noticed that she didn't smile as she greeted them, although they were obviously expected. She left them to wait in a lofty, black and white tiled hall with several large doors opening off it and a wide, shallow staircase covered in thick Turkey carpet curving up to the floor above, where a gallery ran round three sides.

Lucy had no time to take in more than this before the woman came back and led them along a short corridor to a room at the back of the house. Her first impression was of a large, very light room with blue and gold striped wall-paper and a blue carpet and several pieces of elegant, rather spindly furniture covered in blue brocade. It seemed a bit like a room in a stately home. But there was no time to take in much more before Ben led her across to the elderly lady sitting in a deep armchair in the sunshine, beside long windows open on to a formal garden that was also badly in need of attention from a gardener.

Lady Bucknell was thin and rather sharp-featured, and had the whitest hair Lucy had ever seen piled up into a soft bun on top of her head. She was wearing a dark violet-coloured dress with a white frill at the neck and seemed to have a great deal of gold hanging about her person; a double gold chain round her neck, a gold-rimmed lorgnette hanging from another gold chain, a gold fob watch pinned to her collar and several gold bangles at her wrists. The rings on her fingers looked too heavy for her fragile hands to support.

'Your visitors, M'Lady,' the housekeeper announced. 'Shall I bring the tea now?'

'Yes, thank you, Bessie.' Her Ladyship's

voice was low but she spoke very clearly.

Ben went across and took the hand she offered. Lucy had the fleeting impression that he was going to kiss it, but he didn't. He released it, turned and introduced Lucy as his assistant. Lady Bucknell looked her up and down, narrowing her eyes a little. 'And are you as knowledgeable as this young man about antiques?' she asked, with a wry smile.

'Not yet,' Ben quickly answered for her. 'But she's learning.'

'Let the gel answer for herself, young man,' the old lady said with some asperity. 'Well, Miss...?'

Lucy stepped forward. 'Armitage. Lucy Armitage,' she said with a nervous smile. 'And as Mr Manton said, I don't know very much yet but I'm very keen to learn. Particularly about china and porcelain,' she added, although the idea had only just occurred to her.

'Well, sit down, both of you. I'm getting a crick in my neck looking up at you. And – ah, yes, here's Bessie with the tea. I always drink Earl Grey in the afternoon. I hope that's to your taste?' She looked questioningly from one to the other.

'Earl Grey's fine,' Ben said and Lucy smiled in agreement. Since she'd never drunk Earl Grey tea she didn't know whether it was to her taste or not. In fact, when she tasted it she found she didn't like it much; she found it too aromatic. But the cups were small, and between bites of tiny cucumber sandwiches and a slice of delicious lemon cake she even managed to drink a second cup, which clearly pleased Lady Bucknell.

When the tea things had been removed Ben said, 'Before we begin to talk business, Lady Bucknell, I have something I'd like to show you.' He turned to Lucy and said with a suspicion of a wink. 'Did you bring those photographs that my father found in the bureau he's just restored, Lucy?'

'Yes. Yes, I've got them here.' She unzipped her handbag and gave him the two photographs, glad that he had taken the initiative and hadn't revealed that they belonged to her.

He handed the picture of the house to the old lady.

'Hm.' She picked up her lorgnette and held it to her eyes, squinting a little. 'That was taken a good many years ago,' she remarked drily. 'In the days when the fountain worked and there were several gardeners to look after the grounds.' She lowered the lorgnette to look at Ben. 'Where did you say it was found?'

'In a secret drawer in an oak bureau.'

'I wonder how it got there,' she said without much interest, handing it back.

'Perhaps you once sold a bureau and it found its way to my father's workshop,' Ben suggested. 'Stranger things have happened.'

She shook her head. 'No, that's not possible. I've never owned an oak bureau. I'm told that mine is made of walnut and exceptionally small, less than three feet wide. Your father told me years ago that it was a rare piece of furniture. I've never parted with it and I don't think I ever shall.' She handed the photograph back. 'No, wherever this was hidden it has nothing to do with me, though I'm mystified as to how a picture of my house could have got there.'

'This was found with it.' Ben handed her the photograph of the three girls.

She picked up the lorgnette again and held the picture close, staring at it for a long time, then she looked up and Lucy saw tears glistening in her eyes. 'Now, I do find this strange. Very strange indeed. I simply cannot imagine how this could have been found in somebody's bureau, or anywhere else, for that matter. You see, it is a picture of my three daughters, Mr Manton.' She turned away and dabbed her eyes with a tiny lace handkerchief. 'And you say the two photographs were together?'

'That's right.'

'Then it really is most strange.' She handed the picture back to him.

'Wouldn't you like to keep it, Lady Bucknell?' he asked gently.

She shook her head again. 'No. As you can see, I already have one.' She nodded to the wall behind where they were sitting. 'Not that I can see it very clearly, these days. My eyes are not what they were.'

Lucy stood up and turned to look at the picture on the wall behind her. Hanging there was the same picture, greatly enlarged and in a gilt frame. For the first time, Lucy was aware of

43

the likeness. It was unmistakable, like looking in a mirror. But for the hair and the Edwardian dress, the girl standing behind the chair could have been Lucy herself. It was quite uncanny. She felt a chill down her spine and a shudder ran through her.

Ben had obviously seen it too. He put his hand on her arm briefly and whispered, 'Are you OK?' When she nodded, her mouth too dry to speak, he said in a louder voice, 'Three lovely girls, Lady Bucknell. And all very like their mother, if I may say so. Where are they all now? Married and with equally lovely children?'

Lady Bucknell shook her head sadly. 'Would that they were, Mr Manton. Would that they were.' She turned her head away a little. 'No, they all died before the bloom of youth was past. They died too young. Far too young. Only a few years after that photograph was taken, in fact.' She gave a deep sigh. 'It was a bad time. A very bad time. For all of us.'

Ben bowed his head a little. 'Forgive me. It was wrong of me to ask.'

She waved away his apology. 'It's all in the past. All many years ago.' Her voice became brisker. 'But I've still got Peregrine, my son. He looks after the estate, what there is left of it. He and his wife live separately from me in the west wing. Unfortunately, they have no children so I've lost any hope I might have had of grandchildren.' She reached for her stick and got stiffly to her feet, ignoring Ben's offer of help.

'But I mustn't keep you, I've taken up enough of your time. I invited you here today to ask your opinion on my longcase clock. Not that I wish to sell it, of course...'

Ben looked at Lucy and raised his eyebrows. 'Of course not, Lady Bucknell. But let's go and look at it, anyway. As I remember, it's a Tompion. They're worth a lot of money, you know.'

'Yes, I know. But I'm not quite destitute. When I am I'll let you know and you can have first refusal.' She pointed her stick at a small piecrust pedestal table. 'But since you've taken the trouble to come and see me today I might consider selling you that, if the price is right,' she said, a trifle grudgingly. 'Now, come and look at my clock. It loses three minutes in twenty-four hours. That's rather a lot, isn't it? Do you think you can adjust it? I do like my clocks to keep accurate time.'

'I'll have a look.'

'You'd better come too,' she said over her shoulder to Lucy. 'You might learn a few things.'

On the way home some half an hour later, the piecrust table safely stowed in the back of the car, Ben said, 'I'm sorry, Lucy, I didn't handle that very well. It was very clumsy, the way I asked about grandchildren, but that girl in the picture – enlarged like that it could have been you and I wondered...'

'Yes, I know. Thank you for trying, Ben, but I couldn't possibly have any connection with that place. Remember, Lady Bucknell said all tho girls died soon after that photograph was taken. And I've told you, I know my history. My mother was brought up in a slum, for God's sake, not in a posh house like that. I guess it's only thanks to her determination to rise above it that I'm not already married to some drunk and with three or four kids hanging round my apron strings.' She paused. 'When you look at it like that I suppose I've got quite a lot to thank her for, haven't I?'

'Yes, I suppose you have,' he said absently. 'I find it very odd, though,' he went on, frowning at the road ahead. 'You're so like that girl in the picture.' He glanced at her. 'Are you sure you didn't feel anything ... an affinity with the place, perhaps?'

'No. I didn't. Not a thing. I've never ever been there before. I'd stake my life on it.'

'It's just so strange...'

'Oh, it's strange, right enough,' Lucy agreed. 'But don't they say everyone has a double somewhere in the world? Mostly they never meet but it's been just my luck to come face to face with mine.' She gave a little shudder. 'All I can say is I'm glad it was only on a photograph.'

'It was probably just as well that the old lady's eyesight wasn't good so she couldn't see the likeness,' Ben said thoughtfully. 'I wonder what she would have said if she had.'

'I don't know and I don't want to risk finding out. All I can say is, if you have to go there again, Ben, I'd rather not come with you,' Lucy

46

replied a little shakily.

He glanced at her. 'Oh dear. I'm sorry it's upset you so much.'

'I'm not upset,' she said a little too firmly. 'I just don't want to go there again. Ever.'

Four

Ben seemed reluctant to let her go when they arrived back outside the antique shop and Lucy had the feeling that he was on the point of asking her to have dinner with him. But she realized it was only that he was feeling sorry for her because he thought she was upset, so she got out of the car quickly, only stopping long enough to thank him for taking her to Rookhurst Hall.

But to her consternation, before she could hurry away he had got out too and was standing in front of her. 'Are you quite sure you're OK, Lucy? You've had rather a shock this afternoon and you still look a bit shaken. We could...'

'No, no, I'm perfectly all right,' she said, smiling brightly. She gave a shrug. 'It was silly of me, really. I let my imagination run away with me. Heavens, if I'd really looked so much like the girl in the picture Lady Bucknell would have recognized the likeness, wouldn't she? After all, those girls were her daughters, for goodness sake!' She shrugged again. 'I admit it was an odd coincidence that the photographs were in my bureau, but that's all it was, a coincidence. I shall put them back where they were found and forget about them.'

He still appeared doubtful so she looked pointedly at her watch. 'Goodness, look at the time. I've got loads of things to do this evening and I'm sure you have too. Thank you again for taking me to the Hall, Ben. Now I must fly.' She escaped up to her flat, leaving him looking after her with a puzzled expression on his face.

Back in her flat, she flung her handbag on to the settee and sank into an armchair, staring into space. This afternoon she had seen a different side to Ben Manton. Gone was the suave, polished salesman bent on making a sale or bargain purchase and in his place was quite a different character. Remembering how insistent he had been that Lady Bucknell shouldn't sell him the little piecrust table unless she was certain she was happy to part with it, and then, in the car, musing that he had probably offered her a bit over the odds for it, she realized that underneath the brittle, professional exterior was a warm, quite soft-hearted man.

And she knew he had been reluctant to leave her when they arrived back, obviously thinking she was still shocked over her likeness to the picture on Lady Bucknell's wall. Well, she was. Wouldn't anybody be? She bit her lip. Ben must have thought her a little odd, dashing off like that; but she didn't want his concern. She couldn't manage concern, she wasn't used to it. In the whole of her life nobody had ever shown much concern for her; her feelings had never been important and so she had learned to hide them. Now, she couldn't believe that anybody could genuinely care about how she felt and she was determined not to allow herself to be patronized. Nor pitied. By anybody. Especially not by Ben Manton.

Having resolved that in her mind she took out her handkerchief and wiped her eyes and blew her nose. Then, with a sniff, she reached for her handbag and drew out the two photographs. Without even looking at them she took them over to the bureau and put them back in the secret drawer where they had been discovered.

'And that's an end of it,' she said aloud as she closed up the bureau. She made herself some cheese on toast, switched on the television and sat with her eyes glued to *Dixon of Dock Green.* But when George Dixon repeated his usual catchphrase 'Evenin' all' at the end of the programme, she had no idea what it had all been about and the cheese on toast was a congealed heap on the plate. She got up and scraped it into the bin and made herself another cup of tea.

But of course that wasn't the end of it. When she got to work on Monday, Janice was avid to hear all the details of her visit to Rookhurst Hall and Lucy had to relive it all again. Or, at least, part of it.

'And was the house exactly like the one in the picture?' Janice asked eagerly.

'Yes, except that the garden was a bit over-grown and the fountain wasn't working. And there was grass growing in a crack in the steps up to the house.'

'And what did the old lady say about the pictures?'

'Not a lot. She didn't want to keep them, anyway.'

Janice's face fell. 'So didn't she know who those girls were?'

'Which girls?' Bernard Foster came into the office with the letters he had signed ready for posting.

'You know which girls. The girls in the photographs Lucy brought into the office,' Janice said a trifle impatiently. 'Ben Manton took her to see the house in the picture last Saturday.'

'Ben Manton?' A look of annoyance crossed Bernard's face. 'Why did he take you, Lucy? I would have taken you, if you'd asked me.'

Lucy frowned at him. 'I could never have asked you, Mr Foster,' she replied, shocked.

'Why ever not?' he said, putting on his most charming face. 'I would have been delight-ed—'

'Three reasons,' she cut sharply across his words. 'One, as a secretary I would never dream of asking my employer to take me any-where; two, as neither you nor I knew where the place was it would have been pointless, any-way; and three, most importantly, you have a *wife*, Mr Foster. I haven't forgotten that, even if you have.'

He waved his hand. 'Oh, you don't need to worry about Felicity. She's in a nursing home having tests for something or other.' He sighed. 'She's always having tests, she enjoys it, sometimes I think it's the only thing she's interested in. She certainly isn't interested in me or what I do.' He smiled at her. 'So Felicity is the least of our worries, Lucy.'

'She may be the least of *your* worries, Mr Foster, but please don't include me in such a cavalier attitude towards your marriage. And now, if you'll excuse me, I have work to do.' She began typing furiously and didn't stop, even when he left the office, because she didn't want Janice to repeat her question about the three girls.

Fortunately Mr Payne, Janice's boss, called her in to take dictation soon afterwards, so the moment passed.

Although Lucy wrote to her mother every week or so, Margaret's replies were spasmodic, to say the least. She was clearly enjoying her life in Australia with her new husband and when she did write her letters were full of the places they had been to and the things they had seen. Added to this, sometimes their letters crossed, so it was not until early in September that there was a brief postscript at the end of Margaret's letter, most of which had been given over to a trip to Sydney. It said,

In answer to your query I've no idea whether your grandmother is alive or dead

51

and I can't say I care. The last I heard, which was years ago, she had moved to some God-forsaken place by the sea, Crawford-something or other, I believe it was called. I can't remember more than that and I threw the address away. Goodness knows why she bothered to send it to me in the first place. Anyway, she's probably gone from there by now. Or died. If she is still alive she's probably ga-ga and living in some dreadful old people's home. Can't imagine why on earth you want to know.

She obviously didn't care, either. Lucy wondered anew what it was they had quarrelled about but knew better than to ask her mother.

The following Saturday Lucy was invited to supper with the Mantons again. Ben was there when she arrived, having called to see his father and been persuaded to accept his mother's invitation to stay for supper, much to Martha's delight.

Throughout the meal, a delicious pot roast followed by apple pie and cream, talk was kept to general topics and Ben sustained an affectionate banter with his mother, who insisted that he didn't look after himself properly in that old flat of his.

'It's not an old flat, it's a very nice flat in an old house,' he told her.

'I don't know why you didn't move into the flat over the shop where I could keep an eye on you,' she complained.

'You've just answered both questions. I didn't move there precisely because I didn't want to live "over the shop" and at my age I don't need an eye kept on me, Mum, thanks all the same.' He spread his hands. 'How do you think I could live my life of decadent debauchery with you watching my every move?'

'Now you're being silly.' She ladled an extra dollop of cream on his apple pie. 'But I'm sure you don't feed yourself properly.'

'Well, when I'm starving I can always come here for a meal. That keeps me going for a fortnight.' He grinned at Lucy as he spoke.

Afterwards, when he insisted on driving her home although it was not far for her to walk, he said thoughtfully, 'I expect you're thinking from the broad hints my mother kept giving me that I don't visit her as much as I should.'

'I know she's always pleased to see you,' she answered carefully.

'Yes, but the trouble is, she smothers me, or she would if I let her. She seems to forget I'm nearly twenty-six, she tries to treat me as if I'm still a twelve year old. "Do you make sure your socks are aired before you put them on?"' He gave a passable imitation of his mother's voice. '"Do you put a clean shirt on every day? Are you getting enough to eat?" It drives me mad.'

'You get on well with your father, though. Have you always worked with him?' she asked.

'More or less. I stayed at school until I was eighteen, thinking I might go into teaching. But after two years' National Service in the army I'd changed my mind, so I went to help out at the shop while I looked round and decided what I wanted to do.' He pulled up outside the shop and gave a little laugh. 'It took me six months to realize I didn't need to look any further because I'd already found it. I have what's called in the trade a "nose"; I can tell the genuine from the fake just by handling it and I love buying and selling. But that's another thing, I couldn't work with Dad and continue to live at home, both for his sake and mine. And with Mum's fussing as well I just had to get out.' He sighed. 'I suppose it's partly because I don't have any brothers and sisters, so all their concern is channelled in my direction.' He gave an apologetic smile. 'Sorry. I know I shouldn't complain, they're wonderful parents. But I expect you know what I mean.'

'Not really,' she answered soberly. 'I don't have any brothers or sisters, either, but my mother wasn't a bit like that. She didn't fuss over me. In fact, I think it's fair to say she wasn't the least interested in me. There was always a maid to make sure I was fed, so she didn't have to bother about that, but if I'd worn the same clothes for a month she wouldn't have noticed.' She gave a little laugh. 'On the other hand, I suppose, like you, I shouldn't grumble because she was always buying me expensive presents and new clothes that either didn't fit or weren't to my taste.'

'Conscience gifts?' he asked quietly.

'I guess you could say that.' She was quiet for a moment, then she said with a smile, 'So, I must say, it's very nice when your mother makes a fuss of me. It might irritate you, but I'm not used to it so I like it.'

'Ah, yes, but that's because you don't have to live with it all the time.' He pulled up outside the flat and turned towards her in his seat. 'Do you mind living alone? In this day and age it's quite unusual for a girl—' He broke off. 'Oh, I'm sorry, it's none of my business.'

She smiled at him. 'No, I don't mind at all. I like being independent and having my own flat. Not that I had any choice, since Mummy upped and went off to Australia.'

'Couldn't you have gone with her?'

'You must be joking! What, and play gooseberry to a couple of middle-aged lovebirds? No thank you.'

'Does she write to you?'

'Oh, yes. I get a letter from her about once a month, something like that. She tells me about all the wonderful places she's visited with her beloved Harold.' She grinned. 'Is that the end of the third degree?'

'Oh, sorry. I'm interested, that's all.'

'That's all right.' She hesitated. 'I don't know why, well, I suppose it was because I was telling you and your parents about my family history, or what I knew of it, but when I wrote to Mummy several weeks ago I asked her if she knew where my grandmother was living.'

'And?' he prompted.

'She wasn't a bit interested. And she was pretty vague. Said the last she'd heard my grandmother was living in a place on the coast called Crawford-something or other, but she thought she was probably dead by now.'

'Why? She wouldn't necessarily be that old, would she?'

She frowned. 'No, I suppose not. I'm twenty. My mother isn't much over forty, so I guess it's quite possible she's still only in her sixties.'

'Did your mother say which coast this Crawford-something or other was on?'

'No, that was all she said, except that she'd thrown the letter away.' She shrugged. 'Could be anywhere, couldn't it? Like looking for a needle in the proverbial haystack.'

He drummed his fingers on the steering wheel, staring out into the fading light across the square. After a little while he said, 'Come to think of it, there's a place called Crawfordness, on the coast somewhere out in the wilds between Aldeburgh and Southwold. If you were brought up in Norwich and that was where she lived with you, it might be reasonable to suppose she wouldn't have moved to the other side of the country. It could be worth looking at, anyway.'

'Is there a bus service?'

He laughed. 'Probably one a fortnight, from what I know of the area. But I wouldn't really know, since I mostly travel by van.'

She pinched her lip. 'I wonder if it might be the place.'

'And if it is, she might have moved away by now,' he said, anxious not to raise her hopes too much. 'Anyway, I'll check it out if I happen to go that way.'

Lucy thanked him and got out of the car. It was a long shot. Crawfordness might not be the right place and even if it was Alice might no longer be there. From what Ben said the place was in such an isolated spot it wasn't likely that his travels would take him there so, simply out of curiosity, she decided to check the local bus times. A trip into the country might be a pleasant way to spend an autumn Sunday.

She was poring over the bus times one evening during the following week while half-listening to *The Goon Show* on the radio. It didn't take long to discover that Ben was quite right, the buses ran infrequently, something like two a week, and never on Sundays. There was a knock on the door and she went to open it, hoping against hope that it wouldn't be Bernard Foster, her boss. He had half-jokingly promised (threatened was the word she would have used) to call on her and take her for a spin in his car and she was busily composing a suitably scathing refusal. But when she opened the door it was Ben and not Bernard Foster who stood there, a bunch of chrysanthemums in his hand and a wide smile on his face.

'I thought if I brought you these and told you I had some interesting news you might ask me in and offer me a cup of coffee,' he said as he handed them to her.

'If you've got some interesting news I would have asked you in without the flowers, but thank you, these are lovely,' she said, going over to switch off the radio.

Five minutes later, with the mop-head chrysanthemums in a vase on the table and two steaming mugs of coffee between them on a low stool, she curled up in a corner of the settee opposite where he sat in her deep armchair.

'Let me guess. You've been to see Lady Bucknell again and she's told you something about her daughters,' she said, her eyes shining in anticipation.

He shook his head and picked up his coffee. 'No. Better than that.' He smiled at her over the rim of his coffee mug. 'I've found out where Alice lives.'

Lucy's eyes widened. 'My grandmother?' She uncurled her legs and leaned towards him. 'You mean she's still alive?'

'Very much so. I've discovered that she lives at number six Denton Gardens, Crawfordness, and also that she's a pillar of the local church.'

'Gosh! That was clever of you.' She took a sip of her coffee, never taking her eyes off him. 'How did you find all this out?'

'The obvious way. I went to Crawfordness and asked at the post office. It's not a very big place so when I said I was looking for somebody called Alice, somebody who would probably be in her sixties, the postmistress said did I mean Alice Clayton. I said probably but I wasn't entirely sure.' He paused and drank some of his coffee. 'Is that right? Alice Clayton?'

Lucy's face lit up. 'That's absolutely right. Now you come to speak of it, I've got a copy of *Jane Eyre* with that name in it and I've always known it had belonged to Granny, although I don't know how I knew.' She glanced up at her bookshelves. 'It's up there somewhere. Goodness, I'd quite forgotten.'

'Well, it looks as if we may be on the right track, then.'

'So did you see her?' she asked eagerly.

'No, the postmistress wouldn't give me her address, said it wouldn't be right, seeing that she didn't know me from Adam. I couldn't really blame her because I'd declined to tell her why I wanted to see Alice, knowing how quickly rumour spreads in small villages. In the end she suggested that the best thing would be for me to go and see the vicar, which I did. I didn't mind telling him why I was there and eventually he gave me her address. They're pretty cagey in that neck of the woods, but I suppose you can't blame them for that.'

She wriggled excitedly in her seat. 'So did you go and see her? What's she like? Was she pleased?'

He held up his hand briefly. 'Hang on a minute.' He drained his coffee mug. 'No, I didn't go and see her. After a lot of discussion the vicar and I decided it might not be wise. So he's going to talk to her and then, if she's agreeable, he'll telephone me and we'll make a date for me to take you to see her.' He leaned back in his chair. 'Now, was that worth a cup of coffee? Very nice coffee, too, I might add.' He held out his mug for more.

She refilled it. 'Oh, thank you, Ben. It was very kind of you to go to all that trouble,' she said warmly. She hesitated. 'But I wouldn't want you to ... I mean, there's no need...'

'It was no trouble.' He cut across her words. 'I was in Southwold and I called there on my way back. And before you say anything else I shall be more than happy to take you to see your grandmother. There's a very nice little café on the sea front where we can have morning coffee or afternoon tea, too. I checked that while I was there. It'll make a pleasant Sunday out.' He drank his coffee and got to his feet. 'Now, I must go. I've still got work to do tonight. This antique dealers' fair is less than a fortnight away and there's still quite a bit to be done before the stuff will be ready for it.'

'I'm very grateful to you for sparing the time for this when you're so busy, Ben,' she said. 'You're very kind.'

He stood looking down at her, grinning. 'No, I'm not. I'm intrigued. Having got this far with the story, I want to be in on the "happy ever after" bit.'

She accompanied him to the door. 'I hope you won't be disappointed,' she said quietly.

'I hope *you* won't be, either.' He dropped a kiss on her cheek and left.

After he had gone she curled up again in the

corner of the settee and mulled over in her mind what he had told her. She realized that in thinking that the smooth and suave businessman was the real Ben she had done him an injustice. He was actually very nice; just the sort of man she would have liked for a brother.

Five

Lucy didn't tell Janice anything about her grandmother. Janice was too inclined to romanticize, she had already woven several unlikely stories round the photograph of the three girls; moreover she was more than a little nosey. Added to that Lucy was reluctant to share too many confidences with her because she was seriously thinking of looking for another job. Although she enjoyed the work at Payne and Foster she was beginning to find Bernard Foster's attentions very annoying, and the fact that Janice seemed to find it all so funny even more so.

'He clearly thinks he's God's gift to the female race, just because he fancies he looks a bit like Clark Gable,' she complained. 'He really gets on my nerves, the way he always manages to stand just that little bit too close so I have to keep moving away and the way he feasts his eyes on my legs while I'm taking dictation. Heavens, it's not as if I give him any encouragement. I don't even like the man.'

'No, he must think you're the original Ice Maiden,' Janice laughed. 'That's probably what makes him so keen. He's trying to thaw you out.'

'Well, I'm fed up with him trying to touch me; he's always putting his hand on my arm and trying to hold my hand. If he does much more of it I shall leave.'

'Where will you go?' Janice wasn't taking her seriously. 'Behind the till in the little self-service grocer's in the square?'

'I might, at that.' Lucy picked up her note-book and headed for her boss's office. 'At least I wouldn't have to keep watching where old Foster's hands were.'

'No, you'd just have to listen to all the old biddies complaining that it was better in the old days when somebody served you instead of having to pick the stuff off the shelves for your-self.' Janice gave a complacent shrug. 'Nah, you won't leave. You like this job too much.'

'Just watch me. If he tries anything on once more...'

Two days later Lucy was taking dictation from Bernard Foster, concentrating on her shorthand, when he leaned over and squeezed her knee to draw attention to a particular point. This was the last straw. She got up from her chair and flung her notebook and pencil on to his desk.

'That's enough, Mr Foster,' she said icily.

'You've no right to touch me like that. You know I don't like it.'

He looked up at her in feigned surprise. 'My dear girl, I was only drawing your attention—'

'I am not your dear girl and you already had my full attention, Mr Foster,' she replied, her eyes flashing. 'This is not the first time you've tried to be over-familiar with me but I can assure you it will be the last. I've had enough of you trying to paw me.'

He got up from his desk. 'Don't be silly, Lucy. I wasn't trying to paw you, I was only being friendly.'

'You're not my friend, you're my employer. The fact that you pay my wages doesn't give you the right to take liberties with me and I'm having no more of it. I'm leaving. Right now.' She marched to the door.

He was there before her, his hand on the doorknob so that she couldn't get out. 'Don't be silly, Lucy,' he repeated in a wheedling tone. 'You're not going to leave over a silly little thing like that, are you?' He shrugged. 'All right, I admit I may have overstepped the mark, but you know how much I admire you. You're a very attractive young lady, you know.' He made a deprecating gesture. 'Things aren't good between Felicity and me. Her health's very fragile so it's months, no years, since I ... we ... since we shared a bed ... and a man needs ... You understand what I'm trying to say...' He tried to take her hand.

She snatched it away. 'I know perfectly well

what you're trying to say, but what goes on between you and your wife is no concern of mine and of absolutely no interest to me, Mr Foster. I'm leaving right now so please open the door. I'll collect my cards on my way out.' Her voice dripped ice as she tried to push past him.

'Not so fast, young lady.' Suddenly his tone changed and became hard. 'You can't just walk out on me like that. I shall need at least a week's notice.' A wolfish smile spread across his face. 'Either that or a kiss.' He leaned towards her and she could smell his breath, rank with tobacco.

Her eyes widened and she took a step back. 'Don't be so ridiculous. I wouldn't kiss you if you were the last man on earth,' she said, disgusted. 'And you can keep my week's wages in lieu of notice; it'll be a small price to pay. Now, please open that door or I shall scream, and that will put you in rather an awkward position, won't it?' She was terrified inside but she managed to keep her voice level and look him straight in the eye.

He hesitated a moment, then moved away from the door. 'You're a little ... you led me on,' he accused, his face red with rage and frustration.

'You know perfectly well that's not true, Mr Foster,' she said quietly as she walked past him. 'Janice knows it, too, so it's no good trying to blame me for your fantasies.'

She went back to her room and started clearing her desk, throwing things alternately into her bag and the waste paper basket, her face like thunder.

Janice looked up in surprise. 'What's up?'

'I'm leaving. Now. Right this minute.'

'Ooh, so the worm really has turned.' She leaned back in her chair. 'I never thought you'd do it, Lucy. What will you do now?'

She shrugged. 'I shall go back to my flat and make myself a cup of tea. When I've calmed down a bit I'll have to start looking for something else to earn a crust.'

Janice put her elbows on her desk. 'I shall miss you, Lucy.'

'I'll miss you too, Janice.' But she said it without enthusiasm. She gathered the rest of her things into her bag and left without a backward glance.

It was strange, riding her bike across the square in the middle of the afternoon when everybody else was at work and there were only a few housewives and mothers with small children about. She felt a bit peculiar, slightly disoriented and still trembling a little from her altercation with Bernard Foster.

Ben's van was outside the antique shop and he was talking to his father on the pavement, so there was no chance of slipping up to her flat without speaking.

'Well, I can't manage it on my own,' Ben was saying. He turned when he saw Lucy dismounting from her bike. 'Hullo, Lucy, have you got the day off?' he said in surprise.

Before she could answer Alec looked up at

her and frowned. 'What's up? Aren't you well, dearie? You're looking a bit peaky,' he said.

She managed a shaky smile. 'No, I'm not ill. But to tell you the truth I am feeling a bit odd. You see, I've just walked out on my boss because he tried to make a pass at me and it's left me feeling a bit ... well, a bit funny, really.' She gave a sniff, realizing suddenly that she was very near to tears, which was strange, since she had no regrets at parting company with Bernard Foster.

'I reckon what you need is a nice cup of tea,' Alec said gently, giving her a fatherly pat on the shoulder that was quite the opposite of the way her ex-boss had tried to paw her.

'Yes, and we've got a pot just brewing in the office. So why don't you join us?' Ben said, trying to make amends for the fact that he hadn't noticed her distress. 'I'm afraid the mugs are a bit thick and agricultural but as long as you don't mind that...'

'Not a bit, as long as it's not the tea that's thick and agricultural,' she said with a shaky attempt at a laugh.

'No, it's good old PG Tips.'

She followed them through the shop to the office at the back. It was hardly big enough to hold the roll-top desk and chair, let alone the heaps of paper, account books and catalogues that appeared to cover practically every surface. An ancient typewriter stood on a shelf beside the desk but it was so dusty it didn't look as if it was often used.

'Sorry about the mess,' Ben said, fetching her an elegant Victorian chair from the shop and jamming it into a corner. 'It's not always like this.'

'Yes, it is,' Alec contradicted him, handing her a mug of tea.

'Well, all right then. Yes, it is,' Ben agreed, looking a little sheepish.

'It's nice and cosy,' Lucy said, sipping the deliciously scalding tea as they bickered gently between themselves. It wasn't long before she found herself telling them not only what had happened that afternoon but also of the harassment she had suffered ever since she had worked at Payne and Foster's. She felt no embarrassment as it all spilled out; she was simply relieved at being able to talk about it to these two friends who she knew cared about her well-being.

'I'm not surprised,' Alec said when she had finished. 'Old man Foster was just as bad. Had a terrible reputation with the women. Obviously his son takes after him. You're well out of it, my dear.'

'But now you've got to find yourself another job,' Ben said when she had finished.

She nodded. 'I'll start looking.' She yawned and got to her feet. 'But not till tomorrow. I've had more than enough for one day.' She smiled at them both. 'Thank you for letting me share your tea break and listening to my troubles. I feel a lot better now.'

'Good.' Alec took off his apron. 'And we

must be...' He cleared his throat and said tentatively, 'Um ... I suppose you wouldn't like to sit in the shop for half an hour while I go with Ben to pick up some furniture, Lucy? We usually have to shut if we both have to go but as you're here...'

'Oh, come on, Dad!' Ben said, clearly embarrassed. 'That's not fair. Lucy's just said she's had enough for one day.'

'No, really, it's all right, Ben.' Her smile widened. 'After all, you've listened to all my troubles and plied me with tea so the least I can do in return is mind the shop for a while. But what happens if customers come in?'

Ben spent a few minutes showing her the pricing system, then gave her a pile of *Antique Dealer and Collectors Guides* to look through, assuring her that things were very quiet and it was unlikely she would be called on to make a sale. After they had gone she explored the shop. There was one large showroom on the ground floor and three smaller, open-sided rooms upstairs. Each room appeared to be set out with furniture of a different period: in one room the furniture was made of oak like her own bureau; in another it was pine, and included a small four-poster bed; a third, practically empty because of the coming fair, was reserved for walnut pieces. Downstairs most things were labelled mahogany. Pretty china was set out to advantage and she spent a happy time finding objects in the shop that matched some of the pictures in the magazines.

Then the shop bell jangled and she went forward with her heart in her mouth to deal with her first customer, an elderly lady in a felt hat looking for a present for her niece. She went away very happy with a small Wedgwood jug which Lucy had pointed out to her with confidence after sneaking a quick look at the labelled price tag.

It hardly seemed any time before the van arrived back at the shop.

'Sorry we were such a long time,' Ben said when they returned with an enormous wardrobe. 'But Dad had to take it apart before we could get it down the stairs.'

'Have you been gone long, then?' Lucy asked in surprise. Looking at her watch, she saw they had left nearly two hours ago. 'I was quite enjoying myself. I didn't realize how the time had gone. You've got some lovely things here.'

'Mm, but a lot of the really nice stuff is in the back room, ready to be taken to the fair,' Alec said.

'Well, it still looks good.' She picked up her bag and prepared to leave.

'Are you free on Sunday?' Ben called as she went towards the door.

She looked back and grinned. 'I'm free all the time, now,' she said, spreading her hands. 'Until I find another job, that is.'

'Good. Then I'll ring the vicar at Crawfordness and see if we can pay your grandmother a visit.'

'Oh.' She hesitated. 'Well, yes, OK. If you're

sure you can spare the time.'

'You're the one who doesn't sound very sure. Getting cold feet?'

She ran her tongue round her lips. 'I just wonder what she's like, that's all. She may not want to see me.'

'In that case she'll tell the vicar and we won't go. But I'm pretty sure she won't do that.' He patted her arm. 'Don't worry. With any luck you'll only have to wait another five days to find out what she's like,' he said cheerfully.

Lucy dressed very carefully for her visit to her grandmother. It was a sign of her apprehension that she changed her outfit three times before she was satisfied. In the end she wore a green tailored skirt and a cream frilly blouse, with a boxy jacket in green check. A glance in the mirror satisfied her that she looked confident and at ease even if she didn't feel it.

She was waiting on the pavement when Ben drew up. She put the large bunch of autumn flowers she had bought from the market on the back seat and got in beside him.

'Still nervous?' he asked, smiling at her.

She nodded. 'A bit.'

'Well, if it's any consolation, you don't look it.' He let in the clutch. 'Have you brought the photographs?'

'Photographs? No.' She looked at him in surprise. 'Why? Do you think I should?'

'Wouldn't hurt. Better to take them and not need them than the other way round.'

'Yes, I suppose so. But I can't believe...' She

70

saw the expression on his face and opened the car door. 'I'll go and get them.'

Five minutes later, the photographs safely in her handbag, she climbed a little breathlessly back into the car.

They drove out of the town, through little villages and past fields of golden stubble behind hedgerows dotted with red berries and leaves that were just beginning to turn from green to yellow and russet. Then on, past heathland purple with heather, a golf course and an occasional spinney bright with autumn colours. Now and then a car passed them going in the other direction and they saw the odd horse and cart, but for the most part they had the road to themselves.

But Lucy hardly noticed as she was too busy wondering what sort of reception she would get from her grandmother.

'Have you found yourself a new job yet?'

Ben's voice, cutting across her thoughts, made her jump. 'Pardon? Oh, no, not yet. To be honest I haven't really started, apart from looking at the jobs advertised in the weekly paper.'

'Well, think about this, then. It'll take your mind off worrying about your grandmother.'

'I wasn't worrying...' she began.

'Oh, yes, you were. I could see by the way you can't keep your hands still. Now, where was I? Oh, yes. Dad and I have been talking. We've thought for some time that we could do with someone to mind the shop and do a bit of clerical work for us – well, you saw the state of the office – but we've never got round to actually doing anything about it. Now the answer seems to have dropped into our laps – metaphorically speaking, that is. Would you like the job?' He gave her a quick, smiling glance.

'Me?' Her eyebrows shot up in surprise. 'But I don't know the first thing about antiques.'

'You'll learn. And the way you were going round the shop with those *Antique Dealer and Collectors Guides* you're obviously interested. Presumably the clerical side wouldn't be a problem?'

'Oh, no, that's no problem.' She was quiet for a moment. 'Yes, I think I might like that. I'd like to try it, anyway. Thank you, Ben.'

'Don't you want a little time to think about it?'

'Why would I want to do that? I'm looking for a job and you're offering me one. I don't need to think about it.'

'Good. We'll discuss salary and hours when you come in tomorrow morning. Can you start tomorrow?'

She burst out laughing. 'You don't waste any time, do you?'

'No. Can't afford to. We're too busy getting ready for the London fair. Look, we're here.' He pulled up outside a small bungalow. Lucy realized she had been so busy thinking over his words that she hadn't even noticed that they had arrived at the village, let alone reached their destination, a neat little bungalow at the end of a fairly new estate.

'I think this must be the one,' he said as he got out of the car. 'Yes, this is it, number six. The vicar said it was right at the end of the road.' As he waited for Lucy to alight he stood looking towards the huge expanse of the North Sea.

She went and stood beside him. 'Oh, listen, you can hear the sound of the waves on the shore,' she said.

'Well, it's just across the field and over the dunes.' He took her arm and looked down at her. 'Are you ready?'

She nodded. 'I think so. I wonder...'

'You won't need to wonder in a minute, because you'll know,' he said, gently propelling her up a garden path between neat lawns and borders bright with autumn flowers.

Six

The door opened almost before they had time to ring the bell; clearly their arrival hadn't gone unnoticed.

Lucy's first impression of her grandmother as she stood at the door was of a slim, still attractive-looking woman of about sixty. She was of medium height and her hair was a faded chestnut colour, now liberally streaked with

grey, which waved softly back from her forehead into a thick French pleat. Like Lucy, she
had dressed carefully, anxious to look smart but
not too formal, and was wearing a well-fitting
dress of crushed strawberry colour with a flared
skirt, softly draped neckline and three-quarter
length sleeves; plain black high-heeled shoes
completed the picture.

For a moment she just stood looking at Lucy,
her brown eyes sparkling with a mixture of
pleasure and apprehension and a hint of tears.
This was quite obviously an important occasion
for her, too.

Then she stepped forward and held out both
hands.

'Lucy?' she said, her voice rising on the question, as if she couldn't believe her eyes. 'Is it
really you? After all this time ... But, yes, I can
see ... you're so like ... Oh, my dear, I can't tell
you how pleased I am to see you at last. And
what a lovely girl you've grown into.'

Lucy went forward to kiss her and received a
faint waft of lavender that reached back into the
dim recesses of her mind with a sudden warm,
comforting feeling that surprised her. 'Oh, it's
wonderful to have found you, Granny,' she said,
hugging her.

'And this is your young man?' Still holding
Lucy by the hand, Alice turned to Ben, who was
standing a little to one side, watching.

'Oh, no,' Lucy answered, a shade too quickly.
'This is Ben. He's just a friend. He discovered
your address from the vague details Mummy

74

gave me when I wrote and asked her where you lived. All she could remember was that it was Crawford-something or other, so he thought it might be Crawfordness, came here and made enquiries, discovered he was right and' – she spread her hands – 'here we are.'

Alice smiled at him. 'Then I can't thank you enough, Ben,' she said warmly. 'You'll never know how often I've dreamt of this day.' She shook her head disbelievingly. 'And now my dream has come true.'

She took the flowers Lucy handed to her. 'Carnations! At this time of year! Oh, thank you, my dear.' She buried her head in their fragrance. Suddenly, she looked up. 'Oh, goodness, what am I thinking of, keeping you standing on the doorstep. Please, do come in. I've already put the kettle on and it will have boiled by the time I've put these beautiful flowers in water.'

She led the way along an immaculate parquet-floored hallway with several doors leading off it into a large, airy room with French windows that overlooked the sea. The room was very comfortably furnished; the three-piece suite had predominantly rust-coloured loose covers and ruched green scatter cushions, there was a television in one corner by the fireplace and in the other stood a dark oak, heavily carved book-case, crammed with books. A quite expensive-looking, pre-war dining-room suite, comprising a bulbous-legged draw-leaf table with four chairs, also in dark oak, stood against the wall

75

opposite the French windows and two cut-glass bowls and a clock with Westminster chimes that struck every quarter hour stood on the matching sideboard. A green Persian-style carpet covered most of the room and there were stained boards round the edges where the carpet didn't reach. On the mantelpiece, under which a fire was laid but not lit, there were several pieces of china; two matching Staffordshire dogs stood guard, one at each end, and between them a few odd pieces that had obviously been picked up at random because they matched neither the dogs nor each other. A single-bar electric fire stood in the hearth. A couple of cheap landscapes hung on the walls either side of an oak-framed mirror but there were no photographs as far as Lucy could see. The room was comfortable, very neat and well polished, but it had the air of being furnished by someone without money to spare on unnecessary trappings.

As they ate wafer-thin sandwiches and melt-in-the-mouth scones, Lucy tried to find something in her newly discovered grandmother that she could remember from her childhood: a mannerism, an inflection in her voice, an expression on her face, perhaps. But apart from that fleeting, warm feeling at the scent of lavender, there was nothing. She was looking at a perfect stranger. Yet, she was sure she could sense an affinity with the older woman; although her common sense told her this was probably only wishful thinking.

'I had hoped I might recognize you,' she

admitted as she accepted a second cup of tea. 'But...'

'No, of course you couldn't,' Alice replied, smiling and shaking her head. 'You wouldn't remember me at all. You were only three when ... when I left.' She shook her head. 'Eighteen years is a long time. A lot has happened. I've changed; you've grown up – into a lovely girl.' She put her head on one side. 'But most of your curls have gone, Lucy.'

'Oh, did I used to have curly hair?'

She smiled. 'Yes, but I suppose it was only because I used to curl it round my fingers every time I washed it.' She gave her head a little shake and changed the subject. 'Margaret ... your mother, is she well?'

'Yes, she's very well. She recently remarried and she and her new husband have gone to live in Australia,' Lucy told her.

'Only recently? You surprise me,' Alice said drily. 'As I recall she was never a girl to be without an escort for long. Didn't they ask you to go to Australia with them?'

'Yes, but shall we say my refusal was more sincere than their invitation,' Lucy said with a smile. 'I really didn't want to trail round Australia behind a couple of middle-aged love-birds. Although, come to think of it, I believe Harold would have been quite happy for me to go with them.'

'But not Margaret?'

'My mother always preferred my room to my company,' Lucy said honestly.

A look of pain crossed Alice's features briefly but she made no comment. Lucy shot her a questioning glance, afraid she had said something out of place; afraid it had been a mistake to even hint at a criticism, even if what she had said was no more than the truth. But her grandmother's expression was once again serene as she dispensed home-made shortbread. As they reverted to talking generalities Lucy wondered if she had imagined it.

'Have you lived in Crawfordness long, Mrs Clayton?' Ben asked, declining a third piece of shortbread.

'Let me see, about fourteen years, I think. I came here when these bungalows were first built, two years or so after the war ended.'

'What made you choose Crawfordness, Granny?' Lucy asked.

Alice shrugged. 'Pure chance. My friend was looking for somewhere to retire to and I decided to come with her. And these bungalows were being built, so this is where we came.'

'Where is your friend now?'

'Dead. She's been dead, oh, over two years now. I still miss her. She used to live in the bungalow opposite, because we decided it would be nice to live near each other when we left Norwich but we didn't want to live together. It worked very well.'

There were a few minutes of comfortable silence. Then Ben said, 'You mustn't forget to show your grandmother the photographs, Lucy.'

Alice's face lit up. 'Photographs of Margaret's wedding? Oh, yes, I should very much like to see them. I'm making a wedding dress for the vicar's daughter at the moment, so I'll be very interested.'

'No, they're not wedding photographs. I'm not even sure there were any taken,' Lucy said apologetically. 'And if there were I didn't see them because they rushed straight off to catch the boat.' She rummaged in her bag and brought out the two photographs. 'These are the ones Ben meant. I don't suppose you know anything about these people. Or this house, do you?'

A delighted smile spread across Alice's face. 'Oh, yes. Yes. Of course I do! They're my photographs! I was really upset because I thought they must have been thrown away. How on earth did you come across them?'

Lucy smiled at Alice's obvious delight. 'Ben's dad found them. They were hidden in a secret drawer in my bureau. They must have been there for years.'

'*Your* bureau? You mean you've got my old bureau? Oh, Lucy, I'm so pleased you've got it,' she said excitedly, adding almost as an after-thought as she looked down at the photographs, 'I quite thought Margaret would have sold it, since it had belonged to me. She must have forgotten it was there.'

'Quite possibly. It was tucked away in a corner of one of the spare bedrooms. But I often used to play with it when I was home. I called it my office. Now I've got it in my flat.'

'Oh, that's good. I'm so glad.' She shook her

head as she held up the photographs. 'Goodness, just imagine, these pictures must have been lying there all those years, ever since I put them in that secret place.' She sighed. 'I was very upset when I realized I had forgotten to bring them with me when I left. But everything happened so quickly at the end ... there was no time.' She gave a sigh.

Lucy leaned forward. 'Why? What happened, Granny?'

'Your mother and I had a disagreement,' Alice said briefly. She turned back to the photographs, swiftly changing the subject. 'Oh, I can't tell you how pleased I am that these have come to light again after all these years.'

'So you know who these girls are? Or were?' Lucy asked, taking the hint.

Alice smiled. 'Oh, yes. I knew them all. Very well indeed.'

Lucy leaned forward. 'And the house? You recognize the house? Ben has taken me there, it's where Lady Bucknell, one of his clients, lives. She's got a large framed version of this picture,' she said excitedly.

'Lady Bucknell is still alive? Goodness, she must be well over eighty by now,' Alice said, looking up in surprise from the photographs she was still studying.

Lucy put her head on one side and said hesitantly, 'People say one of the girls, that one, there, looks very much like me. Is that possible?'

Alice glanced at her and then at the photograph again. She nodded. 'Yes, there's a definite likeness to Miss Vonny. It's the first thing that struck me when I saw you.' She spoke without surprise.

'But that's impossible. I'm not related to these people. I don't know them from Adam and my mother certainly never spoke of them. As far as I know she didn't even know they existed.'

Alice frowned. 'No, I don't think she did,' she said thoughtfully. 'I don't believe I ever told her.'

'Told her what?' Lucy's tone was a mixture of curiosity and impatience. Ben shot her a warning glance and put his hand on her arm to calm her.

But Alice didn't appear to have noticed. 'Anything,' she said with a shrug. She spread her hands. 'Everything. Well, there was no point, really, since they were all dead.'

Lucy was impatient to know what her grandmother was talking about, but Ben's warning hand was still on her arm so she curbed her impatience and took a deep breath. 'Do you think perhaps you might tell me, Granny?' she asked carefully.

Alice smiled at her. 'Oh, yes, dear, of course I will. Now that I've found you, or rather, now that you've found me, I think it's only right that you should know the whole story. I've started to write it all down so that I shouldn't forget any of it and so that...' She hesitated. 'So that you would understand that even if what I did was wrong it was what I thought was for the best.'

She paused, then went on. 'I've been busy going over everything in my mind ever since the vicar came that day...'

'What did he say when he came, Granny?' Lucy asked.

Alice smiled again. 'He told me a young man had visited him with a fairly implausible story about my long-lost granddaughter. But since the vicar wasn't aware that I had any family he'd quite rightly refused to let him come to see me until he'd checked with me. When I asked if the long-lost granddaughter was called Lucy, he looked quite astonished and said she was. After that, as you can imagine, I couldn't wait for him to get in touch with you again to arrange a visit.'

Lucy spread her hands. 'And here we are.'

'Yes, my prayers have at last been answered and here you are,' Alice said quietly. Her mood changed and she went on, her voice brisk, 'As I said, I've been going over everything in my mind and so that I should get things in the right order I've started to write it all down. In any case, it's better that you should read it than that I should try to tell you because it's quite a long story.'

'Gosh, that must have taken some time,' Lucy said, full of admiration.

'Oh, gracious me, it's not finished yet, although I might tell you it's already kept me burning the midnight oil on a good many nights!' Alice said. 'But it's good for me to set it all down. It's ... what's the word? ... therapeutic. It's clearing my mind and putting everything in ... well, in perspective.' She got to her feet. 'I'll go and get it now.'

It must have been right to hand because Lucy and Ben had hardly time to exchange puzzled glances before she was back, with two large loose-leaf exercise books in her hand. 'I hope you'll be able to read my spidery writing,' she said apologetically. 'I'm not used to writing at quite such length and my Biro kept clogging up. They do, don't they?' She looked at the books in her hand. 'This is only part of it; I've still got a lot more to write.' She saw a look of consternation cross Lucy's face. 'Oh, I don't want you to read it right now, dear,' she assured her. 'I want you to take it home and read it. When you've got time. There's no hurry.' She handed her the two exercise books.

'But what about the rest of the story?' Lucy asked eagerly. 'You said it wasn't all here.'

Alice smiled. 'Don't worry. I'll send it to you when I've done it, if you leave me your address.'

'So it's just a case of being patient and waiting for next week's thrilling instalment,' Ben said with a laugh.

'Yes, I'm afraid it is just a case of waiting,' Alice replied, laughing with him. 'But I'll leave you to decide just how thrilling it is.' She became serious and twisted her hands together in a nervous gesture. 'I hope you won't think I'm being silly but I don't want you to come back until you've read the whole story, Lucy.

When you've finished it, if you feel like coming back to see me again I shall be only too delighted.' She added quietly, 'But if you never want to see me again, believe me, I shall quite understand.'

'Whatever do you mean, Granny?' Lucy asked, puzzled.

Alice laid a hand on her arm. 'You'll know exactly what I mean when you've read my story.'

'That was a strange thing to say, wasn't it, Ben?' Lucy said, on their way home. 'Why do you think she doesn't want to see me again until I've read the whole story?'

'I think maybe she's afraid of getting to know you again and then losing you when you've read it,' he said thoughtfully. 'But why she should think you might turn against her when you know her history I can't begin to imagine.'

'Perhaps it's got something to do with the quarrel she had with Mummy,' Lucy speculated.

'Maybe,' he said. 'No doubt you'll find out when you start to read those.' He nodded towards the exercise books she was holding carefully on her lap. 'And I hope you'll tell me.'

'I've got a better idea. Why don't you set the neighbours talking by coming and having supper with me when we get back? Then you can read them for yourself.'

He glanced at her and grinned. 'Oh, la, miss, you'll ruin my reputation.'

84

'Mine too. Can't you hear the gossip? "What's a young woman living on her own doing entertaining a man in her flat?" So if you see lace curtains twitching when you leave you'll just have to pretend you were working late in the shop.'

'That won't be difficult, I often do.'

They both kept stealing speculative glances at the two notebooks that lay on Lucy's settee as they ate the omelettes she had cooked, and washed them down with the wine Ben had been to buy from the off-licence. When they had finished and stacked the dishes in the sink, Lucy made some coffee and they settled down and began to read what Alice had written in her neat, round handwriting.

Seven

I suppose the right place to start is at the beginning; that's where most good stories start, although there's little that's good about this story. Except you, Lucy. Except you, my dear. But I'll come to that later.

I was born Alice May Clayton on July 12th, 1898. My mother died when I was born and my father soon after, either of a fever or a broken heart, I was never sure which. Either way I was left an orphan. But not an orphan in the usual, miserable, deprived and abandoned sense. Quite the opposite, in fact.

I had a very happy childhood because I was taken to live with Aunt Maud, my father's sister. She was a lovely lady, who since she was unmarried, and therefore had no children of her own, showered me with affection. Not that Aunt Maud was rich, we lived in a tiny cottage in the village of Rookhurst and she made a living as best she could with her needle. Indeed, she was a fine needlewoman and she tried to teach me to sew and she even let me use her sewing machine, which was her pride and joy. But although I tried very hard to learn I was never as skilled as she was because I didn't have her patience.

She also made sure that I was educated, insofar as the village school was capable of educating. When I left, the Christmas before my fourteenth birthday, I could read and write tolerably well and had a reasonable grasp of arithmetic.

At the time, it seemed to me that my schooling was ended rather prematurely – I liked school and enjoyed learning and was expecting to stay on at least until my fourteenth birthday and perhaps to become a pupil teacher after that, so I was disappointed when Aunt Maud told me I was to leave because she had found me a position as kitchen maid up at 'the Hall'. This was Rookhurst Hall, a large estate on the edge of the village where Sir George and Lady

Bucknell lived.

I didn't want to go. I didn't want to leave school and I said so. But she pointed out what I already knew, that any position at the Hall was coveted in the village so I was lucky to be taken on, even at the expense of my schooling. No doubt her years of making dresses for the three Bucknell girls had helped in securing me a place there.

Of course I was not unfamiliar with the Hall. Ever since I could remember I had often gone there with Aunt Maud to fit one or other of the girls for a new dress. Sometimes she would even bring one of their cast-offs home and make it over for me. While she was occupied I would sit in the big, busy kitchen being fed bread and jam or morning buns by Mrs Platt, the cook, or I would wander in the beautifully laid-out gardens, being careful not to incur the wrath of one of the gardeners by walking on the grass. But the thing that always stuck in my mind was the long walk up the wide, tree-lined drive and coming out on to a circular, smooth-as-velvet lawn bordered by flower beds – and the large stone fountain that had water coming out of the mouth of a stone lion sitting on its haunches in the middle of the bowl. I thought that was magical. I didn't know at the time that people like us were supposed to go up the back drive to get to the tradesman's entrance. Dear Aunt Maud only took the risk of using the front drive and then skirting the house to reach the back door because I wanted to see the lion.

When I began work at the Hall I was quite unaware that Aunt Maud was mortally ill. It was only at her death, some three months later, that I understood that this was the reason I had been taken away from school early. It was then that I discovered she had been anxious to make sure I was settled in employment before she died from an illness she had been careful to hide from me. To my shame I had been so full of resentment at my schooling being ended that I had never even noticed how thin she had become.

Under Aunt Maud's care I had grown into a reasonably attractive girl, with large brown eyes, a ready smile and a good complexion. But what she always called my 'crowning glory' was my hair, which was long and thick and the colour of ripe chestnuts. I was given a uniform to wear, a blue striped dress which reached my ankles, making me feel very grown-up, and large white apron and cap. The only thing I minded was the cap. I had to make sure it covered my beautiful hair, with not a wisp showing, in case a single stray strand should find its way into the food I helped to prepare.

Nevertheless, I was happy at the Hall. I had plenty to eat and a comfortable bed and the other servants were friendly enough, although I had to be careful not to get on the wrong side of Arthur, the butler, who was very conscious of his position as head of the men servants. There seemed to be an army of servants, both 'indoor' and 'outdoor' staff, and it took me a long time to get to know the names of all of them. Of course I missed Aunt Maud, but everything was so new and there was so much to learn that I had very little time to grieve for her.

Except, that is, on my afternoons off. The other servants had places to go in their free time, parents or other relatives to visit or, in the case of some of the younger men, a trip to the Bucknell Arms in the village. I had nobody in the world now that Aunt Maud was dead, the other servants at the Hall became my only family and belatedly I realized how wise Aunt Maud had been to secure me a place there. In my free time I would walk through the fields to the woods and sit by the stream if the weather was suitable, or put a muffler round my throat and walk for miles round the estate if it wasn't. As I walked, with tears streaming down my face, I would talk to Aunt Maud in my mind, thanking her for her love and care and telling her all that had happened in the past week. But gradually, as my new life at the Hall took over I let her go. But I have always retained fond memories of dear Aunt Maud. She has been a great influence on my life.

Oh, I haven't told you about The Family (I always thought of them in capital letters). There was Sir George Bucknell, who owned the estate and was treated more or less as the squire in the village, and Lady Bucknell, his wife. She was a gracious lady; tall, elegant and very quietly spoken, although she could be very sharp if things displeased her. In contrast, Sir George was a large, red-faced man with untidy whiskers and a booming voice, which you could hear all over the house. He could be very bad-tempered if he was crossed. Sir George and M'Lady had five children. Giles, who was seventeen when I first went to work at the Hall, then three girls, twins Vera and Veronica – Vonny for short – who at fifteen were very alike but not identical, and were rarely seen apart, and Eliza, usually known as Lizzie, a few months younger than me. Lizzie was always a bit wild. It seemed to me that this was her way of making sure she was not overlooked in the wake of the twins. After them came Peregrine, who was nine, a rather spoiled brat, the apple of his mother's eye.

Being the kitchen maid I had very little to do with The Family, except if I was called on to provide an extra pair of hands waiting on table when they had a dinner party or to help carry and serve the picnic at shooting parties. I quite enjoyed that although I didn't like seeing all the dead birds and animals lined up.

It was during my first summer at the Hall that I came to know Master Giles a little. I knew from kitchen gossip that he was rather a quiet boy, more interested in books than sport, much to his father's disgust. Sir George was never happier than when he was astride a horse, or shooting at some poor innocent creature, which didn't interest Giles in the slightest. But he was at boarding school, so he wasn't there much, only during school holidays, which was when I first met him.

When the weather was good what I liked to do most on my afternoons off was to sit by the stream in the little wood at the edge of the estate and let my hair down. I had always been used to wearing it loosely tied back with a ribbon and I hated having to plait it and screw it up under my cap every day, it felt all wrong and uncomfortable. So it was a real luxury to unpin it and let it fall loose over my shoulders and I would often take my hairbrush with me and give it the hundred strokes Aunt Maud had always insisted on every night. Since working at the Hall I never had time to give it more than a perfunctory few strokes to get the tangles out in the mornings because I had to be up to take the early morning tea to Sir George and M'Lady and to help Cook with the breakfasts. And after a day spent on my feet I was always too tired for hair brushing at night. So this was the only chance I had to do it.

One afternoon in late spring I was sitting in my favourite spot. It was under an old oak tree at the top of a grassy bank, where I could hear the stream murmuring gently over the pebbles not far away and the last few primroses were showing spots of bright yellow in the grass. I had finished brushing my hair and had tied it back with a green ribbon so that it didn't get in the way of the book I was reading – of course I would have to plait it and screw it up under my cap again before I went back to the Hall – when I heard a twig crack. I looked up guiltily. Not that I was doing anything wrong, the servants were allowed to walk where they liked in the grounds in their free time if they wanted to. Of course not many chose to because they all had families to go back to. And nobody ever came to this isolated spot, which was why I had chosen it.

'Oh, you're real! I thought for a moment it was a mermaid sitting and sunning herself on the banks of the stream.' Master Giles, still at home from school on his Easter holidays, was coming through the trees towards me wearing a white open-necked shirt and flannel trousers. At seventeen he was tall and athletic-looking, his face tanned through hours of tennis. I thought he looked incredibly handsome with his deep blue eyes, and quirky smile.

I scrambled to my feet, tossed back my hair and smoothed down my skirt, glad that I was wearing my favourite – made by Aunt Maud, needless to say – a dark green serge with three rows of darker braid round the hem. 'I wasn't doing any harm, Master Giles,'I said anxiously. 'It's my afternoon off and I was just sitting here reading my book.'

He came over to me and as I took a step back I registered that he was well over half a head taller than me. He smiled again and I noticed that one of his front teeth was slightly crooked.

'It's perfectly all right. I wasn't for a moment suggesting you might be,' he remarked. 'I just didn't expect to see one of our servants sitting by the stream with her head in a book.' He looked at me more closely. 'You *are* one of our servants, aren't you? It's difficult to recognize you with all that lovely hair hanging down your back. Where on earth do you manage to put it when you're at work?'

'I twist it up under my cap, of course, Master Giles.' I couldn't help smiling back at him.

'Oh, what a pity to have to hide it.' He craned his neck a little. 'And what are you reading, little mermaid sitting by her stream?'

'*Jane Eyre*, sir. My late aunt gave it to me as a present when I first came here. I've already read it twice.'

'You like reading?'

I nodded. 'Very much.'

'Then you must come to the library and take whatever book takes your fancy to read. You might find something you like even better than *Jane Eyre*.'

'Oh, I could never...' I began shaking my head.

He held up his hand. 'Of course you can. I'll tell my father I've given you permission. Not that he'll mind, I've never in my whole life seen him pick up a book. Oh, by the way, what's your name?'

'Alice, sir.'

He grinned delightedly. 'It gets better and better.' He leaned forward and before I realized what he was doing he whisked the green ribbon away so that my hair tumbled forward over my shoulders. 'Alice in Wonderland. Yes, you're just like her.' He put his head on one side. 'And

93

I wonder who I am. The white rabbit, do you think? Or the dormouse?'

'The Mad Hatter, I should think,' I said rashly, joining in his game. 'First you imagine I'm a mermaid, then Alice in Wonderland. Whatever next, I wonder? Sir.' I added as an afterthought.

He didn't seem to notice my lack of deference. 'We should have a tea party,' he announced, brushing his fair hair back from his forehead in what I was to learn was a characteristic gesture. 'If you're Alice and I'm the Mad Hatter we simply must have a tea party. Don't you agree? Shall we have a tea party?'

'Oh, I don't know about that, sir. I don't think it would be at all proper. After all, you're the young master and I'm only a kitchen maid.'

'You're not *only* anything, you're Alice in Wonderland and if I invite you to join me in a Mad Hatter's tea party will you accept my invitation?'

I dropped a curtsey and smiled. 'I should be delighted, sir,' I said, knowing full well that nothing would ever come of it.

'Good. A tea party it shall be,' he said firmly.

'Oh, goodness!' I looked at the little fob watch I was wearing, a treasured possession inherited from Aunt Maud. 'That's reminded me, I promised I'd go back and help Cook with afternoon tea. I shall be late if I don't hurry.'

He brushed his hair back. 'But I thought you said it was your afternoon off?'

'It is. But Cook's busy with tonight's dinner party so I said I'd go back and help with afternoon tea.'

'Oh, yes, the dratted dinner party, where I'll have to be pleasant to people I don't know and wouldn't like if I did.' He rolled his eyes. 'But never mind that. Next week then. Will you be here next week at this time?' He was quite persistent.

'I come here most weeks on my afternoon off, if it isn't raining,' I told him, gathering my things together.

'Then I shall bring us a picnic. Make sure you're here, Alice.' He raised his hand and called after me as I hurried away. 'Don't forget.'

As if I would! Does anybody ever forget the time and place where they first fell in love?

Eight

I had to smile to myself. On my next afternoon off Cook was grumbling because Master Giles had asked her to make him up a picnic, of all things.

'Whatever next, I should like to know. I wonder where he's going? But that's what he says he wants so that's what he must have,' she said with a sigh. 'Can you just make up a basket for him before you go off, Alice? I want to put my feet up for five minutes.'

I didn't mind. I smiled to myself as I put in the things I liked best, sausage rolls, ham patties and chocolate cake, and things that I guessed would appeal to him, too, and left the basket on the hall table for him to pick up.

I was waiting under the oak tree when he came through the wood, swinging the basket, and he laughed when I told him I had packed it myself.

'Oh, you've chosen all the things I like, Alice,' he said as we laid everything out on the red checked cloth.

'I chose the things I liked, too,' I said shyly.

'Then we're obviously compatible, Alice,' he said, reaching for a cheese scone. 'Because we like the same things.'

I thought I knew what compatible meant but I wasn't quite sure so I went and looked it up in the dictionary in the library later. When I read 'capable of existing together' I felt a warm glow spread right through me.

After that, we met by the stream almost every week on my afternoons off until his holidays ended and he had to go back to school again. Sometimes he brought a picnic – I always knew when he was going to do that because it was usually me that packed it – sometimes he brought me a book he thought I would like, sometimes we just sat and talked.

It was all very innocent. He asked me about my upbringing with Aunt Maud and I told him how kind and loving she had always been to me and how I had often come to the Hall with her when she made the girls' dresses. I told him how I had always regretted my sketchy schooling but when we compared it to his boarding school, which was a cruel sounding place where the teachers thought the best way to make a boy learn was to beat him, I realized that perhaps I hadn't been so badly off.

'Fortunately, I learn very quickly so I escape the worst of it,' was all he would say when I tried to question him further. I got the impression that he had never had much love in his life, he admitted his father discouraged any show of affection and couldn't wait to pack him off to school, although I knew he was very fond of his mother.

In the summer we walked through the wood and he taught me the names of all the flowers and butterflies. Occasionally, when it was very hot, we even paddled in the cool, clear water of the stream. I knew that it was wrong to meet like this and that if we were caught he would be severely reprimanded and I would be instantly dismissed. Yet I couldn't help myself, I was always there, in the same spot – *our* spot – when he arrived, as he invariably did. He seemed somehow lonely, despite the tennis parties and croquet tournaments that were often arranged in the summer, and I felt privileged that he sought my company.

It was, as I said, all very innocent. After I had plucked up the courage to choose books from his father's library we discovered that we often liked the same authors, Sir Walter Scott, Robert

Louis Stevenson, Charles Kingsley, and we had happy times discussing the merits of one against another. All very erudite for a mere kitchen maid, you might think, but Aunt Maud had always encouraged me to read and to question and Giles was happy to share his superior knowledge with me.

We both knew that Sir George would have raised the roof if he'd known that his son and heir was consorting with the kitchen maid but fortunately for us he never found out.

Of course, it had to end.

When he was eighteen Giles left boarding school and under the Estate Manager's wing began being groomed to run his father's estate. He no longer had free afternoons when he could meet me by the stream and we could talk, although there were times when he happened to be in the part of the wood where I was sitting and reading and we would have a few precious minutes' conversation. Precious to me, at any rate. At the time I didn't dare to think he might have engineered it but I realized later that he had done just that.

By this time I had been promoted from kitchen maid to parlour maid so I often saw him as I was about my work in the house, but of course that was different. He was Master Giles to me then, not the Giles who laughed and teased me by the stream. We were both very careful to preserve the formalities in the house. I made sure I never raised my eyes in his presence and his tone to me was always brisk and businesslike because young Perry, his little brother, was a sneaky little imp, always hiding and spying on people, to the great annoyance of his three sisters, who couldn't wait for him to be packed off to his brother's boarding school. I marvelled that he had never discovered that Giles and I had met so often in the woods.

That makes it sound all very clandestine, but it was not. As I have said, my friendship with Giles was just that, friendship. And if in my silly little heart I dreamed of something more, that's all it was, all I knew it could ever be, a dream. I knew that one day he would marry, he was so handsome with his fair hair and twinkling blue eyes and that funny crooked tooth. I could see how popular he was with friends of his sisters, and the girls who came to tennis parties or dances at the Hall, who all flirted outrageously with him. The twins and Lizzie teased him unmercifully about his conquests and the hearts he had set a-flutter, predicting he would be engaged before he was twenty. Maybe they were right, they probably were, but I tried not to think about it.

Then everything changed. Everything in the world, everything in the country and certainly everything in my life.

I don't suppose many people realized that the assassination of Arch-Duke Franz Ferdinand, heir to the Austro-Hungarian throne, and his wife on that fateful June day in 1914 would have such far-reaching effects. But within a matter of weeks we were at war.

I couldn't understand what it was all about although Arthur pontificated about it at great length over supper every night. I must admit I didn't try very hard because I didn't imagine that it would affect us much. But in that I was totally mistaken, as I found out the day I saw Giles down by the stream and he told me he was going to enlist in the army.

'Don't look so crestfallen, Alice in Wonderland,' he said with a smile – I hesitate to say that was his pet name for me, it seems too presumptuous, but I suppose, on reflection, that's what it was – 'Everyone says it will all be over by Christmas, so I want to join up and do my bit before it's finished. I'd be furious with myself if I found I'd left it too late.'

I bit my lip. 'Will it be very dangerous?'

He took my hand and gave it a little shake. 'Now, now, you're beginning to sound like my mother, Alice. That's all she can think about, will I be in any danger.'

I hung my head. 'I'm sorry, Giles.' I looked up at him and managed to smile. 'I'm sure you'll be very brave and I shall be very proud of you.'

'That's better.' He grinned. 'Just wait till you see me in uniform. It'll knock you out.'

It did, too. He looked so smart in khaki, with his gleaming leather Sam Browne and gaiters, his cap set at just enough of a rake not to cause comment among his superiors, that my heart swelled with pride. And love. But of course that was my secret.

The next thing we heard was that he was in France. It was frustrating, having to wait for news of him to filter through from 'upstairs' and not to appear too eager to hear it when it did. But I could legitimately rejoice with the rest of the staff when we heard he had been promoted to Captain.

'Ah, the war'll soon be over now he's been made Captain. I give it till Christmas,' Thomas, one of the gardeners said, smacking his lips over his beer.

He meant Christmas 1915, Christmas 1914 had long since gone. But it wasn't over by that Christmas, either. It was dragging on and on, getting worse and worse and didn't look like ending.

At the Hall life went on very much as usual, although with fewer men servants in the house. Most of the younger ones had seen the war as an opportunity to escape, to swap the drudgery of life 'downstairs' for a life of adventure, and had gone off full of optimism and hope. Some of them didn't return and those that did were changed for ever. Several of the younger farm workers followed suit and went off in high spirits to enlist. They came back furious, having been told that their work growing food was vitally important, just as important to the war effort as fighting at the Front. But there was no smart uniform for farm workers, no glamour in hoeing turnips. It didn't help when one of them was given a white feather, for cowardice, the next time he went into the nearby town, by a young woman who should have known better. He told me about it, his mouth twisted with bitterness, when I went for a walk with him one Sunday evening. I think he would have liked to think we were 'walking out' with a view to getting married but although he was a nice enough young man and I went out with him several times I couldn't see myself as his wife. Maybe it would have been better if I had.

When the twins had their eighteenth birthday M'Lady decided to send them with Lizzie to Ipswich to have their photograph taken. I was sent with them, oh, not to have my photograph taken, too, but to hold wraps and handbags while they were being posed in the studio. We were all excited, the girls because they were to be photographed by the best photographer in Ipswich, me because I was going for a ride in Sir George's Bentley motor car.

I had never been to Ipswich before, never seen so much traffic, never heard so much noise. The clop of horses' hooves, the rumble of iron-shod cart wheels mingled with the noise of motor cars and the wonderful electric trolley buses that ran attached to overhead wires, which I had heard about but never before seen. And in amongst it all were people risking life and limb on bicycles, weaving their way along to miss the horse droppings and trying to avoid the other traffic.

It was a relief to walk into the photographer's studio where it was quiet. The photographer was a flamboyant man with a silly little beard, fuzzy hair that needed a good trim and a floppy cravat. He took ages to pose the three girls, deciding which should stand and which should sit. Then he had to get the lighting right and then to make sure they were all smiling, that Vonny was standing just so and Vera had her hand in exactly the right place on the back of the chair and that Lizzie had stopped wriggling with excitement before he was satisfied. And all the while I was able to sit there, holding their belongings and watching. I think I was nearly as excited as they were although I got a bit fed up with the photographer's antics. Afterwards the three girls went for afternoon tea at a posh tea shop while I waited in the Bentley with John, the chauffeur. He was a rather pale young man, quite nice looking, with dark brown eyes and a neat moustache. While we waited he spent the time telling me how motor cars worked and how stupid the recruiting office had been for rejecting him when he went to join the army, just because he'd had rickets as a child.

'But I'm as strong as a horse now.' He flexed his biceps to show me. Then he tried to hold my hand. I was glad when the girls came back.

It caused quite a stir when Vera and Vonny announced that they had both volunteered for the Red Cross. M'Lady cried. She said Giles was already fighting at the Front, why did the twins need to put themselves in the way of danger, too? Vonny said they were going nursing, not fighting and Vera pointed out that with zeppelins coming over and dropping bombs all over the place nobody was safe anyway. King's Lynn and Great Yarmouth had already been bombed and who knew where the next one would fall? M'Lady refused to be comforted by that so Sir George told her not to be silly, gave the twins twenty pounds each, patted them on the back and wished them luck.

So they went away to train as nurses and were then sent to work in a hospital on the south coast. Occasionally, one or other of them got leave and came down to the kitchen to give us graphic accounts of the things they had seen as they tended the wounded soldiers coming off the troop ships. The poor girls needed to tell somebody of the horrors they had witnessed but they were forbidden by their father to speak of it in front of M'Lady. They had both grown up and grown thin and Vonny in particular seemed to be living on her nerves.

Although we didn't lose many of the farm workers most of the indoor servants had gone by now, either to enlist in the army or to do war work in the munitions factories where the pay was so much better. I considered doing the same, but foolishly I remembered the words Giles had said to me down by the stream on his last leave, 'I often think of you here, Alice, sitting by the stream with your glorious hair round your shoulders. It helps to keep me sane when things get tough.' I felt, in a funny kind of way, that while I was where he remembered me he would be safe. Ridiculous, I know, but that's how I felt. So although the other young servants had all gone I remained at the Hall, doing three people's work and knitting balaclava helmets and socks whenever I had a spare minute, which wasn't often.

The war dragged on. The farms on the estate were kept busy growing food which was then mostly taken to feed people in the big towns, leaving us just enough for our own needs. Meat was rationed, but this didn't affect us too badly because there were plenty of rabbits and pheasants in the fields so we didn't go short. And neither did the villagers, to which Sir George uncharacteristically turned a blind eye.

Each day we read about the carnage at the battle-front in the newspapers and I worried about Giles. Whenever I had the opportunity I would go down to the stream and recall his words to me, 'Thinking about you here keeps me sane when things get tough.' It was pure superstition on my part, I knew that, but miraculously, his letters kept coming and he even came home once for a few days' leave, which he spent mostly sleeping.

But of course, it couldn't last. In April 1918, on a balmy spring day, just like the day I had first met him, a telegram came to say that Major Bucknell (he'd been promoted yet again due to the death toll among officers) was missing, presumed dead, at Ypres.

Nine

To say that the whole household was distraught at the news that Giles was missing would be an understatement. With the news of the dreadful carnage still taking place in this awful war, four hundred thousand men had been lost in only three weeks, we all realized that these words were only a way of avoiding stating the stark truth – that in all probability his body had never been found because it had been blown to pieces. It was a probability I couldn't bear to contemplate.

M'Lady was distraught and took to her bed for a week, lying in a darkened room, unable to eat, her grief too deep even for tears. Sir George manifested his grief by being even more bad-tempered than usual and taking it out on whoever happened to be near at the time. The servants – or those of us left who remembered Master Giles – reminisced sadly, as people do after a death in the family, talking about the things he used to say, the kindness and consideration he showed to everyone. I kept quiet, my grief was too deep and my memories of Giles were too precious to share with anyone.

But to everyone's amazement, it soon became

evident that it was not so much grief from which Sir George was suffering, it was anger. He was blatantly furious at the loss of the heir he, or to be more precise, Mr Baines, the Estate Manager, had been grooming to take over the estate.

'It's all the fault of this damn war, Baines,' I heard him saying, as I took them in their morning mug of beer. 'Patriotism's all very well, but blood's thicker than water. If Giles hadn't had the damn-fool idea of doin' his bit for King and Country and then goin' an' gettin' himself killed in the process he could have taken over the running of this lot,' he waved his hand vaguely out of the window, 'and I could have retired and put my efforts into huntin' and shootin'. But now it looks as if I shall just have to carry on, in spite of my damned gout. Young Perry's still at boardin' school so he won't be old enough to start to learn the ropes here for another two or three years. It's damned annoying.'

'Yes, it's a great loss to us all. Master Giles was shaping up real well,' the Estate Manager said with genuine sorrow in his voice. 'He'd got a feel for the land and he was always ready to listen to the men and to take on board what they said.' He didn't add 'Unlike his father', but I knew that's what he meant. 'It's a great pity he's gone. Like so many of our young men...'

'Pity? Pity?' Sir George interrupted rudely. 'It's a great deal more than a pity as far as I'm concerned, man. It's a damnable confounded nuisance.'

I didn't hear any more but from the expression on Mr Baines' face I could see he was as shocked as I was at Sir George's callous words. We were both appalled and disgusted that the selfish old man hadn't shown a bit more compassion towards his eldest son, so cruelly cut off in his prime.

But compassion wasn't in Sir George's nature. Not even for his youngest child. It was a real bone of contention between Sir George and his wife that Perry had been packed off to boarding school before his twelfth birthday – 'to make a man of him', according to Sir George, who insisted that his mother spoiled him. I had to admit that this was one instance when I heartily agreed with Sir George, to my mind M'Lady had always been far too indulgent towards Peregrine. But I suppose it was understandable. He was her last-born so it was only natural she would lavish so much affection on him. Heaven knows, Sir George wasn't exactly a lovable man.

A telegraph message was sent to the hospital on the south coast where the twins were both nursing, and as soon as they received the news about their elder brother they managed to get leave and came home briefly in order to comfort their parents. This was something of a lost cause, since M'Lady was inconsolable and Sir George was too bad tempered to even talk about Giles. Their father's reaction shocked the girls, they found his behaviour quite unforgivable and they ended up avoiding him as much as they could. They were both looking tired and gaunt and they slept a lot, so the few days at home did them good even if it didn't help their parents. They had both taken up smoking, too, they said it helped to calm their nerves – which rather shocked their mother and disgusted their father, who thought smoking should be the sole prerogative of men. In his view, women who smoked were 'fast'. Nothing could have been further from the truth as far as Vonny and Vera were concerned.

Cook tried to feed the two girls up with nourishing soups and stews – in spite of all the shortages it was amazing what tasty meals she managed to concoct. Of course, a good deal of the farm produce had to go to feed the outside world and Sir George smugly regarded this as his personal 'War Effort'. Not that he put any effort into it at all.

Just as when they had come home before, what Vonny and Vera needed more than anything was to talk. Being able to recount some of the worst of their experiences in the military hospital where they worked helped to make them more bearable in a funny kind of way. However, Sir George forbade them to even speak of it in the presence of their mother and younger sister 'in case it upset them' and he himself simply wasn't interested. He said he knew perfectly well what was happening without them going on at great length about it. In truth, I suspected he only read as much as he wanted to in the daily newspaper, taking in anything that might affect him personally and glossing over the less savoury aspects.

Because they couldn't talk to their parents and needed to tell somebody, the twins spent a good deal of their time whilst they were at home sitting at the kitchen table, drinking innumerable cups of tea and picking nervously at Cook's morning buns or tea scones while some of the terrible things they had witnessed spilled out. The rest of us, including their young sister, Lizzie, listened in horror as they poured out their sad and terrible stories. Stories of young men – some of them little more than boys – left maimed for life, limbless, blinded, or shell-shocked and mentally scarred for ever by the devastation and horrors they had seen, the mud and rats in the trenches, and the constant barrage of shellfire they had been subjected to.

Lizzie had recently been pestering her parents to let her go and join her sisters, but I noticed that she was turning pale at hearing what the two girls were saying. It wasn't many days before she stopped coming to the kitchen at all. After the girls had gone back she never again mentioned joining them, contenting herself instead with the everlasting khaki knitting and helping with the money-raising events.

Although we thought little about it at the time, one thing the twins said proved ominous. It was on the day before they were due to return to their hospital that Vonny said, almost casually, 'And as if the poor fellows in France haven't got enough to contend with there's some kind of influenza, they call it Spanish 'flu, that seems to be going around in the trenches. Doesn't last long, from what we hear, the doctors have labelled it three-day-fever, but by all accounts it's pretty nasty when you get it.'

Vera nodded as she stubbed out her cigarette and lit another one. 'And it seems to be affecting both sides, from what we can make out. It's as bad for the Germans as it is for our boys. Mind you, you can't wonder at it, the mud and filth they have to exist in. A breeding ground for germs if ever there was one.'

'Perhaps if they all catch it the fighting will stop. That'd be one way of putting an end to this dreadful war.' Vonny stretched her arms above her head and yawned widely. 'Everybody's had enough of it, food shortages, never knowing where the next zeppelin raid will be. It's getting to be almost as bad for people at home as over in France.'

'No, Von, I don't think so,' Vera said quietly. 'From the terrible things we're hearing and seeing nothing could be as bad as that.'

'No, you're quite right, Vee, it was a stupid thing to say.' Vonny lit another cigarette with hands that shook slightly and took a drag. 'Nothing could be as bad as that.'

'Well, all I can say is I hope you two young ladies don't catch this ... what did you call it?' Cook looked from one to the other.

'Spanish 'flu,' they both said together.

'Not that it comes from Spain,' Vera added. 'I believe the Spanish call it French 'flu, but nobody seems to know where it came from in the first place.'

'Well, French or Spanish, wherever it comes from, I hope it stays there.' Cook held up the teapot. 'Another cuppa tea, girls?'

The twins went back to their hospital and we thought no more about it. Life at the Hall returned to what now passed for normal, with everybody doing two people's work and all the indoor staff, except for Cook and me, untrained and under fourteen. As soon as they were old enough, everyone else went off to earn better money in the munitions factories. Arthur, of course, was too old to join up, but wouldn't admit it, instead telling everybody he couldn't go because he had bad feet. Now that Giles was dead I thought about going into a munitions factory myself, but Cook was getting on a bit and I felt she needed my support. Added to that, the Hall was now the only home I knew and I was afraid that if I left it I would never be able to return. And then what would I do? Where would I go? So I stayed. A good thing I did, really, because I was the only one who could persuade Lizzie to lend a hand with some of the lighter tasks.

Well, I didn't see why she should sit around while the rest of us were worked off our feet. But she was a lazy little minx, never around when she was needed most. Often it was quicker to do the job myself than go looking for her.

It was rather strange how often the word influenza began to crop up after the twins had

112

gone. Before they came home it had hardly ever been mentioned – after all, why should it? It wasn't like the scourge of scarlet fever or consumption, the two dreaded diseases that were a constant threat everywhere. But suddenly, influenza was a word that seemed to be on everybody's lips. Everybody knew somebody who knew somebody else who had a member of the family who had suffered from it. Sometimes whole families were said to have gone down with it and we even began to hear that people were dying from it, which did seem a bit of an exaggeration.

Arthur always ironed the daily paper and stitched the leaves together before taking it up to Sir George every morning – it saved a tirade over crumpled or misplaced pages. Arthur never minded this, it gave him a chance to read the headlines and the more interesting items so he could recount them to us over breakfast. But it seemed a little ominous when even the newspapers began to report how many people had died from influenza.

'Are you sure that's right, Arthur?' Cook asked, frowning. 'The papers don't usually report things like that.'

'Well, that's what it says here,' Arthur repeated, as he folded the paper carefully ready for Sir George. 'And it also says the death toll is growing, especially in the big towns.' Affronted that his word should be doubted he glared at Cook over his spectacles.

'Well, we're not near any big towns,' Cook

said complacently. 'Our nearest big towns are Ipswich and Norwich, and they're a long way away so we're all right.'

I said nothing. It was true, the influenza scare was not much of a threat to us in our little village, but nevertheless, from what Arthur was saying it did seem to be spreading at quite an alarming rate.

Ten

We knew things must be getting serious when Perry was sent home from boarding school in the middle of term. He came with a letter saying that it had been decided to close the school for the time being. Although so far nobody at the school had been affected, in the light of what appeared to be turning into an influenza epidemic this was deemed to be the wisest action to take. Perry, being Perry, was delighted with this extra holiday and went round regaling everybody with gory tales of people dropping dead in the street with blood pouring from every orifice. Of course, nobody took him seriously.

Except his father.

One morning in late September – I'll never forget that day – Sir George called everybody, including the farm workers, together in the servants' hall.

He began with much clearing of his throat and hrrrumphing, 'I'm sure you have all read – or been told – what's been written in the newspapers about this Spanish 'flu, during the past weeks,' he began. 'We're told that thousands of people all over the world are dying from it. China, India, Australia, it appears that no country can escape. If we are to believe what we are told more soldiers at the Front are being killed by influenza – on both sides – than are dying in battle. And even here, in our own fair land, this scourge has reached epidemic proportions in the big towns. As you all know, Perry, my son, has been sent home because his school has been closed and I have spoken on the telephone to acquaintances of mine in both Ipswich and Norwich who tell me that things are becoming very worrying there.' He lowered his voice. 'In both towns undertakers and gravediggers are becoming so overworked that the dead—' Here he was cut off by M'Lady, who cleared her throat warningly.

'The point is,' he continued, slightly flustered at having been interrupted in his flow, 'the threat of this influenza is growing ever closer. Soon, I fear, it is inevitable that it will reach our village, if indeed it hasn't already done so. Thank God it hasn't affected us here at the Hall.' He paused, looked round at the assembled faces and continued in a louder voice, 'And I have no intention of allowing it to. In

115

fact, I feel it is my duty to do all I can to prevent it.' He banged his fist dramatically on the table. 'I am determined to keep my family and all of you who work on the estate safe from this terrible scourge.' He paused again for effect, then continued, 'To that end I have decided that this Hall and grounds will be isolated from the outside world until the danger is past. Nobody will be admitted past the Lodge gates and nobody will leave.' He looked round at the assembled company. 'Unless, of course, you choose not to stay and prefer to take your chance in the outside world. In which case, naturally, you will not be allowed back.'

A gasp went round the room and a buzz of surprise and fear. Then everybody glanced round to see the reaction of the rest.

'I have given long and careful thought to this matter,' Sir George went on, after more hrrrumphing and blowing his nose on a large red handkerchief. 'And after consultation with Mr Baines,' he nodded towards the Estate Manager, 'I have decided that this is the best – indeed, probably the only way to prevent this Spanish 'flu reaching us here at Rookhurst Hall.' Once again he banged his fist down on the table. 'As well as protecting all of you I have a duty to protect this place. It has been in my family since the eighteenth century, passed down through the generations to the eldest son. As you are all aware, I have already lost my eldest son, killed under who knows what dreadful circumstances in the Flanders mud.' Here he paused and blew his nose again. 'Therefore, I have an added duty to protect my only remaining son, Peregrine, who is now of course my heir, in order to preserve Rookhurst Hall for future generations.' He paused, looked round at us all then went on, 'I don't need to tell you that it is in everybody's interests to comply with the measures I have worked out with the help of Mr Baines. If our instructions are carried out to the letter then you will have nothing to fear from the scourge that is sweeping the country.' He raised his eyebrows and looked over at the short, balding figure in a shabby tweed suit and gaiters. 'Baines? You can carry on.' He sat down at the head of the table, mopping his forehead with his handkerchief.

Percy Baines stood up and cleared his throat. He was a stocky man, full of his own importance. 'I don't think there's a lot to add to what Sir George has told us,' he said briskly. 'Nobody is to be allowed outside the grounds and nobody is to come in, it's as simple as that. The farm workers' cottages are all well within the estate boundary so there's no problem there. The children, of course, won't go to school, but I believe the school is shortly to close anyway.'

'Beggin' yer pardon, Mr Baines, sir, thass already closed,' a burly red-faced man said. 'My littl'uns hev bin at home since last week.'

'Well, there you are, then.' He looked round. Several people appeared rather perplexed. 'Does anyone want to ask a question?'

'When does this all start? This isolation or

whatever it's called?' an old bewhiskered cow-man called from the back of the hall.

'Right now. From now on nobody is to leave and nobody will be allowed in. Mrs Diggens at the Lodge has already been told to keep the gates locked.'

'What about our families, Mr Baines?' Cook asked anxiously. 'We ought to be able to tell our families. I go to visit my sister in the village every week on my afternoon off. She'll wonder where I am. And how will I know she's all right?'

'Ah, yes. That's all been thought of. Any messages can be left at the Lodge,' Mr Baines said. 'Any letters or parcels, together with the supplies that have to be brought in from out-side, will be left there to be collected and brought up to the house. Likewise, the milk churns and all our surplus fruit and vegetables, whether to be sold in the local shop or taken to the town by the carrier, will be left there. Anything that either goes out or comes in will be left at the Lodge.'

Agnes, the fourteen-year-old scullery maid, twisting her apron in large, raw hands, anxi-ously whispered something to Cook.

'Agnes is worried about her mum getting her wages, Mr Baines,' Cook spoke up for her. 'She takes them home when she goes every week.'

'They too can be left at the Lodge,' Mr Baines said. 'Duly sealed and labelled, of course.'

'But I can't write,' Agnes protested, her voice rising with her fear, tears running down her cheeks, 'and my mum needs my money to feed the little 'uns now dad can't work with 'is consumption. An' she'll wonder where I am if I don't go 'ome reg'lar.'

I leaned over and squeezed her arm. 'I'll write a letter for you, Agnes,' I said. 'And I'll make sure your money is properly labelled, don't worry.'

'Oh, thank you, Alice.' She sniffed and gave me a watery smile.

'What about the laundry women?' Cook then asked, folding her arms across her ample bosom. She was obviously pleased with herself at having found a chink in the armour of isolation. 'We have two of them every Monday to do the laundry and two more on Tuesdays to do the ironing. And the scrubbing woman comes on Fridays. What about them?' She glared at Sir George, but when she saw he was looking at her she quickly slid her glare towards Mr Baines.

Mr Baines didn't notice. He was looking to Sir George, his eyebrows raised questioningly. Clearly, this hadn't been considered.

Sir George hrrrumphed and shifted in his seat. 'Well...'

Cook gave a shrug. 'I suppose the laundry could all be bundled up and left at the Lodge, to be collected again when it's all done and ironed,' she muttered to me.

'What will happen,' Sir George repeated in a loud voice, as if he'd thought of it himself, 'is that the laundry will be bundled up and taken to the Lodge to be collected by the laundry women and left there for collection when it's done.'

'But you can't pick up floors to be scrubbed and take them to the Lodge,' Cook said flatly.

'I'm afraid you'll have to manage as best you can over that, Cook,' Mr Baines said impatiently, annoyed that a flaw had been found in his arrangements. 'I'm sure Sir George will reimburse the kitchen and scullery maids for the extra work?' He looked enquiringly at Sir George.

Sir George scowled. 'No doubt we can come to some arrangement,' he mumbled into his moustache.

'There we are, then,' Mr Baines said. 'I think the scheme should work perfectly well, but I must remind you all again that once you leave these premises you will not be allowed to return. Is that clear?'

John Theobald, who was both chauffeur and under-groom, had married in something of a hurry some six months earlier. Now he stood up, looking uncomfortable. 'I'm not quite sure what I should do,' he began. He turned red to the tips of his ears. 'My wife is, as you all know – well, she...'

'Out with it, man,' Sir George barked impatiently.

Lady Bucknell put her hand on his arm and he leaned down for her to whisper to him.

'Oh, I see.' He hrrrumphed. 'Well, if you think it would be better for you and your wife to leave my employment I shall have no objection. After all, I shan't be needing the Bentley for a week or two.'

Mr Baines was clearly horrified at Sir George's callous treatment of his young chauffeur. He spoke up. 'Begging your pardon, Sir George,' he said, 'but I reckon it's only natural that John is anxious about his wife since she's to become a mother within the next month or so. And I would respectfully remind you that if John goes there'll be nobody but Henry to look after your horses and help with the garden because all the young gardeners have gone to the war.' He laid a slight emphasis on *your*. 'And with all respect to Henry, he's not as young as he was.'

Henry chewed his gums. 'No, thass right. I couldn't be doin' wi'out young John. He'm a good lad.'

John looked worried. He knew he had no choice. If he left the flat over the garage he would have nowhere for himself and his wife to live and no money to live on. On the other hand, if Sheila were to be confined who would look after her?

Agnes sidled round to him and whispered, 'I know what to do when a baby comes, Mr John. I was there when me mum had her last two.'

John looked doubtful. 'You sure?'

She nodded. 'Yes. I know ezzackly what to do.'

He smiled at her with relief. 'Thanks, Aggie.'

Sir George lifted his chin and looked round.

'Well, then. Are there any more questions or is it all settled? I can take it you'll all be staying here, where it's safe, under my wing, so to speak?'

There were murmurs of assent and slightly reluctant nods all round.

'Good.' There was the sound of chairs scraping back and everyone got to their feet as Sir George and M'Lady left the room, followed by Mr Baines.

'It'll never work. You mark my words,' Cook said, ever the prophet of doom.

But surprisingly enough, it did. At least, for a time.

I have to admit keeping the Hall isolated didn't affect me too much. After all I had nowhere else to go, no relatives to visit, and my friends were the people I worked with, especially Cook, who although she was several years my senior was nevertheless a very good friend to me. As long as I could still wander in the woods or walk in the fields that were all part of the estate on my afternoons off I was happy enough. (It sounds a bit as if I had never left the Hall since the day I went there to work, which was far from the truth. I used to go into the village sometimes and several times I had a trip to Saxmundham on the carrier's cart. Then of course there was the time when I went to Ipswich with the girls to have their photograph taken and another time I went there with just Miss Lizzie in the motor car, but only as chaperone because M'Lady wouldn't let her go alone with John, the chauffeur, even though she was only going shopping. I didn't care what the reason was, I had a real exciting time, sitting in the back of the Bentley like a lady, wandering round all those big shops, although Miss Lizzie complained there was nothing in them because of the war. I shall never forget that day.)

The farm workers, too, in their estate cottages were all anxious to comply with Sir George's ruling. Several of them had small families to protect and news was beginning to filter through that this influenza epidemic was not only becoming more and more serious, it was getting closer to home. So, although it might have seemed an impossible task to isolate us from the rest of the village – indeed, the rest of the world – in truth it was not that difficult. None of us wanted to leave. We felt safe at the Hall. And we still got news of what was going on from the newspapers that were left at the Lodge every day and fetched up to the house by Henry or John, along with the post and any deliveries that had been made. Plus, of course, all the local gossip.

Eleven

The daily papers came back to the servants' quarters when Sir George had finished with them. Arthur, who now that most of the indoor staff had gone to war combined his duties as butler with being Sir George's valet, then took them to his room and read them from cover to cover. Of course he didn't have time to do this until he had finished for the day and could relax while he soaked his feet in a bowl of water, which meant the news, apart from the headlines we had heard at breakfast, was always a day late by the time we got it.

Not that it mattered. The news didn't change that much from day to day.

It always fell to me to read the newspapers aloud. The kitchen girls couldn't read and Cook could never find her spectacles. I suspected this was only an excuse on her part, I never saw her pick up a book of any kind, not even a book of recipes, and she always got me to read any necessary instructions, saying the print was too small. But that's by the way.

The news about the war was gradually becoming more cheerful. When I read out that the Germans were retreating, the girls always cheered and we speculated that it would all be over by Christmas with an end to rationing and shortages.

But now what everyone wanted to hear about more than anything else was what was happening over the 'flu epidemic. Apart from Cook and me and Mrs Parkes, the housekeeper, there were now no servant girls left at the Hall over the age of fifteen. As the weeks went on the young girls became restless and homesick and worried about their families, missing their mothers and younger brothers and sisters. The men on the estate began to chafe at missing their evenings at the pub with a glass of beer and a game of shove ha'penny and the younger farm workers missed their evenings chasing the village girls. But no one dared to disobey Sir George, jobs weren't that easy to come by. And nobody wanted to risk catching the dreaded 'flu.

Of course, there were no more organized shoots, no more dances or tennis parties, so we didn't see the usual crowd of young people. Most of them by this time had gone to war, anyway. This lack of young company irked Miss Lizzie more than anything. I began to notice that she was spending quite a lot of her time lurking round the stables, long after she had had her daily ride round the estate on Becket, her horse. Her excuse was that she was bored so she went there to help John polish the Bentley, or to help Henry muck out the stables – which last, knowing Miss Lizzie, was not very likely. But of course, it was not for me to say anything, whatever I might think. I did tell her that if she was bored I could always find her some work to do in the house, but her reply was that she preferred to be out in the open air.

I tried not to sound too gloomy at what I read in the newspaper each night but there was no hiding the fact that the news from France seemed to be getting more and more depressing. But this wasn't because the fighting was going badly, it was because large numbers of troops were now dying from what appeared to be a particularly virulent strain of influenza.

'I'm not surprised,' Cook remarked complacently, rocking in her chair as she knitted yet another khaki balaclava helmet. 'It's living in them trenches, that's what it is. It's no wonder they catch their death of cold.'

'It's not cold they're dying from, Cook,' I explained. 'It's 'flu.'

'Same thing,' she said with a shrug. 'I've heard tell they have to slosh about with their feet in muddy water all the time. No wonder they're ill.'

'I don't think it is the same at all, Cook,' I said, uncomfortable at having to contradict her. 'It's this Spanish 'flu the men are dying from. I've never heard of anyone dying of a cold.'

She shrugged again. 'Well, anyway ... Go on, what else does it say?'

'It says that it's affecting people in India and China ... in fact people all over the world...'

'Oh, it's not just in the trenches, then,' Cook

said, surprised.

I shook my head. 'No.' I tried not to sound impatient but sometimes Cook's grasp of anything that didn't go in the oven was at best a bit slow. 'Don't you remember? I read out only last week that over a hundred thousand people had died in this country. That's why Sir George has been keeping the Hall isolated all these weeks. So none of us catch it.'

'Ah, yes.' She nodded. After a minute she looked over her spectacles and said, 'Do they put any recipes in that paper?'

I gave up, folded the newspaper and went back to darning my stockings, which had been cut to ribbons by the stubble as I helped with the harvest, even though I had been wearing boots.

It had been a good harvest and as usual we had all been called in to help. Of course, there were not many horses left on the farm now, most of them had been requisitioned for the army, much to Sir George's fury. But the few that were left did sterling work, plodding back and forth to take the sheaves to the barn. With Sir George's ban in force there was no gleaning for the villagers this year so there was no need for one last sheaf – known as the 'policeman' – to be left in the middle of the field until it was taken away as a sign that gleaning could begin. Instead, we on the estate did the gleaning and the gleanings were taken to the Lodge and distributed from there among the villagers.

Although that was all weeks ago I still hadn't

finished darning my stockings.

It wasn't many days later that Henry, who had the responsibility of taking the trap every morning to fetch and carry between the Hall and the Lodge, came into the kitchen with the grim news that Ellen Trubshaw from the village had been brought home with a bad throat and a cough. I remembered Ellen from school, she was the brightest girl in the class and had gone on to be a pupil teacher in the next village.

'I expect she caught it from the children at school, they're always coughing and sneezing all over the place,' I said, trying not to think the worst.

'I shouldn't wonder,' Henry agreed, chewing his gums and slurping the tea Cook had poured for him. 'They was sayin' down at the Lodge there was talk of sprayin' the classrooms with a mixture of paraffin and menthol in one school. I think it was out Sudbury way but I ain't sure.'

'What? Spraying it all over the children?' Cook asked, horrified.

Henry frowned. 'I 'speck so. Wouldn't be no good if the childer weren't there, would it? Wouldn't kill the germs.'

'But surely if the fires are alight they could all be burnt at their desks!'

Henry took a bite out of a morning bun fresh out of the oven. 'That don't seem a wunnerful idea to me, neither, Mrs Platt,' he agreed, spraying crumbs all over the table. 'Strikes me they dunno what to do next for this 'flu business.'

'Better to close the schools altogether, I

should think,' I said, 'like they've done here in the village.'

'Reckon you're right,' Henry said, looking hopefully at the batch of morning buns, a look Cook ignored this time. He gave a wheezy chuckle. 'Mrs Diggens at the Lodge told me the childer got a little chant what they sing as they skip in the road. She sang it to me. Now, let me see if I can call it to mind.' He thought for a minute and then began to sing in a quavery tenor voice, *'I had a little bird an' its name was Enza. I opened my window and in flew Enza.'* He grinned as he finished. 'There, I didn't misremember it, did I? Mrs Diggens told me they sing it all the time. In flew Enza – influenza, see?' He beamed at us all.

'Whatever next?' Cook tutted. 'Fancy making a rhyme out of that. What is the world coming to?'

There was a sniff from Agnes, polishing knives at the table.

'And what's the matter with you, Miss?' Cook said, looking at her sharply. 'You haven't got a cold. Have you?'

Agnes shook her head. 'No. I was jest thinkin' about my sisters playin' in the road and singin' that little song,' she said, tears spilling down her cheeks. 'I heven't seen them for nearly a month. I'm afeared the baby won't even rekernize me when I see him.'

'Well, I'm sure it won't be for much longer,' Cook said more kindly. 'This 'flu scare will soon be over, I'll be bound.'

129

She was wrong, of course. Things got worse, not better. The newspapers began to report that so many people were dying of influenza in the big towns that undertakers couldn't cope and coffins were piling up waiting for burial. Soon after that there were urgent cries for carpenters in some places because they were running short of men to make the coffins. There were reports of skilled coffin makers being released from the army and getting soldiers to help with grave-digging in order to keep up with the demand. The numbers reported dead were rising all the time. Shops, even some departmental stores, were forced to close because the staff were either ill or dead and people were urged always to wear a mask against infection. There were pictures in the newspaper of people in the street, all of them with white masks covering their noses and mouths, hurrying about their business. People were urged to eat porridge, lentils, mackerel, milk and a host of other un-likely preventatives and there were countless advertisements for the prevention or cure of the disease.

'Goodness knows where it'll all end,' Cook remarked, smug in the knowledge that we were safe at the Hall.

Yes, we were safe, but even at the Hall we weren't immune from the results of the epidemic.

One afternoon a telegraph boy came cycling up the drive. He was the only person who had got past the Lodge gates in over two months, but telegrams couldn't wait and it was common knowledge that they never contained good news.

This one didn't, either. It was from the hospital where Vonny and Vera nursed, and it stated in bald terms that Sister Veronica Bucknell had succumbed to the influenza virus and died on October 31st 1918. We were all shocked and appalled. Vonny had worked all through the war caring for injured troops, it just wasn't fair that she should die. But war wasn't fair. Even cocooned in their self-imposed prison at Rookhurst Hall Sir George and M'Lady were paying the same price as millions of other parents all over the country, losing first their eldest son and now one of the twins. Sir George tried to telephone the hospital where the twins had spent the war together but couldn't get through. We were all worried about Vera. How would she cope, separated by death from the twin she had never been parted from before?

We needn't have worried on that score. The very next day the telegraph boy brought an identical telegram – identical, that is, except that the name on it was Vera instead of Veronica.

It was a terrible blow to us all and I feared for M'Lady's sanity. But to my amazement she remained calm.

'I was expecting it, Alice,' she said, dry-eyed now, although her red-rimmed eyes told their own story. 'I knew Vera couldn't exist for long without Vonny. I couldn't bear the thought of

131

losing them both, yet I couldn't bear to think of them being separated. I didn't know which would be worst.' She closed her eyes briefly and nodded. 'It's best this way.' She paused. 'I just hope the authorities will be sensitive enough to give them a double funeral.'

I didn't answer. From what I was reading in the newspapers so many people were dying now that they were being forced to bury them in mass graves. The best that could be hoped for was that the twins would lie side by side in one of those.

For some time now I had felt restless. Reading about the dreadful things that were happening in the outside world and now with the awful news of the twins, I felt very guilty remaining isolated in the haven of Rookhurst Hall. It wasn't right that I should stay here, cocooned and safe. I was healthy and able-bodied, I had no family to worry about me, so I ought to be out there in the wide world, helping to nurse the sick or looking after motherless children, not cosily sitting and reading about the lack of nurses in overcrowded wards.

I went about my work, my conscience troubling me. Anybody could do what I was doing, looking after M'Lady, making sure that the house ran smoothly – I'd taken on the work of housekeeper in place of Mrs Parkes, who had elected to leave after only a month's confinement to the Hall. She said it gave her claustrophobia, although how that could be in such a large house with big, open grounds was something of a mystery. But she had been very friendly with the butcher who used to call twice a week and no longer came at all, so perhaps that was the reason she left. I don't know whether she was friendly with his wife as well. I suspect not.

One wing of the house had been shut completely. We no longer had any visitors and what few staff remained had quite enough to do without the extra cleaning. True, I had no time to sit about twiddling my thumbs, in fact I fell into bed most nights too exhausted even to say my prayers, which would have shocked Aunt Maud, but at the same time the feeling was growing that I ought to be doing something more useful 'out there', as I had come to think of the outside world.

But I have to admit I was nervous. I had never been the adventurous type and the Hall had been my home ever since I was fourteen. It would be hard to leave it. Strangely, the risk of catching 'flu never crossed my mind.

It was my afternoon off, an afternoon of hazy sunshine after morning mist had cleared. The leaves had mostly fallen and I scuffed my way through a carpet of yellow, red and brown that reflected the sunlight and lent the wood a bright, almost fairy-like atmosphere. As I walked, hands deep in my pockets, I realized it was almost a week since news of the twins' deaths and I still hadn't decided what to do, whether I should go to Ipswich or Norwich to offer my services at the hospital, or whether I should try to find an orphanage where I could help to look after motherless children. The news was coming through that the war would soon be over, but that didn't mean there wouldn't be work for me to do, after all, people would always be ill and there would always be motherless children. And there was nothing to keep me here at the Hall now that Giles was dead. Maybe out in the wider world I might even find somebody else ... No, I knew that could never be. Young as I was, Giles had been the love of my life, there could never be anyone to take his place.

Almost without thinking, I turned my steps to the place by the stream where we used to meet.

And there he was.

Twelve

'Oh!'

Ben looked up from the page he was reading and reached for the one Lucy was holding in her hand. 'What's the matter? Something wrong?'

She handed it to him. 'No, nothing's wrong, but this is the last page Granny's written. Talk about a cliffhanger! I just want to go on reading...'

'Hang on.' Ben read the final page as she watched. 'Ah, yes, I see what you mean,' he

134

said, handing it back when he'd finished.

She scanned the page again. 'Do you think Giles really has come back, Ben? Is he really there, or do you think it's a trick of her imagination?'

He lifted his shoulders. 'Who can tell? Wishful thinking can play funny tricks. And they did spend quite a lot of time at that spot together, it was what you might call their special place, so it would have been a magic place for her.'

She pinched her lip. 'It could have been his ghost, I suppose. Do you believe in ghosts, Ben?'

'I've an open mind on that subject. I've certainly heard some strange tales in my time but I can't say I've ever seen one,' he said. 'But aren't you forgetting? Giles was posted missing, *presumed* dead, so I suppose he could have come back.'

'Yes, but surely he would have gone straight to the house. He wouldn't have waited in the wood. After all, Alice might not have gone there for ages.'

'That's true.' He slapped his knees. 'Lucy, we could sit here and speculate all night and we still won't know till you get the next bit of the story.' He looked at his watch. 'A night that's already half over! Do you realize it's nearly one o'clock?'

'Gosh, is it? I don't feel in the least sleepy.' She yawned widely, giving the lie to that statement.

'I'm not surprised, the amount of coffee

we've drunk.' He got to his feet. 'But like you, I'm intrigued and I can't wait for the next bit to arrive. I hope you'll let me read it?' There was a question in his voice.

'Of course I will. You're in this every bit as much as I am, Ben. I'll let you know as soon as it arrives and we'll read it together, just like this time. To be perfectly honest it's nice to have someone to share it with.'

'Good.' He smiled. 'Now, I really must go. Apart from ruining my reputation and yours as well by staying here till the small hours, I've got a lot of work to get through before the carriers come on Thursday to collect the stuff for the fair. And, if my memory serves me aright, I believe you're starting a new job to-morrow morning, Miss Armitage. Nine o'clock. Sharp.' He grinned down at her as she accompanied him to the door. 'And no oversleeping! Don't forget the boss will be there to check up on you.'

She laughed. 'At least I haven't got far to go to the office.' She became serious. 'Thank you, Ben. Thank you for finding Granny, thank you for coming with me to see her. Just ... well, thank you for everything.' She stood on tiptoe to give him a peck on the cheek at the same time as he bent his head to do the same to her. But somehow their aim got misdirected and their lips met. It was only a brief kiss but they both parted as if they had been scalded.

'I'm sorry,' he said quickly. 'I didn't mean...'

She pressed the back of her hand to her mouth

guiltily. 'No, neither did I.'

'Goodnight, Lucy.' He turned quickly and hurried down the steps and out to his car.

She locked the door and went back to gather up the loose sheets of Alice's story that were strewn over the settee and clip them back into the folder. She read the last page again, but there was no clue as to whether Giles was really alive or not. If it was only Alice's imagination and he wasn't there at all, she mused, what had she done next? Had she left the Hall and gone to work in a hospital? Or in an orphanage? Thoughts and speculations began spinning round in her head and she knew that if she continued with this train of thought she would never sleep. So she carried the folder over and laid it carefully in a drawer in the bureau that had once belonged to Alice.

'And that's exactly the right place for it,' she said aloud. Then she went to bed.

But what kept her awake was not Alice's story; it was the memory of that brief, unintentional kiss she had exchanged with Ben as he left. Nothing more than a peck on the cheek was what they had both intended, but brief as it had been, for her it had turned into something more. It had shown her that she had been deluding herself in thinking her affection for him was purely sisterly; it was not sisterly at all, the sensation that had shot through her at the touch of his lips had proved that.

But tomorrow she would begin work at Rosewood Antiques, Alec and Ben Manton would be her employers. There was no way she was going to allow herself to fall in love with the boss.

She slept badly and didn't hear the alarm; neither did she hear Alec arrive and open up the workshop. What woke her was the sound of Alec calling to Ben to be careful as he helped him to carry something out of the workshop. She looked at the clock; it was eight forty-five. She leapt out of bed and by dint of skipping breakfast managed to walk into the shop on the stroke of nine o'clock, her hair still wet from the shower. She had been apprehensive, fearing that what had happened last night might alter her relationship with Ben and make things awkward between them. But he immediately put her at ease, because he came through from the back and glanced pointedly at his watch as she walked in.

'Congratulations,' he said with a grin. 'You've made it on time. Just. Although I can see your hair's still wet.'

'And I didn't have time for any breakfast,' she admitted ruefully.

'That'll teach you not to oversleep. Never mind, we'll have sticky buns at eleven, if you can last that long.' He led the way to the office, a small room at the back of the main showroom, into which a large window had been inserted so that the whole of the showroom was visible from the desk. 'I shall be around most of the day today. I've got to catalogue and label all the stuff that's going to the fair. Most of it's stacked

138

in the storeroom at the back, so if you have a problem you can always give me a shout.'

She spread her hands. 'So what do you want me to do, sit in the office here and wait for customers to come in?'

He looked round. The office was something of a shambles; invoices, receipts, letters, catalogues from firms specializing in handles and escutcheons, leaflets on wax polishes, samples of stains, bulging folders were all stacked on the desk, on the shelves above it and on the floor. There was a light patina of dust over everything.

'To tell you the truth I'd rather you grabbed an overall and did a bit of tidying up in here. Mrs Wills, who keeps the shop clean, doesn't "do" in here so it's got a bit dusty over the years.'

'Over the *years*?' she gulped, raising her eyebrows.

He gave a sheepish shrug. 'Well, perhaps it's not quite that long. But as you can see, it is in a bit of a mess. Dad and I always seem to have more important things to do than tidy up.'

'But I'll bet you know where everything is,' she guessed.

'Most things.'

'Well, I don't make any promises that you'll be able to find anything by the time I've finished.'

'No, but with any luck you'll still be here so you can tell us where to look.'

She smiled. 'OK. Where's the overall?'

She donned the green nylon wrap-over overall and began by clearing a space on the desk, then she sorted things into piles: catalogues, invoices, bills, receipts, advertisements, letters, putting anything that didn't fit into these categories on the floor to be dealt with later. There were several box files on the shelf, most of them empty, although one contained a dead mouse, and she cleaned them out and labelled them so that she could put the relevant piles of papers away.

At the same time, whenever the shop bell rang she whipped off the overall and went to deal with the customers. It was Monday morning so the shop wasn't busy; a couple of people just came in to browse, with no intention of buying anything although it wasted nearly twenty minutes of Lucy's time.

But three times during the morning customers asked to see Mr Manton himself and she had to go and fetch Ben from the back room where he was busy with labels and lists. It amazed her that although he was clearly annoyed at being disturbed, he was invariably patient and charming to the people he was dealing with. She was full of admiration that he allowed his valuable time to be wasted by people who had only come in to pick his brains over the best way to remove a heat mark or to ask whether Aunt Matilda's bedroom commode might be worth a fortune.

'If anybody else wants to see me tell them I'm out on a call, will you,' he said as he took five minutes to drink a cup of Maxwell House coffee and eat the sticky bun he'd promised her in the office. 'If I keep getting called away from what I'm doing I shall never get it finished before Pickfords arrive on Thursday to take it all to London.'

'Where do they have to take it?'

'To the town hall in Chelsea.'

'Oh, posh place.'

'Yes, it's becoming quite an important fair. Dad and I have to go up as well to set up our stand and make sure that the things we take to replace items that are sold are put in the store the way we want them. It's chaos, I might tell you, because everyone else, all the other dealers, are doing the same thing – wanting the lifts, shouting for porters, complaining their stall isn't where they wanted it, moaning if they think somebody else has got a more advantageous position, greeting old friends. It's quite funny. Some of them are real prima donnas.'

'You sound as if you enjoy it, though.' She licked her fingers.

'Yes, it's good fun. Exhausting, mind you, but good fun.'

'And do you have to stay in London all the time the fair is on?'

'No. Dad does the first week as a rule and I do the second. Mum usually stays up there with him and she goes shopping and visits museums and art galleries while he's on the stand. Sometimes they go to a show in the evening. They make a bit of a holiday of it, which is nice for them.'

'And what about you?'

'No. More often than not I come home every night. Not really any point in staying up there on my own.' He went over to the tiny sink in the corner, which was the first thing Lucy had attacked when she had located Mrs Wills' store of cleaning materials. 'My word, this looks different,' he said admiringly as he washed the sticky sugar off his hands. 'I can see you'll be a real asset to the firm.'

'I do typing as well as cleaning wash basins, sir,' she said modestly.

'Ah, a woman of many talents, just what Rosewood Antiques needs.'

'Yes, well, don't trip over that pile of invoices on the floor, or you may find one of my talents is to use strong language. I've spent the last half-hour sorting them chronologically. I've left out the ones that need to be paid.'

'You amaze me.'

'Well, now go and be amazed somewhere else.' She made a shooing gesture. 'Oh, thanks for the sticky bun.'

'My pleasure.'

She went back to work. It was all right, there was no embarrassment between them; last night's ... mistake ... was forgotten. She didn't know whether she was glad or sorry.

She sat down at the desk to sort through yet another pile of papers. Every now and then she looked up through the office window to the showroom. Even though the two large windows at the front and the glazed door threw plenty of light, there were strategically placed lights and mirrors throughout the showroom so that all the furniture and pictures were placed to the best advantage. Another thing she noticed was that each item had plenty of space round it. Some antique shops she had seen looked more like glorified auction rooms at best and junk shops at worst, but this could never be said of Rosewood Antiques. And even though there were later, less valuable pieces upstairs on the next floor, they were still set out carefully. She suspected all this was Ben's doing. There was no doubt he had a real flair for it.

Alec came through from the workshop during the afternoon, wiping his hands on his work apron. He stood in the office doorway and gaped. 'Goodness me, it hasn't taken you long to clean the place up,' he said in amazement.

'I found this old typewriter in the corner.' She pointed to an ancient Remington she had cleaned up and placed on the desk. 'I don't think it's much use though.'

He went over and pressed down a few keys. 'I'll have a look at it. I dare say I can make it work. You'll need a typewriter, won't you, so I'd better see what I can do with it.'

'Well, yes, I will, but...' She looked at it doubtfully.

'Don't worry, it'll be as good as new by the time I've finished with it,' he assured her. He picked it up and turned to leave the office.

On the way back to his workshop he met Ben.

'Where are you going with that?' Lucy heard Ben ask.

'I'm going to take it into the workshop and have a look at it. Lucy will be needing a type-writer, won't she?'

'Yes, but not that one, Dad. You can do it up and we might be able to pass it on to a museum or something, but you surely don't expect Lucy to use it! We'll get her a new one.'

'What's wrong with it?'

'Dad! It came out of the Ark.'

'Yes, I suppose it is a bit elderly. Anyway, I'll have a look at it when I've got time.'

'You said that when it came in after we'd done a house clearance five years ago. That's why it's been stuck in that corner.'

Ben was still shaking his head as he came into the office. 'It's a good thing my father is in the antique trade,' he said with a smile. 'I sometimes think that's exactly where he belongs.'

Thirteen

When Lucy had set the office straight, which had taken her the best part of two days, she went through to the storeroom to help Ben. The furniture, which was mostly mahogany and walnut but with a few early oak pieces, was ready and waiting for collection, everything waxed and gleaming, the brasswork bright. She was amazed at how many different items there were; it was like a house removal on a grand scale, except that each piece was in immaculate condition. As well as unusual items she couldn't even put a name to there were tables of all shapes and sizes, chairs both wooden and upholstered, several chests of drawers of varying sizes, a large sideboard, two flat-topped desks, a bureau similar to Lucy's but bigger, a magazine rack which Ben told her wasn't originally a magazine rack at all but a Canterbury for storing sheet music ... the storeroom was full, with hardly room to move between the carefully stacked pieces.

Ben looked tired, even though it was first thing in the morning. She knew he'd been working late every night apart from Sunday, when he had been reading Alice's story with her, and that had kept him up till the small hours.

'There's just the china and glass to wash and pack now,' he told her, running his fingers through his hair in a tired gesture. 'I would have asked Mrs Wills to do it, but she's not here today.'

'I don't mind doing it. I've come through to see if I could help,' she said.

He looked relieved. 'Well, if you wouldn't mind washing it all in hot, soapy water and rinsing it, that would be great. Then, when it's completely dry I can wrap it in newspaper and pack it in these tea chests.'

As they worked together he told her how to distinguish one make of china from another; the colours used, the designs, the little individual touches, as well as the makers' marks on the underside. He used words like slipware, earthenware, porcelain and names like Wedgwood, Chelsea, Derby, Staffordshire, till she was so confused by it all that she laughed and said she would never sleep with all this information going into her brain.

'Yes, I'm probably trying to teach you too much, too soon. It's taken me years to learn and I'm still learning,' he said.

She leaned her arms on the sink. 'One thing I am confused about,' she said, 'is the word commode. I always thought a commode was something kept in the bedroom for...'

He grinned. 'A kind of posh chamberpot.'

She nodded. 'Yes.'

'That's a night commode,' he explained. 'A commode is also another name for a rather superior chest of drawers. Like this one.' He pointed to a chest of drawers, the front of which was ornately decorated in brasswork he called ormolu.

'Oh, I see.' She pushed a strand of hair away from her forehead with her forearm and went back to the task in hand. In between looking after the shop and digressions to discuss china and furniture it took the two of them all day to wash and pack the china, but Lucy had never before enjoyed washing up so much and she felt she had learned a great deal while doing it.

'I suppose you haven't heard anything from your grandmother yet?' Ben asked as they were drinking a well-earned cup of tea when they had finished.

She shook her head, smiling. 'Give her a chance, Ben. It's less than a week since we were with her.'

He raised his eyebrows. 'Heavens, is it? I've been so busy it seems like half a lifetime to me. No, of course, she's hardly had time to write much more.'

'I must confess I look out for the postman every day, though,' she admitted with a half-guilty smile. 'I'm still wondering whether Giles could have been a figment of her imagination...'

'Be patient. You'll find out before too long.'

'We'll find out, you mean. I've promised I won't read it till you're with me.'

He grinned. 'Good. Let me know and I'll

bring another bottle of wine.'

There was no danger of Lucy being late for work the next day because not long after seven thirty a large Pickfords furniture van was backed expertly into the yard of Rosewood Antiques. Alec and Ben were already there and there was a great deal of good-humoured wise-cracking between them and the two Pickfords men as the furniture for the fair was expertly wrapped and stacked into the van. It was a task that, with a good many tea breaks provided by Lucy, took most of the day.

When it was finished the van was locked up and left in the yard, which would also be pad-locked for the night, and the two men drove off in the car belonging to the driver's mate. Alec and Ben came into the office where Lucy was entering the sale of a small table in the ledger. They both looked exhausted.

'I'll just finish this, then I'll make you both another cup of tea. You may have drunk a gallon or so during the day but I expect you can drink another cup,' she said, looking up.

'I'll put the kettle on,' Ben replied. 'And I don't care if I never hear "Mack the Knife" again as long as I live. Stan, the driver's mate, seemed to have that tune on the brain, he was whistling it the whole day.'

'Oh, is that what it was?' Alec asked. 'I didn't recognize it.'

'I did. It got on my nerves, too,' Lucy said. She finished writing and closed the ledger. 'There. I've sold that little Chippendale side table and the Staffordshire toby jug in the window today,' she said proudly.

'She's really beginning to get the hang of things, isn't she?' Alec said to Ben, making sure he spoke loudly enough for her to hear as she poured the tea. 'Quite an asset to the firm.'

'She'll be even more of an asset when she gets a decent typewriter,' she said over her shoulder, winking at Ben.

'We're working on it,' Alec said. 'These things take time.'

She swung round. 'Oh, surely you're not doing up that old Remington for me,' she said, horrified.

'Well...' Alec shook his head sagely. 'You work in an antique shop, you know...'

'Yes, but just because it's an antique shop it doesn't mean we have to use antique equipment. You'll be handing me a chisel and asking me to chip the invoices out in stone next,' she argued, not quite sure whether or not he was serious.

'Don't tease her, Dad,' Ben said, laughing. 'It's all right, Lucy. I've been in and ordered a brand new Olivetti for you. It should be delivered next week.'

'Thank you, Ben.'

'Don't mention it.' He took the mug she was offering and turned to his father. 'I'll go up in the van with the furniture tomorrow and you can follow a bit later on the train. Is that OK?'

'Yes. What time are the boys coming?'

'Seven thirty.'

149

Alec grinned. 'Suits me. I needn't catch a train till after nine.'

'Don't gloat. I just hope Stan will have forgotten "Mack the Knife" by tomorrow or I might be tempted to take one to his throat.'

'That's a bit extreme. What about the shop?' Lucy asked.

'What about it? You'll be here. You can manage perfectly well,' Ben said. 'And Mrs Wills will be here for at least part of the time. Thursday's still her cleaning day, isn't it?'

'Yes. But if...'

'If you have any problems ask them to leave their name and address and we'll sort it out.' He smiled at her. 'You'll be fine. Don't worry. And I'll be back tomorrow night.'

'Would you like me to cook supper for you?' she asked tentatively. 'Then you can sort out any problems for me.'

'That would be very nice, although I'm not anticipating problems.' He paused. 'I may be a bit late.'

'What's late?'

'Half eight? Nine? Past your bedtime?'

'I think I can probably manage to stay awake.'

Neither of them noticed Alec's smug expression as he picked up his mug and drained his tea. He'd have something to tell Martha, who he knew was already quietly match-making.

Lucy felt more than a little apprehensive as she opened up the shop the next day. She hadn't overslept, for which she was relieved. In fact, she had been woken before half past seven by the sound of Ben and the two Pickfords men greeting each other and the sound of Stan whistling a different tune. Not long after that the motor started up and the huge van was driven out of the yard and down the road, packed, as Ben had told her the previous day, with the fruits of a whole year's searching for suitable bargains on his part plus six months' cleaning and restoration work on his father's.

With some trepidation Lucy went down and opened the shop. She was busy sorting through the post when Mrs Wills arrived.

'Goodness, you've made a clearance in here,' she said as she tied on the green nylon overall Lucy had borrowed. She shrugged. 'I don't do in here, they say they on'y want the showrooms kep' nice, but sometimes my fingers itch to give this place a good turn out, I can tell you.'

'I hope you don't mind. I borrowed your overall. And I used some of your cleaning materials and your rubber gloves,' Lucy said. 'But I put everything back where I found it.'

'Reckon you needed rubber gloves in this office,' Mrs Wills remarked gloomily, leaning on the doorpost and folding her arms.

'I'll make you a cup of tea at ten thirty,' Lucy said pointedly. Alec had warned her that Mrs Wills would spend half the morning talking, given half a chance. Fortuitously, just then the phone rang so Mrs Wills took herself off. Lucy picked it up.

'This is Lady Bucknell.' She would have

151

recognized the imperious voice even if she hadn't identified herself. 'I wish to speak to Mr Manton.'

'I'm afraid neither Mr Ben Manton nor his father are here today,' Lucy replied. 'Can I be of any help?'

'Are you Mr Manton's assistant? The gel that came with him last time he visited me?'

'Yes, Lady Bucknell. I am.'

'Well, when he comes back tell him I wish to see him.'

'May I give him any indication of what you'd like to see him about?'

'No. You may not. Just tell him to call on me at his earliest convenience.'

'Very well, Lady Bucknell, I'll give him your message. But I should warn you that he is very busy for the next fortnight. Most of the time he'll be in London at the antique dealers' fair.'

'Well, tell him to come as soon as he gets back.'

'Very well, Lady Bucknell. Good morning.'

The phone went dead.

Sometimes, Lucy marvelled at Ben's patience with the imperious old lady.

On the dot of ten thirty Mrs Wills came for her cup of tea. She sat down and made herself comfortable and lit a cigarette, obviously preparing for a lengthy chat.

'You used to work for that solicitor chap down Lane End, didn't you?' she said, blowing smoke in Lucy's direction.

Lucy coughed pointedly. 'Yes, that's right.'

152

'He's a right one for the ladies, that one. Did you know?' This time the smoke was directed towards the ceiling.

'I had heard.'

'Reckon you're well out of that place.'

Lucy bit her tongue against retorting that it was none of Mrs Wills' business whom she worked for.

But Mrs Wills was oblivious of the fact that she might be causing offence and went on smugly, 'But you'll be all right here. Mr Alec's ever such a nice man and Ben's all right, too.' She frowned. 'I don't know why such a nice young man has never married. He lives in that flat all on his own, you know. Can't understand it, meself. It don't seem right to me, a man livin' all on his own. My Colin still lives at home. Sid, that's my husband, says he ought to fend for hisself a bit more but I say it's a mother's privilege to look after her on'y son. I don't mind doing his washing and cooking his meals an' that. Well, it's a mother's privilege, that's what I say.'

Yes, and you've already said it twice and I'll scream if you say it again, Lucy thought to herself. She pointedly began to leaf through some papers.

Mrs Wills stubbed out her cigarette and finished her tea. 'Well, better get on, I s'pose.' She got to her feet. 'Nice young lady, that's what Ben needs.' She put her head on one side. 'Come to think of it, I believe he did have a young lady once. I saw him with her several times. I don't know what happened to her, though.'

'Married someone else, I expect,' Lucy said shortly, getting to her feet as she saw a customer come in.

'Yes, I expect she did. Pity. He ought to have somebody to look after him.'

'Well, don't look at me,' Lucy mouthed at Mrs Wills' back as she went off to resume her cleaning and polishing.

She sold a pair of silver-plated fish servers to the woman who had just come in and was looking for a wedding present, then she went back to the office. It was the only sale of the day.

Ben arrived at the flat just before nine o'clock, tired and hungry. But when he had done justice to the macaroni cheese with chips and salad Lucy had prepared he looked much better. Yes, it had been a good day, he told her when she asked. Everything was safely stowed and on Monday they would finish setting up the stand ready for the opening by the Queen Mother on Tuesday.

'I'm taking Mum up on the train for that,' he said with a grin. 'She's thrilled at the thought that she might be meeting the Queen Mum; my mum's a sucker for royalty. She watched Princess Margaret's wedding to Tony Armstrong Jones last May on television and then went and saw it at the pictures because she wanted to see it in colour. And she went and bought the book.'

154

Lucy laughed. 'I see what you mean. Will she come back with you?'

'No, she'll stay up there with Dad for the rest of the week.'

'And the following week it will be your turn,' Lucy said, serving up treacle tart and custard.

'That's right. Mm, you're nearly as good a cook as my mother,' he said appreciatively.

'I cannot tell a lie. I only made the custard, I bought the tart from the baker's,' Lucy confessed.

'Well, it's very good.' He held his plate out for more.

When they had finished the meal and were sitting and drinking coffee in more comfortable chairs, he said, 'As you were saying, the second week of the fair it will be my turn to be on the stand. And since you've been so helpful in preparing for it I wondered if you might like to spend the day there with me, say on the Thursday?'

'Oh, yes, please,' she said eagerly. 'Although I wouldn't claim to have done all that much to help.'

'And maybe we could have dinner and if there's time do a show afterwards? Agatha Christie's *Mousetrap* is still running and there's a late train. I've checked.'

'Thank you. Yes. I'd really enjoy that,' she said, her eyes shining. 'But what about the shop?'

'Dad will keep an eye on things and Mrs Wills never minds sitting in for the odd extra morning or afternoon.' He grinned at her. 'It's a date, then?'

'It's a date. I'll look forward to it.'

'And so will I.'

It was after eleven before he got up to go.

'Thanks, Lucy,' he said at the door. 'I've really enjoyed the meal.' He hesitated. 'And the company.'

'Well, I thought it might be better than going back to fish and chips in an empty flat,' she said, remembering Mrs Wills' words.

'That's very true.' He cocked an eyebrow. 'Heard anything from your grandmother?'

She made a face. 'Oh, Ben. Do you think I wouldn't have told you?'

'It could have slipped your mind,' he teased.

'Not very likely, since I'm on constant watch for the postman and I even go through the post at the shop in case it's been delivered there.' She put her hand to her mouth. 'Ah, but one thing I had forgotten. Lady Bucknell phoned, demanding your presence.'

'Well, I'm afraid she'll have to whistle for it for a few days. Did you tell her I was tied up with the fair?'

'I did. She wasn't impressed and said you were to contact her as soon as you were back.'

'It won't hurt her to wait. We'll go in a week or two.'

'Not me,' Lucy said quickly. 'She didn't ask for me. I don't want to go.'

'You're my assistant, remember? She'll expect you to accompany me. And I wouldn't like to disappoint her.' He smiled down at her. 'Now, I really must go. Goodnight, Lucy, and thanks for the supper.' He held her gaze for a second or two longer. She had the impression that he would have liked to kiss her but was afraid of repeating the fiasco of the other night.

'Goodnight, Ben,' she said, wishing he would.

Fourteen

The following week passed quickly for Lucy. There was plenty for her to do, especially after the new typewriter was delivered, because there was a backlog of letters to be answered and price lists to be updated as well as looking after the general running of the shop.

Ben came in every day to sort the post and dictate letters but he didn't have time to stay long. He was out attending sales or driving all over the county and beyond, looking for items to replace the stock that was already being sold at the fair.

'Yes, it all seems to be going very well,' he said when she asked. 'I was on the phone to Dad last night and he's very pleased with the way things are selling. Now, where has this escritoire got to be delivered to?' He looked at the address on the label. 'Oh, that's just the other side of Ipswich. Can you give me a hand to load it into the van, or is it too heavy for you?'

It was a dainty little writing desk, on tapered legs, with one long and two small drawers below the writing fall. It was all heavily decorated with gold, which Lucy could now recognize as ormolu. It didn't look very heavy.

'I think I can manage,' she said.

'Good. Keep your back straight and bend your knees when you lift it. That's it.'

'It's very elegant,' she remarked as he covered it with a blanket and secured it in the back of the van. 'Why didn't you take it to the fair?'

He smiled. 'Because it's been too heavily repaired. You probably couldn't detect it, but Dad made a whole new front leg for it because one leg had been smashed off. They don't allow that much restoration at these fairs.' He noticed that she was frowning. 'It's all perfectly above board, Lucy, the lady who bought this knew exactly what she was buying; and anyway, the amount of restoration was reflected in the price. You wouldn't have got a piece like this in mint condition for the price she's paid.'

Her face cleared. 'Oh, that's all right, then.'

He burst out laughing. 'We're honest men, not wide-boys, Lucy, I promise you that. You don't need to worry. You're not working for some shady outfit on the wrong side of the law.' He was still laughing as he got into the van and drove off.

While he was gone the second post came.

'There's a package for the flat upstairs,' the postman said as he gave her a wad of letters and catalogues. 'Can I leave it here? Save my old legs?'

'Yes. It's for me. I live up there.'

'Oh, that's all right, then.'

Her heart skipped a beat as she recognized her grandmother's writing on the label. The next instalment of Alice's life story had arrived!

All through the day her eyes kept straying to the bulky package but she was determined not to open it until Ben was there. She had promised him that they would read it together and she wouldn't go back on her word.

It was annoying that he didn't come back to the shop that day and didn't make an appearance at all the next day. In fact, she didn't see him again until Friday, by which time she was bursting with curiosity.

'Oh, here you are at last,' she said when he came into the office. 'Where on earth have you been?'

He looked taken aback at her outburst. 'If you must know, I've been to three sales and yesterday I went to London.' A grin spread across his face. 'Have you missed me that much, Lucy?'

'No, I ... well, yes...' Her voice tailed off as she realized what he must be thinking. 'I was beginning to wonder where you were,' she finished lamely.

'That's nice. Well, I'm here now and I'm gasping for a cup of coffee. Shall I put the kettle on? Then I can sort out your problems while we drink it.'

'Oh, I don't have any problems. Everything's gone very well,' she said quickly.

'That's good.' He made the coffee and handed her a mug, then cleared the only other chair in the office and sat down. He raised his eyebrows. 'So?'

'Ah, yes. That's what I've been wanting to tell you.' She leaned forward, her eyes shining. 'I've got the next instalment from Granny.'

'Oh, that's great.' He was nearly as excited as she was. 'What does she say?'

'That's why I've been so anxious for you to come in. I don't know, do I? I promised I'd wait till you were with me before I read it.'

He picked up her hand and squeezed it. 'Oh, Lucy, that's really sweet of you. But I really didn't expect you to wait for three days before you opened it.'

'Well, I did promise.'

He gave the hand he was still holding another gentle squeeze. 'I rather like the sound of that,' he said quietly. 'Do you want to look at it now?'

'I've left it in the flat, but I could go and get it,' she said eagerly. 'Have you got time?'

He glanced at his watch and shook his head. 'Not really, I suppose. It would be pushing it a bit. I've got an appointment in half an hour so I wouldn't have time to read it all. But if you could bear to wait till Sunday we could take a picnic somewhere nice and read it then. How about that?'

160

She smiled. 'I've waited this long, I daresay I can wait a bit longer, especially if an afternoon out and a picnic is involved.'

'Good.' He got to his feet and she did the same. He looked down at her. 'It's a date, then?'

'Yes, it's a date.' She smiled up at him. 'I'll look forward to it.'

He drew her towards him. 'And so shall I.' He bent and kissed her and this time it was no accident that his mouth found hers.

Sunday dawned, a sunny late September day that promised to be unseasonably hot later on. Ben had insisted on providing the picnic and he had promised to pick her up in his car soon after two o'clock.

She was just ready as he pulled up. After spending the morning with almost her entire wardrobe spread over the bedroom in a panic of indecision as to what to wear she had eventually settled for her favourite dress, which had a full red skirt with tiny white spots and a bodice with the pattern reversed, a white background with tiny red spots. The sweetheart neckline and sleeve cuffs were trimmed with the red and white skirt material and there was a wide band of the white and red material three inches from the skirt hem. She wore a wide red belt that emphasized her slim waist and took with her a white woollen jacket in case it turned cold.

From Ben's admiring look she knew she had made a good choice.

'Where are we going?' she asked as she settled into her seat.

'It's such a lovely day I thought we'd go to the coast,' he replied. 'I know a very nice, quiet little beach where we can picnic undisturbed and then read the rest of Alice's story.'

'Oh, I like the sound of that,' she said happily.

They drove along country lanes bordered with fields, which here and there had already been ploughed into stripes of rich, brown earth ready for the sowing of winter wheat. The hedgerows were dotted with red hip berries and twined with the last of the dog roses. Blackberries were beginning to ripen and yellow dandelions smothered the verges. There was a definite hint of autumn in the air despite the warm sun.

As they drove along Ben said, 'I've been looking up the 'flu epidemic Alice speaks about in her memoirs. I'd never heard of it and I had great trouble finding out anything about it, which is surprising, considering what a devastating business it all seems to have been.'

'I'd never heard of it, either,' Lucy said. 'So what did you discover?'

'Well, apparently, it was a world-wide thing, a bit like the Black Death, you might say. Something like fifty million people died all told. I could hardly believe what I was reading. India alone lost sixteen million, which was more than half as many again as died in the Great War. And nearly three hundred thousand people died in Britain.'

'Three hundred thousand! Goodness, that's an enormous number,' Lucy said. 'And to think, we'd never known anything about it till we read what Granny has written.'

'That's why I looked it up.' Ben warmed to his theme. 'Apparently, nobody knows exactly where it started but it spread like wildfire in the trenches, on both sides. That was hardly surprising, I suppose, when you think of the conditions the troops were all living under. One theory is that it helped to shorten the war because so many of the soldiers were ill and couldn't fight.'

'And then I suppose they took the infection home with them.'

'I guess so. Of course, crowded troop ships and trains would help to spread the infection.'

'It must have been a very virulent strain of 'flu if all those people died.'

'Yes, people all over the world.'

'Like you said, a bit like the Black Death. That was world-wide.'

'Yes, but that was carried by rat fleas. This was passed on by coughs and sneezes. Or just by breathing the same air.'

She shuddered. 'Oh, that's really scary.'

'And the trouble was, they didn't seem to have any real idea how to stop it from spreading. Things weren't as advanced then as they are now.'

They drove along in silence, thinking about the shocking statistics Ben had unearthed. After a while Lucy suddenly noticed that the fields had given way on both sides of the road to heathland full of colour. Yellow gorse bushes mingled with purple heather as far as the eye

163

could see, and as Ben turned the car off the road into what was little more than a cart track she could see in the distance the glint of sun on the sea.

'Oh, are we nearly there?' she exclaimed in surprise.

'Yes, but we'll have to leave the car soon, because it's a bit of a scramble to get down the cliff to the beach.' He glanced down at her feet. 'I'm sorry. I should have warned you.'

'That's OK. I'll just take my sandals off and slither down in my bare feet.'

They parked the car and found a narrow track down to the beach, made slightly less steep where a huge chunk of cliff had eroded. Scrubby bushes of wild tamarisk grew all round and each side of the pathway.

Ben gave her his hand to help her down and then went back for the picnic basket and a blanket.

While he was gone Lucy went to the water's edge. The tide was receding and high water was marked by a jagged line of seaweed, shells and dried froth halfway up the beach. Beyond it the sand was still wet and perfectly flat for a short distance; further out it had become corrugated by the action of the sea, now nothing more than a gentle ripple. Some distance further up the beach there were other people picnicking, and there were screams of excited laughter from the children splashing each other as they played in the water.

After a first gasp at the cold, Lucy savoured

the water swirling round her ankles and calves and she turned and beckoned Ben to join her. He took off his shoes and socks, rolled up his trouser legs and ran down the beach, a mild expletive escaping as he too felt the shock of the cold water.

Hand in hand they sloshed at the water's edge, laughing at and with each other, picking up shells and popping seaweed as the fancy took them.

'We're like those children along the beach,' Lucy said, laughing up at him.

'Only we're not so noisy,' he laughed back.

'I don't think I'll ever forget this day,' she said dreamily.

'No, neither shall I.' He slid his arm round her waist. 'Come on, little one. Time to eat and then time to read. I'm looking forward to that.'

They went up the beach with their arms round each other and sat down close together on the blanket he had spread.

'What was it Alice used to pack up for Giles when they had their picnics? Sausage rolls, ham patties, chocolate cake?' Lucy said, as Ben unpacked a bottle of wine wrapped in a wet towel followed by sandwiches and sausage rolls.

'I've managed the sausage rolls and chocolate cake but you'll have to settle for ham sandwiches, I couldn't get ham patties,' he said with a grin. 'Although I did try.'

'They didn't have wine, though, did they?' Lucy said, accepting a glass. She held it up. 'Real glass, too.'

'Nothing but the best for you, my lady,' he said bowing his head.

'Do you think Giles was really in love with Alice?' Lucy mused, as she bit into a sausage roll. 'I know she was in love with him, there's no doubt about that.'

'Oh, yes, I'm quite sure he's in love with her,' Ben said softly.

Something in his voice made Lucy look up and catch his eye. 'Quite sure,' he repeated with a smile and she had the feeling that he wasn't really talking about Giles at all.

'But they would never have been able to marry, would they?' she said after a minute. 'After all, he stood to inherit the Hall and she was only a servant there.'

'Stranger things have happened,' he said handing her a piece of chocolate cake. He smiled at her. 'She obviously married somebody or you wouldn't be here.'

'That's true.' She bit into her cake. 'Unless...'

'No,' he said firmly, reading her thoughts. 'He would never have seduced her. He was not that kind of man.'

'How do you know that?'

'I just do. Now, come on, hurry up and eat your cake or we'll never find out what happened to any of them.'

'Aren't you having any?'

He looked a little sheepish. 'I've already had two pieces while you weren't looking.'

'Piggy.'

He sighed dramatically. 'That's me.'

Together, they packed up the picnic basket, leaving out the wine bottle and glasses. Lucy found a suitable spot where there was a boulder to lean back on and spread the blanket out again. When he came back he poured more wine while she undid the envelope and took out the loose-leaf binder, opening it to find more pages covered with her grandmother's neat handwriting. She settled down and began to read.

Fifteen

I rubbed my eyes. I could see Giles sitting there, his back up against the tree under which we so often used to sit. Of course, I was only imagining it, I knew that. It couldn't be Giles, he was dead, blown to pieces in the trenches. But my heart leapt, all the same.

I stood very still, afraid to break the spell. A dead leaf fluttered down from the tree and landed on his shoulder ... landed on his shoulder ... I held my breath.

Then he turned his head and looked at me. Under a coating of grime his face was pale and gaunt and he looked deathly tired. His cap was pushed far back on his head and I could see that his fair hair had darkened and looked lank and greasy. He was wearing a tattered army uniform, the jacket open, several buttons missing; his boots were scuffed and dirty. A half-smoked cigarette was in his hand.

'Giles?' I whispered, afraid the sound of my voice would break the spell and he would disappear.

He didn't disappear. He smiled. It was his familiar crooked smile, yet it held a weary sadness I had never seen before.

Almost reluctantly, I took a step towards him. 'Are you real?' I said, still whispering. 'Please...'

'Oh, yes, it's me. I'm real, Alice in Wonderland,' he replied quietly. 'I've been waiting for you. I knew you'd come and find me.'

I took several more steps, then stopped as he held up his hand. 'No, don't come too near me, I'm filthy, I stink and I'm covered in lice and fleas. What I need more than anything is a bath and some clean linen.'

I crouched down as near to him as he would allow, longing to go to him, to hold him in my arms. 'We were told you were dead ... well, missing, presumed dead.' I hardly dared to blink in case he disappeared and I found I'd been imagining things after all.

He smiled a smile that held no mirth. 'I'm not surprised. I thought I was dead, too, buried under a heap of poor buggers that were...' He bit his lip. 'When I found I was still alive I crawled out from...' He took a deep breath. 'I crawled away. Been shot in the leg so I couldn't walk. A French farmer found me in a ditch, shoved me in his cart and took me home. I was there for...' He shrugged. 'I dunno. Months? Could have been years for all I know. Apparently, I was unconscious for a long time.'

'But how did you get home?'

'I joined up with a battalion who were passing through making their way back. They didn't care. They were just happy to be coming home. When we got to England I was sent home on sick leave. I didn't argue. I am sick. Sick of this bloody war.'

'Oh, Giles. But why did you come here, to this place? Why didn't you come straight to the Hall?' I said.

'Because I heard that the Hall had been isolated because of this 'flu business and that Father was refusing to allow anybody to come or go from there.' He gave a shrug. 'He's not very popular out there, you know. People are pretty sarcastic when they speak of him.' He nodded vaguely in the direction of the village. 'They say he's too concerned for his own skin to let any of his carpenters go and help make coffins ... that's the sort of thing they're saying.' He gave another shrug. 'So I thought it wouldn't be prudent to walk up to the front door in case I was turned away. In any case, look at me...' He spread his hands.

'How can you think that? You're *Giles*. Of course you'd never be turned away. You'll be welcomed with open arms,' I said, tears running down my face, amazed that he should even think that way. 'We all thought you were *dead* and now you're not ... Oh, how could you imagine everyone wouldn't be overjoyed to see you!' As I spoke I stretched out my hand toward him. He put out his own hand and for a brief moment our hands clasped, sending a tingle straight to my heart.

'And are you overjoyed to see me, Alice in Wonderland?' he asked softly.

'Oh, how can you ask? I've dreamed of this for so long I can't believe it's true. I can't believe you're real.' Rashly, I put his hand to my lips before he drew it away. He smiled and touched it to his own lips.

'Come back with me now, Giles,' I urged.

He shook his head. 'Better not, I think. I've seen too much of what this dreadful 'flu can do to risk inflicting it on my family.' He grinned his tired, lopsided smile again. 'And that includes you, my lovely Alice in Wonderland.'

'But you haven't ... you don't think...' I began, alarmed.

'No, as far as I know I haven't caught it, I don't feel ill, just deathly tired.'

'Thank God for that.'

'And thank God you are all safe, too. Perry?'

I nodded. 'He's growing up. You'll see a difference in him.'

'Lizzie?'

I made a face. 'She doesn't like being confined to the Hall,' I said. 'Although since Vera and Vonny...' I stopped.

'What about Vera and Vonny? Are they still at

the same hospital?'

I hesitated. 'They were, yes. But...' I hesitated again. 'It's no good, you'll have to know sooner or later...'

'Know what?' He frowned.

Still I hesitated. Then it all came out in a rush. 'That a telegram came only last week to say that Vonny had died. From influenza.' I took a deep breath. 'And there was another one the very next day to say that Vera had died, too. From the same thing.'

He took a deep, shocked breath. 'Oh, no! Oh, God. Not my little twin sisters.'

'Your mother took a grain of comfort from the fact that both of them died,' I said, my voice little above a whisper. 'She said one of them could never have survived without the other. They'd never been apart all their lives.'

'That's true. And typical of Mama to have such a generous thought when she herself had lost two daughters.'

'And a son,' I reminded him. 'She still thinks she's lost her eldest son, too. Oh, Giles, she'll be over the moon to know you're still alive.' I couldn't help a smile spreading across my face.

He didn't smile back. He was silent for a long time, dragging on his cigarette until at last he threw it down and ground it under his heel. 'No justice, is there, Alice?' he said bitterly. 'I was the one who went to fight, not Vonny and Vera. Yet I'm alive and they were the ones who died.'

'It was 'flu that killed them, not fighting,' I said. 'I'm sorry they had to die, of course I am,

171

but I just thank God you're still alive, Giles.'

He gave me a brief smile of acknowledgement, then we were both quiet for several minutes, deep in our own thoughts.

I broke the silence. 'So what do you intend to do now?' I asked. 'You can't stay out here in the woods indefinitely.'

He shrugged. 'I don't know. Haven't thought that far.' He felt in his jacket for another cigarette and lit it. 'Just wanted to get home. And to see you, Alice.' He looked up at me through the smoke, his eyes dark. 'Out there among all that carnage I realized that class and station in life don't matter a tinker's cuss. It's people that matter. It's you and me that matter, Alice. Nothing else.' The longing look in his eyes made me want to fling myself into his arms and I could see he wouldn't have stopped me if I had.

'Oh, Giles, if only things were as simple as that,' I said. 'Don't forget I'm only a servant...'

'You're not *only* anything, Alice,' he said roughly. 'You're a woman and I love you and that's enough for me.' He smiled. 'You'll see, things will be easier than you might think. Once this war is over, and I'm sure it won't be many days now before it's all finished, life will never be the same, for women especially. I've seen women driving ambulances in the most appalling conditions, tending the wounded, taking them to field hospitals. I've seen them working in conditions that would make a strong man quail. They're not going to be happy going back

172

to the days of drinking tea and leaving calling cards, they're going to start standing up for themselves.'

'Like the suffragettes?' I asked, humouring him.

'Yes, something like that.' He pinched out his cigarette and threw it down. Then he leaned back against the tree and closed his eyes. 'I'm talking too much. I always do when I'm tired. And God, I'm so tired. I just want to sleep and sleep.'

I dragged my mind back to practicalities. 'Well, it's a sure thing you can't sleep out here,' I said, looking round the clearing.

He opened one eye. 'I've slept out here for the past three nights, waiting for you, Alice. And I must say I've slept in worse places.'

'Well, you're not staying out here any longer. Come up to the house with me, now.'

He shook his head wearily. 'Not wise, I think. You've all been kept away from any infection for this long, far be it from me to risk bringing the dreaded 'flu into the family.'

'But you said you were all right,' I said, alarmed that he might not have told me he was ill.

'I am all right, darling Alice, as far as I know. But what I don't know is if I might be carrying the germ without being infected by it myself. God knows, the ship I came back on was crowded to the gunnels and they say this 'flu thrives in crowds. So it might be best if I hole up somewhere ... in one of the stables perhaps, till I'm sure...'

'No.' I shook my head, my mind racing ahead. 'Listen. I've got a better idea. The east wing has been closed up because we never have anybody to stay now and anyway there aren't enough servants left to look after it. I could let you in there and I could bring you food and clean linen...' I smiled. 'Not that you'll be there for long, not once everyone knows you're home.'

He wasn't listening. 'A bath. That's what I need most,' he said fervently, closing his eyes. 'That, and to sleep between clean sheets.' He opened them. 'And you, Alice,' he added softly. 'I need you. I feel as if I never want to let you away from my side again.'

It was a lovely, impossible dream, to be savoured in the future. But the heir to Rookhurst Hall and the parlour maid? In spite of what he had just said, things like that only happened in fairy tales. But now was not the time for shattering dreams, the most important thing was to get him up to the house and then to tell everybody he was not only alive but home, right here, under their very noses.

I smiled at him. 'Well, my love...'

His eyes were closed but he was smiling. 'I like that. Say it again, Alice.'

'Well, my love...'

He opened them. 'Yes?'

'I'm going up to the house now and I'll unlock the door to the east wing for you. It'll probably be best to wait till after dark before you come up. The blue room's got its own bathroom so you can hole up there. I'll make sure there are towels and food for you. Not that you'll be there long. Not when I tell them you're home.'

I could already imagine the joy and excitement. After the dreadful news of the previous week it would be like welcoming home the Prodigal Son.

Or so I thought.

Sixteen

I hurried back to the house, bursting with the wonderful news, but on the way I decided to wait until the next day before I told anybody Giles was alive and home again. I told myself this was to give him a chance to have a good sleep before being welcomed back into the bosom of his family but that wasn't the whole story. While nobody else knew he was back he was my secret, he belonged only to me.

It was a secret I nearly couldn't keep.

'What's the matter with you, miss?' Cook asked suspiciously, as I actually offered to make the cheese sauce for the cauliflower, a job she knew I hated. 'You look as if you've lost sixpence and found half a crown.'

I smiled at her and shrugged. 'I've had a pleasant walk this afternoon in the autumn sunshine and I feel happy, that's all,' I replied, trying without success to wipe the smile off my face.

As I had promised Giles, as soon as I could escape from the kitchen I unlocked the outside door of the east wing, knowing that he would do the rest, choosing his own time – I guessed it would probably be in the middle of the night. I packed a small suitcase with his clothes and other things he would need, including soap and shaving tackle, and I made up the bed in the blue room. I wasn't worried about the sound of the bathwater gurgling, the plumbing at the Hall was efficient but so noisy that you could never tell which part of the house water was coming from or going to.

I also left hot soup and some bread and cheese. Managing all this was not without its difficulties, but things were much more relaxed at the Hall in these days of staff shortages, and being a senior staff member my movements were never questioned.

Early the next morning I let myself into the east wing, which had been kept locked away from the rest of the house since the decision to close it, and hurried along to the blue room with tea and toast for Giles' breakfast. He was still asleep, lying on his back with one arm flung out. He had bathed and shaved and looked more like the Giles I knew and loved, although his face was still thin and gaunt and there were deep lines etched in his face. As I stood gazing down at him, drinking in the sight of him actually lying there, I realized that he had gone away a boy and come back a man.

Suddenly, his eyes flew open and he was up on one elbow, immediately alert and wary. Then he saw me standing there and smiled.

'Oh, I can't tell you how many times I've dreamt of this moment, Alice.' He reached out his hand. 'Just put the tray down and come here,' he said. 'I want to kiss you. Please, I just want to kiss you.'

I wanted to kiss him, too. It was the moment I'd dreamt of, too. Many, many times. I slipped off my shoes and lay down beside him on top of the covers and he enfolded me in his arms. After all, what harm could a few kisses do?

I don't know exactly when I discovered that he was naked under the sheets, I suppose it must have been when I slid under the covers beside him, my clothes thrown anywhere as he pulled them off me. But it all seemed so right, so natural, as if we were born to love each other. And so we did.

Later, much later, he turned his head towards me on the pillow and stroked my hair, which at some point, I don't remember when, he had freed from its restraining plait. He whispered, 'I didn't intend it to happen quite like this, Alice, but I'm glad it has because I've loved you ever since the first day I saw you, down by the stream.' He kissed the tip of my nose. 'You don't have to worry, sweetheart, I meant what I said, I intend to marry you. I've always intended to marry you, you must have known that.'

Smiling, I put up my hand and stroked his face. 'It's a wonderful idea but I don't know how your parents will take to it, Master Giles.'

'They'll get used to it, my Alice in Wonderland.' He nuzzled my neck. 'They'll have no choice because I can't live without you.' He lifted his head and looked down at me. 'I'm serious, Alice. I can't. I really can't. Now I'm home with you I'm never going to let you out of my sight again.'

I gave him a squeeze. 'I'm afraid you'll have to, my love. And right now, because I have duties to perform. And the first one will be to tell your parents the wonderful news.'

'That can wait.' He began to kiss me again.

A little later, when he at last released me, I slid out of bed and put my clothes back on, twisting my tangled hair back under my cap.

'Oh, dear,' I said, peering at my flushed face in the mirror when I'd finished. 'Do I look as if I've been ravished?'

He leaned back on the pillows, his hands behind his head and grinned at me. 'You look wonderful, and I'm warning you, if you don't get out of here quickly you'll be in grave danger of being ravished again.'

I picked up the tray, then put it down again because his breakfast was still untouched. 'Don't tempt me,' I giggled. 'But you'd better eat your breakfast and make yourself respectable because I'm going to tell your father the wonderful news. So prepare to be welcomed into the bosom of your family.'

'I'd rather be welcomed into your bosom,' he said wickedly.

M'Lady always took her breakfast in bed but Sir George was still in the breakfast room drinking coffee while he read *The Times*. He looked up as I entered the room.

'Ah, Alice. Good. I was just going to ring for some fresh coffee,' he said, glancing up briefly.

'I have something important to tell you first, Sir George,' I replied firmly.

I stood in front of him with my hands clasped together to contain my excitement as I told him the wonderful news that his son had returned, quite literally, from the dead.

His reaction was not at all what I had expected. He didn't even smile, let alone rush off to tell M'Lady. Instead, he sat at the table pulling at his moustache, first one side, then the other, his mouth turned down, a frown drawing his bushy eyebrows together until they nearly met. At last he sniffed, then looked up at me.

'You're telling me Giles is actually here, in the house?' he demanded.

'Yes, Sir George.'

He scowled. 'How the hell did he get in?'

'I – I opened the door to the east wing for him,' I faltered, puzzled and surprised at his lack of enthusiasm.

'Is he ... are you sure he hasn't...?' He could not bring himself to say the words.

Now, I understood. 'He appears perfectly healthy but he's very tired. He's been through a lot, Sir George, and his one thought was to get home,' I answered coolly.

That was not exactly what Giles had said, but I didn't think this was the time to tell his father it was me he was anxious to see.

Sir George hrrrumphed a bit, then got up and paced up and down the room. After more hrrrumphing he said, 'I think it will be best if he stays where he is, in the east wing, for a few days. Just in case,' he said gruffly. He waved his hand. 'Just till any danger of him infecting the rest of us with this confounded 'flu is over.' He must have seen the amazement on my face at his reaction to the news because he nodded several times and added, 'Wonderful news, of course. Wonderful news that the boy is alive after all this time. We shall have to kill the fatted calf, so to speak, when he ... when he joins the rest of us. I take it he's not wounded?'

'No, sir. Just tired. What he needs more than anything is sleep.' And me. But I couldn't say that.

'Hmm.'

'Shall I go and tell M'Lady, sir?' I asked eagerly.

He pulled his moustache some more. 'No,' he said slowly after more thought, 'I think perhaps not. She'll be wanting to go and see him and I don't want to have to forbid her.' He nodded again. 'We'll leave it a week or so, till we know there's no danger of infection. After all, there's no doubt he's been exposed to it, coming home on the boat and so forth and we don't want to run any risks...' He frowned at me. 'Do you think a week is enough, Alice?'

I raised my eyebrows, surprised that he should be asking my advice. 'I should think so, sir,' I said. If it had been left to me I'd have kept Giles to myself, for ever and a day.

He cleared his throat. 'And you'll see he has everything he needs? Food and so forth?'

'Oh, yes, sir. You don't need to worry about that. I'll make sure he has everything he needs,' I said, speaking with total confidence.

'Good. Well, I leave it to you to look after him until this day next week.' He nodded several times. 'That should be long enough to be sure it's safe,' he muttered into his moustache. He looked up at me and smiled briefly. 'Capital news, of course, Alice. Absolutely capital news.' But his voice held more anxiety than enthusiasm.

It was then that I realized, with something akin to disgust, that Sir George's decision to isolate the Hall during the 'flu epidemic had had nothing at all to do with preserving Peregrine, his heir, from infection and everything to do with preserving his own skin. Sir George was a coward, terrified he himself might catch the dreaded Spanish 'flu and prepared to go to any lengths to avoid it and keep himself safe.

But I didn't care what his motives were, that week was a magic time for me. And for Giles, too, I like to think. I obeyed Sir George's instructions to the letter and made sure that he had everything he needed. Everything. I believe I can say without fear of contradiction that I never left him alone long enough for him to get bored.

I had to confide in Cook, of course. I could never have kept him supplied with food without her knowledge. As it was, she entered into the conspiracy and cooked the kind of food she knew Giles liked best and made sure he had all the tastiest titbits, so she made a good ally. She also covered for me when I was with him, although she could never have guessed the things we got up to.

Of course, it had to end, our few days of magic. At the appointed time Giles came out of hiding, looking rested and well, to be welcomed back into the bosom of his family and I, for the moment, sank back into the obscurity of servant. He still had quite a limp from his injury but he had put on a little weight. Not that anybody but me knew that because this was the first they'd seen of him. Thankfully, he was showing no sign of the dreaded 'flu that was still ravaging the country, indeed the entire world.

M'Lady's tears this time were of sheer happiness at the return of her firstborn. Lizzie, who had hidden herself away to grieve over her sisters, came back to us almost manically excited at her brother's return. Sometimes I worried a bit about Lizzie. She was an odd girl, these days you never knew whether she would be flamboyantly happy or quietly miserable. She hated being confined to the estate and spent a lot of time either out riding her horse, Becket, or grooming him in the stables.

Peregrine, not unnaturally, I suppose, would not leave his big brother's side, bombarding him with questions, even trying to emulate his limp, which made it difficult for Giles and me to even share a surreptitious kiss. Everyone was so overjoyed to have Giles back that the atmosphere everywhere, even in the kitchen, felt more like Christmas than November.

And then, to cap it all, on the eleventh hour of the eleventh day of the eleventh month of that year the armistice was signed, Germany admitted defeat and the guns were silenced. The terrible war was at last at an end.

Cook managed to make a marvellous celebration meal, using up practically everything from her marble-slabbed larder. There was a delicious game soup, followed by roast turkey, rabbit pie, a whole cold turbot and tiny little whitebait in aspic. There was jam roly-poly because she knew it was Giles' favourite, plus trifle, meringues, and towering multi-coloured jellies that wobbled but miraculously didn't collapse.

And all for only five people.

Vonny and Vera were conspicuous by their absence. Although we were used to them not being there because they had both been away from home for nearly four years, the fact that they were both dead and would never be coming back meant that their absence was felt more keenly than ever before. It was as if we could all cope with the fact that they weren't here because they were somewhere else and would be returning sometime, but we couldn't cope with knowing they would never be back because they were dead. It wouldn't have been quite so bad if other people could have been invited to share in the celebrations, but with the wretched 'flu epidemic still raging Sir George insisted on keeping the Hall isolated.

I could tell from the expression on Giles' face that evening that he wasn't at all happy seeing me waiting on table and hearing the peremptory way his father ordered me about, but as I told him later, lying in his arms, I was still a servant in the house. It was my job to wait on table if that was what I was required to do.

'Even so, that doesn't give him the right to treat you as if you were a slave,' he said furiously. 'I could have knocked him down, the way he was speaking to you, Alice. I would never treat a servant like that.'

'We might not be able to afford any servants, Giles. If you marry me and your father disowns you we might have to live in a barn.' I laughed, but I was serious.

'If you knew some of the places I've lived in during the past four years you'd know you couldn't frighten me with that, Alice in Wonderland.' He kissed me briefly. 'I'd live in a ditch as long as I could be with you.'

'I hope you'll find us something better than that,' I told him, tracing the line from his ear to his chin with kisses. 'But in case you think the life of a servant is all drudgery, let me tell you we had a real feast in the servants' hall finishing up all the leftovers.'

He rolled over so that he was on top of me. 'You shouldn't be eating leftovers in the servants' hall, Alice, you should be sitting at the dining table with me. As my wife,' he said fiercely. 'And before long that's what you will be doing. I promise you that.'

'Oh, dear, then I shall have to mind my manners,' I said with a sigh.

'Rubbish.' He began to cover me with kisses, which naturally put an end to the conversation.

Seventeen

The next day I took some of the leftovers from the celebrations to John Theobald, the chauffeur, and his wife in their flat above the stables. John's wife was getting near her time so she didn't venture outside the house much. It looked to my inexperienced eye as if she might be needing Agnes any day now. It was ironic that the fifteen-year-old kitchen maid was the only one of us who had any experience of childbirth.

'But where is Agnes?' I asked Cook as I helped her to clear the table after we had finished our meal. 'Why wasn't she here to dinner tonight?'

Cook looked over her shoulder to make sure nobody was listening.

'I've let her nip home,' she whispered. 'When he came back from the Lodge with the newspapers this morning Henry brought news that her mum and dad were poorly. She was worried sick about the little ones so I said she could go home, just to make sure they was all right and that there was someone to look after them. I packed up a bit of food for her to take and told her to slip out the back way so she wasn't seen.'

'Oh, dear, do you think that was wise, Cook?' I asked anxiously.

She shrugged. 'Can't see no harm in it. After all, Master Giles is back and he's all right, though God knows all the places he's been where he could've caught it. Anyway, I told her not to stay long. Poor little mite was worried out of her mind so I thought she'd better go and see they was being looked after all right. Put her mind at rest. Anyways, I reckon the papers have made too much of this so-called 'flu epidemic. Meself, I don't reckon it's been as bad as they make out.'

She was soon to find out her mistake.

Agnes slipped back into the kitchen the next evening after dark. She was looking white and shaken and she brought with her the mask that she had been given to wear against the spread of infection.

'They all wear them. Everybody,' she said, showing it to us. 'Not that there's many people about. I don't know where everybody's gone.'

'What about your family?' I asked.

She bit her lip. 'Dad's died,' she said, her eyes filling with tears. 'He never stood a chance, not with him already hevin' the consumption. Our Billy's dead, too. He was never very strong. Mum an' the other three little ones seem all right so far, although Ella's got a dreadful cough and she's a funny blue colour round her mouth, I don't know if that means anything.' Her face crumpled and her voice began to rise. 'But Dad an' Billy, they're still lying in the bed covered up with a sheet. Mum's called the undertaker but he can't get round fast enough to measure people up and get the coffins made, the rate people are dying. They're dying so fast they can't get them buried. I saw for meself all the coffins piled up in Mr Radford's under-taker's shop, they was piled one on top of another, all with bodies in them. I swear he'll have to leave 'em outside the door if he gets many more. And Mum said both the grave-diggers have died so anybody who can dig is asked to go and help dig the graves. The poor vicar's run off his feet, trying to help people. And there's a horrible sickly sweet smell hang-ing over the whole village.' She hung her head, sobbing. 'I never thought it would be like that. It's dreadful.'

'Well, you're back now, love,' Cook said,

patting her shoulder with unusual affection. 'You're safe enough here.'

Yes, I thought bitterly, we're all safe enough here. John, spending his time polishing a motor car that was never used or flirting with Lizzie while his wife waited for the birth of their child. He was able-bodied enough to dig graves. But he wouldn't go, he wouldn't risk it because if he went he couldn't come back. And the rest of us, we were all living in something of a glass palace, cocooned from the realities of life. And all because of Sir George's fear of catching the disease that was sweeping the country. It made me feel quite sick.

But even life at the Hall wasn't without its excitement. Early in the morning two days later, when Agnes was still busy lighting the fires in the breakfast and morning rooms, I had just carried up morning tea for the family and Cook was preparing M'Lady's breakfast tray, John came over looking worried and unshaven.

'Can somebody come? I don't know what to do. Sheila's not well,' he said, prowling round the kitchen and running his hands through his hair, which was already standing on end.

Cook looked up sharply. 'Are you saying her time's come?'

'Yes, I think that's what it is.' He stopped prowling and leaned his hands on the back of a kitchen chair. 'I knew this would happen,' he said savagely. 'We're all stuck here in this bloody place and nobody knows what to do. We can't call on Mrs Carter who looks after these things because nobody's allowed to come here and all the while my Sheila's in dreadful pain.' He straightened up. 'I don't care what Sir George bloody says, I'm damn well going to fetch Mrs Carter.' He started for the door.

'Don't be daft, John,' Cook said sternly. 'And watch your language. You know I won't have bad language in my kitchen. Sit down.'

He came back and sat down, knowing better than to disobey Cook.

'Now,' she said. 'You can't fetch Mrs Carter. For one thing, if what we hear is right she'll be much too busy laying out the dead to come up here. Not that she'd come anyway, from what Master Giles told us nobody in the village would cross the road to help anyone from Rookhurst Hall now.' She pursed her lips. 'That's what isolation's done for us, thanks to Sir George. And you wouldn't want to put Sheila and the baby to risk from 'flu, would you?'

He put his elbows on the table, his shoulders slumped. 'I dunno what to do.'

'Pull yourself together, that's what you can do, then I'll pour you a cuppa tea,' Cook ordered. She nodded at me. 'You go and find Agnes, Alice. She said she'd helped her mother so she'd know what to do. And you'd better go with her. Two pairs of hands will be better than one.' She jerked her head towards John, who was sitting at the table looking lost and woebegone. 'And he'll be no use.' She pushed a cup of tea at him. 'Oh, get this inside you, for goodness sake. You'll give us all the jitters. And then you can finish what Agnes was doing, lighting the fires and getting the coal in, it'll give you something to do.'

I fetched Agnes. She washed her hands and took off the sacking apron she wore for cleaning and we went across to the flat over the stables.

I was scared stiff but for a fifteen-year-old girl Agnes was remarkably calm and competent, soothing Sheila and telling me what to do so I soon forgot my fear. I was fascinated, repelled and amazed all at the same time, caught up in the marvel of birth. I did exactly as Agnes told me, fetching water, tying rags to the foot of the bed for Sheila to pull on, helping wherever I could, full of admiration for the young girl so competently in charge. And several hours later, when Sheila held her little daughter in her arms, tears pricked my eyes and I felt privileged to have been present at this everyday miracle.

'I'll make us all a cuppa tea now,' Agnes said, pushing her hair back with her forearm. 'I think we could all do with it.'

'No, you sit down and have a bit of a rest, Agnes, I'll do it,' I said, surprised to find it was the middle of the afternoon.

When I returned, Sheila was dozing happily, the baby snug in her cradle beside her. Agnes was sitting by the fire looking pale and shivering.

'What's the matter?' I asked.

'Don't worry about me, Alice, I'm all right.

It's only nerves.' She gave me a wintry smile. 'I was like this after our little Jimmy was born. I manage at the time, but it hits me afterwards. Me mam says that's what it is. Jest nerves.' She put the cup to her lips and I could hear her teeth chattering against the china.

'Well, when you've finished your tea you can go over and tell John he's got a beautiful daughter and then you can take the rest of the day off. I think you deserve it.' She looked doubtful so I smiled at her. 'Tell Cook I said so.'

She nodded. 'Thanks, Alice. I think I might go and lie down. I must say I do feel a bit weary. It's hard work helping a baby into the world.'

'You can say that again!' I agreed fervently.

'I shall call her Agnes Mary after you, Agnes,' Sheila said sleepily from the bed.

'Oh, thank you, Mrs Theobald. I'd like that,' Agnes said, clearly delighted.

Of course, there was great celebration. The servants all congregated in the kitchen to congratulate John and to 'wet the baby's head' with mugs of beer. Even The Family raised their wine glasses to the new baby at dinner in the evening.

Agnes didn't appear any more that day so I helped Bessie with the washing up before going to bed. Bessie was the daughter of one of the estate workers, she'd only been with us a few months.

When we'd finished I stood in the kitchen for

a moment, undecided what to do. There was no doubt Agnes deserved a good rest but on the other hand she'd had nothing to eat all day. I cut some thin bread and butter and made her a cup of tea and took it up to her in her little attic room before going to my own bed next door.

'Thanks, Alice, but I'm not hungry,' she said when she saw me, without lifting her head from the pillow. 'My throat's too sore to eat anything. I can hardly swallow me own spit. And I've got a dreadful headache.'

I put my hand on her forehead. It was burning. 'I'll get you some water,' I said.

'Put a hanky over your mouth when you come back,' she whispered. 'Just in case...'

I didn't really think that was necessary but I did as she asked. I took her a headache powder as well as the water, made her comfortable and went to bed, hoping and praying she would be better by morning, that she was simply exhausted both mentally and physically by the events of the day. That was probably all that was wrong with her. Heaven knew, my own head was thumping and I could hardly put one foot before the other, I was so weary myself.

But she was no better in the morning. In fact she was worse, because she had developed a rasping cough in the night.

I told Cook but we decided not to frighten the rest of the staff with our suspicions. Instead, Cook made vast quantities of porridge for everyone because we had heard that this helped to stave off Spanish 'flu.

'Better to be safe than sorry,' Cook said, although we still denied this might be what Agnes was suffering from.

John came in to light fires and carry coal while Agnes was ill. He couldn't stop talking about his beautiful daughter, which cheered us up a lot. I kept my distance from him just in case.

But after a couple of days I began to think our fears were unfounded. Although she still would not eat I thought Agnes was looking better. She had a little colour in her cheeks and her cough had loosened. I didn't realize this was not a good sign until a day later she began coughing up blood and the colour in her cheeks turned an alarming violet blue. Even her ears had a bluish tinge. I did what I could for her. I alone nursed her, wearing a gauze mask over my mouth and nose and a camphor bag round my neck. But it was awful to see the poor girl struggling for breath yet knowing there was nothing I could do. Agnes died in my arms. She had been ill for only four days.

I went down to tell Cook. She was sitting at the kitchen table, mopping her eyes with her apron.

'John's just been over. He's in a terrible way. The baby died in the night. They didn't even realize she was ill,' she said, her voice flat. 'And Sheila's got a temperature. But it could be child-bed fever.' We were still reluctant to admit it could be the dreaded 'flu.

'Agnes Mary, they were going to call her. She

was such a pretty little baby,' I said sadly.

'Was she? I never even saw her.' Cook's face was bleak.

'We'll have to tell The Family because of calling the undertaker,' I said.

Her head shot up. 'Don't breathe a word about Agnes going home, will you, Alice? It'll cost me my place if Sir George ever finds out I let her leave the Hall.'

'But how else could the 'flu have got here?'

She shrugged. 'Master Giles?'

'That's not very likely. He kept to his room for a week and he's never shown any signs of it. In any case, Agnes hasn't been near him.' Not like I have, I thought. If Giles had brought infection home it was me that would have caught it, there was no doubt about that.

'The telegraph boy! He came to the house twice. It was him. He must have brought it. Most likely the germs was on the telegram.' Cook was triumphant at having found a scapegoat.

I didn't argue.

Eighteen

Of course, it fell to me to go and tell Sir George. He was in his study opening the mail Henry had brought up from the Lodge. He looked up through a fug of cigar smoke as I opened the door in response to his barked, 'Come!'

'Well?' He was clearly displeased at being interrupted.

I told him the grave news.

His reaction was not what I had expected, although if I'd thought about it I might have known. He showed not an ounce of sympathy or regret for the two deaths, instead he became nearly apoplectic with rage.

'How did the infection get here? Who's responsible for the lapse in security? Someone must have left the place, or come in. Whoever it is will be instantly dismissed.' I almost smiled at his assumption that it must have been one of the servants.

'The only people that have come to the Hall are Master Giles...'

'Couldn't have been him,' he interrupted rudely. 'We kept him in quarantine for a week and he showed absolutely no sign of it. Still doesn't. Couldn't have been him.'

'Or the telegraph boy,' I continued as if he hadn't spoken. 'He came twice, if you remember, Sir George.' As if any of us were likely to forget!

'Hm.' He pulled at his moustache and swivelled back and forth in his chair.

I shrugged. 'The germ could have been on the telegrams,' I suggested. 'I suppose it could even be on the letters or newspapers that Henry brings up every day. If people were to cough their germs over them...'

'Nonsense.' Nevertheless I noticed that he quickly pushed the day's mail away.

'The point is, Sir George, we need the undertaker,' I persisted. 'A funeral needs to be arranged for Agnes and the baby.'

His face went red and I thought he was going to pull his moustache out by the roots the way he tugged at it. 'I'm not having any undertaker coming here,' he barked. 'Don't you realize? Undertakers are exposed to infection all the time. The last thing we want is an undertaker coming here bringing God knows what with him, not after we've managed to keep the blasted 'flu out for all this time.'

I could have killed the stubborn old man with my bare hands. 'But it hasn't been kept out, it's here, Sir George,' I reminded him. 'And Agnes and the baby must be given a decent funeral. We can't just leave them lying...' I swallowed at the picture my words conjured up and went on. 'Perhaps you wouldn't mind telephoning the undertaker and making arrangements for him to

196

come. It'll come better from you, as master of the Hall, than from one of the servants.' At least it would carry more clout, I thought. Sir George was used to people being at his beck and call. Added to that, of course, none of us in the servants' hall knew how to use a telephone.

He must have heard something in my voice that made him realize he was not being reasonable. 'Yes. Yes, of course. I'll do it now.' He picked up the telephone, dropping it twice in his agitation. 'You'd better wait while I telephone, I may need more details.'

At the third fumbling attempt he managed to ring the exchange and ask for the undertaker.

'I'm sorry, Sir George, I've been told not to put any more calls through to Mr Radford,' I heard Mrs Jones the operator, who also ran the post office, say. That was something I'd noticed about the telephone, everybody shouted. She went on, 'Don't you realize what's going on out here? In case you hadn't noticed there's a 'flu epidemic. People are dying left, right and centre and the poor man's being run off his feet trying to help out all over the district. None of the undertakers can cope. Coffins are piling up everywhere – Mr Radford's even got them stacked up on the sideboard in his front room waiting for burial because the gravediggers are all dead and them that are trying to help out can't dig graves fast enough. And now there aren't any coffins left to put the bodies in because the carpenters can't get the wood to make any more. Nobody's ever known anything like it.' Her voice was rising hysterically. 'And you think, Mr High and Mighty Sir George Bucknell, that just because you live in your little ivory castle up at the Hall, isolated from the rest of the world, you can just ring up and snap your fingers and Mr Radford will come running. Well, I'm telling you, if you think that you've got another think coming!' The phone was slammed down before he could speak.

He hung the earpiece up and stared at it for a moment, his mouth hanging open. Then he looked up at me in amazement. Nobody had ever dared to speak to him like that before.

'So what's going to happen, Sir George?' I asked, pretending I hadn't heard the tirade from Mrs Jones. I felt almost sorry for this man who had been so anxious to protect himself and – if I was generous – his family that he had distanced himself from the horrors that were taking place almost under his nose.

He took a deep breath and pulled himself together.

'Apparently, the undertaker can't come just at present so I suppose the only thing we can do is to find someone among the members of staff who can lay people out. Then, as it seems there are no coffins to be had, the bodies will have to be stitched into shrouds and put carefully in the coldest place you can find.' He was silent for a moment, tugging at his moustache as he always did when he was thinking. 'Ah, yes, the old ice house, that would be a good place. It's partly underground and lined with brick. There's no ice in there now of course, but...' He looked at me questioningly, his eyes troubled and uncertain, expressions I had never seen there before. 'What do you think, Alice? Do you think that would be best?'

I gulped. I'd never known Sir George to ask anyone's opinion before, let alone mine. But this was the second time he'd asked my advice and since he had asked I wasn't afraid to say my piece.

'I think it's a very good idea, Sir George. But I also think we should all wear gauze masks over our faces and camphor bags round our necks. That's what it says we should do in the newspaper.' I fingered the bag round my own neck. 'Cook already makes porridge for breakfast every day. That's supposed to be good for preventing infection, too.'

'Good. Good. Whatever you think best, Alice.' He shook his head. 'I don't know what the world is coming to, can't get a decent burial...'

I left him then. He looked quite defeated.

Henry's wife, who like Henry was becoming elderly and arthritic, had once been known as Nurse Willis and in her day had been called on to officiate at all the births and deaths in the village. Now, although she could hardly walk and her hands were so crippled and gnarled that she could hardly use them, she came to the rescue and made Agnes and the baby ready before they were laid carefully and respectfully in the ice house awaiting burial.

The ice house then had to be locked because Peregrine had taken a ghoulish interest in the proceedings, in spite of being warned he might catch the dreaded 'flu.

'Room for a lot more bodies down there,' he remarked cheerfully, trying to peer through the open door.

'You jest watch out yours ain't one of 'em, Master Perry,' Henry said, giving him a scathing look.

M'Lady came down to the kitchen in spite of Sir George's insistence that the infection was confined there. She was wearing a mask and she brought several more with her, together with a little pile of camphor bags.

'I have just stitched these for all of you,' she said in her melodious voice. 'We must all do what we can to prevent any more infection.' She turned to go. 'Oh, Alice, I shall take my breakfast downstairs with Sir George for the time being, not in my room. It'll save work for you.' She shuddered. 'Ugh. I wish I didn't hate porridge so much, it reminds me of my nursery days. But I shall eat it, along with everybody else. Make sure all the servants eat plenty of it as well, Cook.'

Cook bobbed a curtsey. 'Very well, M'Lady.'

'Oh, and I shall send Miss Lizzie down to give you a hand. She can wash up and peel potatoes if she's shown how. It's time she began to make herself useful.'

Sometimes I wondered how such a gracious lady had managed to find herself married to such a boorish man as Sir George. It surely couldn't have been a love match.

Two mornings later John didn't appear to bring in the coals and light the fires, a task he'd taken on when Agnes became ill. With fear in my heart I went over to his flat and found him lying beside the bed in a pool of bloody vomit.

'Can you help him up, Alice?' Sheila said, weak tears running down her cheeks. She'd hardly stopped crying since her baby died and her voice sounded rasping and rough. 'He's been sleeping in the armchair covered with a blanket because of my lying-in and I could hear him groaning in the night. I called out to him several times but he said I wasn't to worry. Then when he tried to get up to make a cup of tea this morning he fell down making a dreadful choking sound. I keep trying to get out to help him but I can't, I haven't got the strength. My limbs all feel like water and my head spins every time I lift it off the pillow. Perhaps you can help him, Alice. Can you help him up on to the bed with me so I can see him and hold him.'

I crouched down beside him and saw that his face had turned a bluish purple. Even his ears were blue although it was worse round his mouth. I'd seen this before, with Agnes, just before she died. John was already dead.

'I'm sorry. It's too late, Sheila,' I whispered, looking up at her. 'He's dead.'

She raised her head a little. 'Dead? No, he can't be dead. Not my John!' Her head fell back on the pillow, which was soaked with sweat and

201

tears. 'It'll be me next, Alice,' she murmured. 'I've nothing left to live for now my baby and my husband are both gone. I shall be next. Please God it won't be long before I join them.'

I looked down at her. Her ears were already blue and the tell-tale blue tinge was creeping across her cheeks and round her mouth. I knew she was right and there was nothing I could do to save her.

I stayed with her all day, sponging her with cool water to bring down the fever, holding her as she coughed black mucus up from her lungs, giving her sips of water until she sank into unconsciousness and died.

I could hardly believe it, the same little family who had been so happy at the birth of their first child now wiped out. And all in the space of a few days. And the same thing was happening all over the country. All over the world.

The little rhyme Henry had sung to us in his quavering voice came back to me:

I had a little bird and its name was Enza.
I opened the door and in flew Enza.

Last time there was a plague like this was back in the seventeenth century. They had a rhyme for that, too:

Ring-a-ring o' roses, a pocket full of posies.
A-tishoo, a-tishoo, we all fall down.

I couldn't help wondering how many more

people would fall down from this dreadful scourge before it was ended.

But all was not doom and gloom. Human nature is such that even the direst circumstances have their compensations and mine was that I saw plenty of Giles, although during the day we could seldom do more than snatch the odd kiss when nobody was looking. However, we made up for it when I went to his room each night, ensuring I slipped back to my own room before anybody was about in the morning. Sometimes I only made it by the skin of my teeth!

Unlike his father, who for the most part refused to leave his study except at meal times, Giles was tireless in helping out wherever he could, from milking the cows to mucking out the pigsties to carrying the dead bodies to the ice house. I wished he wouldn't work so hard and such long hours, although now that he was at home, rested and well-fed, he looked the picture of good health and my heart skipped a beat every time I saw his handsome figure limping about the place. I crossed my fingers and prayed that he would remain that way. I was terrified he would catch the disease; now that he was back with me I couldn't bear the thought of losing him again. It never occurred to me that I was in just as much danger as he was.

But we all did what we could without thought for our own safety because so much help was needed everywhere. Once the dreaded influenza had reached Rookhurst Hall it spread like wildfire over the entire estate, and seemed to attack people indiscriminately.

Yet apparently it was not entirely indiscriminate. It was reported in the newspapers, who of course had access to the wider view, that it was often the young, healthy people, people in their twenties, who were worst hit. Speculation was rife as to why this should be. Medical opinion seemed to favour the idea that children were born with a natural immunity and older people, over years of exposure to infection, had built up their own. Young men and women fell between the two and were therefore more susceptible to infection.

It didn't seem like that to me. On the estate, people of all ages went down with the dreaded 'flu. Some recovered quickly, some were ill for weeks. Some never recovered at all. It was a cruel, unpredictable scourge. Bodies began to pile up in the ice house shrouded in white sheets, waiting for an undertaker who had neither coffins nor gravediggers and was at his wits' end trying to cope. In the end, Jim, the estate handyman, began to fashion coffins out of what wood he could find, aided by Albert, an old farm worker who should have retired years ago and was an expert in hedging and ditching. Giles rolled up his sleeves and helped them.

Nineteen

As well as helping to make coffins Giles organized men to begin digging graves.

'It's no use, we can't go on like this, Father. We shall have to start burying them ourselves, here on the estate,' I heard him telling Sir George as I served dinner one night.

'Is that allowed, Giles?' Lizzie asked.

He shrugged. 'I don't know whether it is or not. But since there's nobody else to do it and we can hardly leave the bodies to rot I don't see any alternative. There are already twenty bodies in the ice house and some of them ... well, let's just say that some of them have already been there too long.'

'I know,' Perry said eagerly. 'I was there the other day...' He pinched his nose with two fingers and made a face.

'That's enough, Perry,' his mother said quickly. 'You know you're not supposed to go anywhere near the ice house.'

'No, young 'un, you know very well it's out of bounds,' Giles said. He turned back to Sir George. 'Well, Father?'

Sir George nodded, prodding at his food without much interest, which wasn't at all like him.

'Ah. Yes. Well, I suppose you'd better call the vicar, then,' he answered at last, looking anxious. All the fight seemed to have gone out of him. He had retired into his shell, his usual bumptious, bullying manner gone. He was a frightened man. In truth, we were all frightened, but the rest of us kept our fear at bay by going about our business as normally as we could. Sir George was still trying to hide and now that there was no place he could hide physically he hid mentally.

Giles sighed. 'The vicar can't come, Father. Don't you remember? I told you, he died last week.'

'Oh, did you? Ah, yes, so you did.'

'But I'm sure we can manage. We'll have our own funeral. You can say the burial service, Father.'

Sir George looked up, alarmed. 'Oh, I don't know...'

'You'll have to, Father. It's your duty, as head of the estate.' Giles' tone brooked no further argument. 'I'm sure it's not illegal under the circumstances and it goes without saying that we shall make sure it's done in a reverent and dignified manner.'

So on a cold, foggy day we all put on our Sunday best and congregated round the graves that had been dug by those able-bodied men that were left on the estate. Sir George, wrapped in a huge black overcoat, took off his top hat and exposed his bald head just long enough to recite the burial service in a nervous, quavery voice quite unlike his usual stentorian tones, his hands trembling visibly as he held the prayer book. As he spoke the bodies, some in coffins, some simply shrouded in white sheets, were slowly lowered into the graves that had been dug. Where whole families had died they were buried together in one grave, otherwise each was buried separately. A rough wooden cross with the names of those buried beneath was placed over every grave. Later, stone crosses would replace them and the whole area would be enclosed by railings.

It was a sobering experience for those of us left and as we walked away we couldn't help wondering who the next victim would be.

We didn't have long to wonder. That night, after feeling vaguely unwell at dinner, Sir George himself collapsed as he got up from the table. He writhed on the floor, choking and clutching at his collar, his eyes bulging and blood spurting from his ears and nostrils. In less than two hours he was dead, an unpleasant, choking death which shocked us all, not least by its violent suddenness.

It fell to Giles to say the burial service over his father.

Yet such was the capricious nature of the disease that while so many died, just as many recovered and some never succumbed to it at all. Bessie, the little kitchen maid, was ill for several days and we feared for her life but she rallied and was soon back to normal. Master Perry was ill for weeks, sometimes lying delirious with fever, at others fretting because he couldn't get out of bed and go out riding on his horse. M'Lady never left his bedside, her young son's illness affected her far more than her husband's death, it seemed to me. But eventually he recovered and his older brother ruffled his hair and remarked, 'I knew you'd get better, young 'un. Only the good die young.' Giles and Perry had a good, brotherly, bantering relationship.

Of course, as I said, not everybody caught 'flu, some of us escaped altogether – Cook, Miss Lizzie, M'Lady, Arthur, me. We all worried about M'Lady, she was so thin and fragile-looking that a puff of wind could have blown her away. Yet she was a tower of strength to us all and able to stay up night after night tirelessly caring for Perry without ill-effect, while Sir George, a big, solid man, had died, killed by the very thing he dreaded and had tried so hard to avoid.

Gradually, thankfully, the epidemic began to ease. The numbers of deaths reported in the newspaper began to fall and people in the towns and villages began to pick themselves up, resuming some kind of normal life despite the gaps left in their families by the scourge of Spanish 'flu.

Even so, it had a cruel sting in its tail.

It was a few days before Christmas, when we were all beginning to relax because there had been no deaths in the village or on the estate for over a fortnight. Sir George's ban had at last been lifted and people could come and go as they pleased to the Hall. The servants were relieved at being able to visit their families again, and despite the mutterings against Sir George there was no difficulty in getting back the scrubbing and laundry women, because they needed the money.

The usual preparations were going on at the Hall. Christmas was Christmas, although nobody had much heart for it and nearly everybody was in black, either through having lost somebody near and dear to them or in deference to Sir George.

However, M'Lady had decreed that Christmas should be celebrated normally as far as was possible, so Mr Baines had brought a young fir tree in to be decorated and we were putting up sprigs of holly and mistletoe in the dining room and drawing room. We were all very conscious that Sir George would not be there, at the head of the table, to carve the turkey and hand out presents to the servants with his usual forced air of jollity, that task would fall to M'Lady. Or Giles. They hadn't yet decided which of them would do it. In the event, Fate decided for them.

Giles was helping put up the holly and mistletoe, and making a great play of kissing all the ladies under the mistletoe. He even caught Cook, which rather flustered her. I made sure he caught me several times. I was excited but not a little apprehensive, because I knew that he was going to announce our engagement as The

Family drank their sherry before Christmas dinner.

'This is what we'll do, darling,' he said. 'You bring in the sherry, I'll pour it and you can take them each a glass then come and stand by my side. That's when I'll tell them all we're to be married and—'

'When they've got over the shock...' I giggled, lying in his arms on his bed when I was supposed to be sorting linen.

'All right, when they've got over the shock, I'll put the ring on your finger and you can go and put your glad rags on and take your rightful place next to me at dinner in the dining room.' He was going to give me a ring that had belonged to his grandmother. I hadn't seen it, it was to be a surprise, but he assured me it was a very pretty ring.

'I do hope they'll accept me,' I said doubtfully.

He gave me a kiss. 'Of course they will, silly. Everybody likes you. How could they not?'

'Yes, but only as a servant, who looks after them.'

'Well, they'll have to get used to liking you as a relative-in-law. I'm head of the house now, remember. What I say, goes.'

I didn't think it would be quite as simple as that but I didn't argue.

When we finished the decorating and were clearing up Giles went over and sat by the fire. He was shivering and complaining of feeling cold although the fire was piled high with logs

210

and the room was warm.

'It's only an excuse to get out of helping with the clearing up,' Lizzie teased him. She had put a bit of tinsel in her hair in an effort to be festive. 'You can't possibly be cold, Giles. Look, the fire is halfway up the chimney.'

'I know it is. But I still feel cold and shivery.' He drew as near to the fire as he could without scorching his trousers.

M'Lady frowned. She looked very elegant in black, relieved only by a double gold chain that hung nearly to her waist. It suited her peaches-and-cream complexion and blonde hair. She went over and put a hand on his forehead. 'I think you're feverish, Giles. Your head is very hot. Perhaps you should take a headache powder and go to bed with a hot water bottle, dear,' she suggested. She spoke calmly enough but I could see the anxiety on her face.

'Yes, I think perhaps I'll do that,' he agreed, which rather surprised me. Giles didn't usually give in that easily. 'I don't want to miss the festivities, do I?'

The next morning when I took him his morning tea – a privilege I reserved for myself – he was shivering under the covers although he was bathed in sweat.

'I think it's got me, Alice,' he said through chattering teeth. 'I feel bloody awful.'

I stroked his sweat-soaked brow. 'I'll look after you, Giles,' I promised. 'I'll make sure you're better soon.' I tried to sound calm but my insides were a churning mass of fear and

211

panic. No, not Giles, I was praying desperately. Not my beloved, precious Giles.

Christmas must have come and gone, but it didn't register with me. I nursed him for three weeks, willing him to get better, bathing his fevered body, caring for him in ways that would have mortified him had he known. I didn't care what the others thought, I never left his side and wouldn't let anybody else nurse him. Sometimes he seemed to be improving, then the fever would return and he would thrash about the bed, delirious. And all the time he had a racking cough that shook his whole body. Then, one evening early in the New Year, he quietened and gave me a lovely smile.

'I'm feeling so much better I do believe I'm on the mend, Alice in Wonderland,' he said softly, 'although I feel as weak as a kitten so I don't think I'll be able to spring our little surprise on the family at Christmas dinner. It'll have to wait a few days longer, I'm afraid.'

I leaned over and smoothed his hair away from his forehead. 'Christmas was a fortnight ago, darling,' I said as I kissed him.

'Good Lord, have I been ill all that time?' He held out his hand to me and I took it. 'Don't leave me, Alice.'

'I haven't left you for the past three weeks, my darling. I shan't leave you now.'

I sat down beside him and held his hand to my heart. All night I held it, dozing by his side, exhausted but happy to think the worst was over.

I was wrong. When I woke in the morning his hand was cold. My beloved Giles was dead. I couldn't even begin to describe the desolation that swept over me. At first I couldn't, wouldn't believe it. I have to confess that I even shook his lifeless body a little, refusing to believe what I knew to be true. Then I sat beside him for a long time, trying to drag myself into some semblance of normality, knowing that somehow I had to summon the strength to go and break the news that Giles was dead without screaming and railing against the Fate that had taken him from me.

Somehow I did it.

It was a sad little group that clustered round as M'Lady read the burial service in her low, melodic, precise tones that nevertheless carried clearly on the frosty air. I admired her self-possession because I knew how much she loved her eldest son. Her voice only broke once and she recovered herself quickly. For my part, I had to pretend that Giles was no more to me than to the rest of the servants, after all, would they have believed me if I'd told them the truth? But inside I was dying. I couldn't even allow myself a quiet tear like Cook and Bessie because I knew that once I started crying I wouldn't be able to stop. My tears had to be reserved for the privacy of my room in the dead of night when I could give vent to my feelings and acknowledge that my heart was completely broken.

I have to admit that I was so busy trying to

hold myself together at the graveside that I hadn't noticed that poor Lizzie was overcome with grief until she fainted and had to be carried away and put to bed. But M'Lady showed no such weakness. It didn't take us long to discover that she had a backbone of steel under her fragile appearance. Now that her husband and elder son were dead she took over the reins in a way that amazed everybody.

Fortunately, Mr Baines had escaped the epidemic and she left him to organize the estate with what men he had left, and to recruit more from the surrounding villages if he needed to. This wouldn't be difficult. In spite of those killed in the war and the influenza cull, there were still soldiers returning who would be looking for work.

Indoors there was just Cook and Arthur, Bessie and me.

'I'm sure we'll have no trouble in finding new staff,' M'Lady said optimistically. 'But until we do I suggest we close both the east and west wings. Indeed, the extra accommodation won't be needed since there will be no more shooting parties now that Sir George is no longer with us.' She didn't sound as if she minded that at all.

So life gradually limped back to something approaching normality.

As M'Lady had predicted, there was no difficulty in finding new staff. The antagonism felt by the villagers towards Sir George when he isolated the Hall during the epidemic didn't

214

extend to M'Lady, everyone knew the ban was not of her making. In fact everyone loved and respected her. And people needed work.

Peregrine, at barely sixteen, proved to be surprisingly mature. He refused to go back to school, instead asking Mr Baines to teach him how to run the estate. Mr Baines was reluctant at first – he couldn't forget what a pest the boy used to be – but was surprised to find him willing and eager to learn. And – the most important thing in Mr Baines' book – not afraid of hard work.

Lizzie was the only one who made no effort to help. She stayed in her room, refusing to eat and complaining that she was unwell. We all thought she was grieving over Giles so we left her alone, but eventually I went up to her and found her lying in bed looking white and ill, her eyes puffy and red because she had been crying.

I frowned. 'What on earth's wrong with you, Miss Lizzie?' I dropped to my knees and put my hand on her forehead. 'Oh, please, not you! I thought this dreadful 'flu was over. Have you got a temperature?'

She dashed it away. 'No, don't worry, I have not got 'flu, and I haven't got a temperature,' she snapped. 'It's worse than that.'

I got to my feet. I couldn't think of anything worse than the dreaded 'flu.

She looked up at me. 'I'm pregnant,' she said flatly.

Twenty

My legs nearly buckled under me, I was so surprised. I sat down on her bed with a thump. 'Pregnant?' I repeated stupidly. 'Miss Lizzie, are you sure?'

'Of course I'm sure. I've got all the signs.' She plucked at the sheet irritably.

'What signs?' I asked blankly. She obviously knew a great deal more about these things than I did.

She shrugged. 'Oh, you know. My breasts are sore, I feel sick all the time. I fainted at Giles' funeral. All the usual signs. And you must have noticed when you sorted the laundry I haven't had my past three monthlies.' A smile hovered round her lips. 'I suppose I shouldn't be surprised. John and I did go at it a bit.' She glanced up at me to see my reaction.

My mouth dropped open. 'John? You've been...? With John Theobald? But what about Sheila, expecting his child?'

She gave a shrug. 'Well, he couldn't do anything ... not with her like that ... and a man has needs...' She sat up in bed. 'It was never anything serious, Alice,' she said, hugging her knees. 'He was never going to leave his wife.

He loved Sheila, I knew that. But I was bored with not being able to leave the Hall and he was ... well, let's just say he didn't need much persuasion.' She sighed. 'We had some really good—'

I put my hands over my ears. 'Stop. Stop. I don't want to hear any more.'

'I just never thought I might get pregnant,' she said, sliding down under the covers again. 'Well, to tell the truth I never thought about anything much except—' She broke off when she saw my expression. 'But now I feel sick and ill and I don't know what I'm going to do.'

I swallowed and shook my head, fear clutching at my insides. 'Have you told M'Lady?'

'Tell Mama? Don't be silly. I can't tell her. She'd go through the roof.'

'Well, you can't stay in bed for the next six months so she'll have to know sooner or later.' Sometimes Lizzie could be remarkably stupid. I might not know much about the finer details of pregnancy but I did know that it was something that couldn't be hidden indefinitely.

'Not if I go away.' Her eyebrows lifted as the idea occurred to her. 'Yes, I could do that. I could go away and have the baby and then come back.'

'And what about the baby?'

'Oh, I don't know,' she said irritably. 'I hadn't thought about that.'

'It strikes me there's quite a lot you haven't thought about, Miss Lizzie,' I said primly.

She shook her head irritably. 'I dunno. I

suppose I'll have to get it adopted. Or put it in an orphanage. There, I've thought about it now,' she said. She sat up and clutched my hand. 'Yes, that's what I'll do. I'll go away,' she said triumphantly. She hesitated. 'But I don't think I could go alone.' She looked at me for a minute. 'Alice, I know it's a lot to ask, but would you come with me? It wouldn't be quite so bad if you were there to...' She didn't say the words but I could hear the unspoken plea, she wanted me there to look after her.

I took a deep breath. 'I don't know. I'll have to think about it.' Why should I give up my safe life, a comfortable home and a regular wage, a good part of which I could put in my growing bank account to save for my old age, in exchange for an uncertain future with this selfish, thoughtless girl?

I left her and went back to my room and sat down on my bed. I didn't want to go with Miss Lizzie. I didn't want to go to a strange town and search for somewhere to live. I didn't want to look after this silly, self-centred girl till her baby was born, nor to worry about what was to happen to it afterwards. I didn't want my life disrupted. Changed for ever. Hot tears dropped on my arms as I rocked to and fro, hugging myself.

But I knew that I would go with her. I would go with her because I had no choice. Because I too had the symptoms she had described. My breasts were sore and heavy, I too had missed my monthlies and I felt lethargic and sick all the time, in fact several times I had had to rush to the toilet and only just got there in time, thinking I had eaten something that didn't agree with me. But now I knew it wasn't that. It wasn't that at all.

Lizzie was not the only one who was pregnant. I was carrying Giles' child.

I folded my hands over my stomach protectively, a ghost of a smile playing round my lips. For a brief moment I could be glad. Glad that I had Giles' baby growing inside me, glad that I would always have this lasting legacy of his love – his child.

I realized that this would mean my life was going to be very different and probably very difficult from now on. But I had no regrets, my child and I would manage somehow. And the first step on the path to our future was being made smooth for me. Because Lizzie wanted me to go away with her.

I waited two days before I told her I would go with her, because I didn't want to appear too keen. To my amazement she already had a plan worked out.

'But how could you be so sure I was going to agree?' I protested.

'I knew you would if I prayed hard enough,' she replied confidently. Lizzie was not normally religious so I realized then just how desperate she was.

She outlined her plan, assuring me that one thing we wouldn't be short of was money, which was a relief.

'Well, I haven't been able to go anywhere to spend my allowance, have I?' she pointed out, adding that when the money eventually ran out she would sell her jewellery.

'And we'll also have the money from selling the Bentley,' she added.

'The Bentley? Your father's car? But you can't do that,' I said, horrified.

'Why not? He's dead so he's got no further use for it, and anyway there's nobody to drive it now John's dead so it'll only be rusting in the garage.'

'But how...? Where...?' I was practically speechless.

'I've got it all worked out. I'll drive it to Ipswich and sell it there. Then we'll take the train to Cambridge. Or Norwich. Or even Colchester, I haven't decided which yet, and find ourselves lodgings. That way nobody will be able to trace us.'

'But you can't drive.'

'Oh, I'll manage.' She waved her hand airily. 'John showed me where the gears are. And the brake. That's all you need to know except how to steer the thing and I'll soon get the hang of that.' She sounded quite excited.

Which was more than I felt. I puffed my cheeks and let out a long breath. 'But you can't just get in a car and drive away. Somebody will hear,' I said weakly.

'No, they won't. We'll go early in the morning, before anybody is up. Then, even if they do hear us, by the time they get their clothes on we'll be well away so they won't catch us.'

'Well, I don't know...' The whole thing seemed fraught with danger to me and I didn't think we'd get away with it. I must confess part of me hoped we wouldn't. I was sure M'Lady would stand by Lizzie and there was just an outside chance that she would stand by me when she knew I was carrying her beloved Giles' child. So I went along with Lizzie's outlandish scheme, almost confident that we wouldn't even get as far as Ipswich.

Miraculously, we not only got as far as Ipswich with nothing worse than a dented bumper and smashed headlamp, but Lizzie even managed to find a garage in a back street where the man was willing to buy the car. I had to admire her, she'd found out what it was worth and she haggled with the man till she got more out of him than he wanted to pay. True, she didn't get as much for it as she'd hoped, but at least she got rid of it with no questions asked.

'You should have joined the suffragettes,' I said admiringly as we got on the train, 'they need women like you.'

'I might do that, when I've got rid of this.' She pointed to her stomach, then saw my expression. 'I mean when it's born, silly.' I wondered if she was thinking she would keep it after all, with the idea that I should look after it while she went her own way. I might, at that. For a price. I couldn't see that looking after two would be any more trouble than looking after one. But she would have to earn the money to

221

keep us all. Whether she realized it or not, her life as a lady was fast coming to an end, I intended to see to that.

We caught the train to Norwich. I would have been excited if I hadn't been so nervous. I had never been on a train before and we seemed to rattle through the countryside at an alarming rate. But Lizzie was quite composed and unaffected.

'So far, so good,' she said smugly as we settled into our corner seats in the otherwise empty carriage, our luggage, most of which belonged to Lizzie, either on the rack above us or beside us on the seat. 'Now, when we get to Norwich we'll find a hotel where we can spend the night before we start looking for rooms.'

'A hotel!' I was horrified. 'Surely, we can't afford—'

'Oh, I've got plenty of money,' she said. 'Don't forget I've just sold a large car.'

'That may be, but we're going to need money for rent and food, as well as things for the baby...' I nearly forgot myself and said 'babies'.

'Yes, but it's only going to be for six months or so. And I shan't need much for the baby. As soon as it's born I intend to get it adopted or put it in an orphanage. Then we can forget all about it and go back home.' She gave me a winning smile, delighted that she had got things so easily worked out.

I couldn't believe she could be so callous. But life had always been simple in Lizzie's eyes. She had only to think she wanted something and it fell in her lap. 'It may not be quite as easy as that,' I contented myself with saying.

'You're afraid we'll run out of money, aren't you? Well, I shall keep a tight rein on the purse strings and if we start to run out you'll have to find yourself work.' She waved her hand. 'Not that you'll need to, of course, you'll be too busy looking after me, but if it became necessary I'm sure there'd be something you could do.'

I took a deep breath. I knew I would have to tell her about my own condition at some point and this seemed as good a moment as any. 'In a few months' time I shan't be in a fit state to go out and find work, Miss Lizzie,' I said quietly. 'You're not the only one who's pregnant.'

'You!' Her eyes widened and her mouth dropped open. 'Why, you little—'

'Be careful before you start calling me a little slut, Miss Lizzie,' I said, icicles dripping off my tongue in my fury. 'It could be a case of the pot calling the kettle black, except that my baby was conceived in love whilst by your own admission yours was the result of nothing more than boredom and lust.'

For a moment she looked shocked. Then her expression hardened and her eyes narrowed in temper. She was not used to being spoken to like that, but I held my ground. 'So, would you like me to leave you and get out at the next station?' I asked, my voice still cold.

She leaned back and closed her eyes. 'No, of course not, Alice. I deserved that,' she said with a sigh. Her eyes flew open. 'So who's the father? One of the farm hands?'

'That's my business,' I said primly. 'All I'll say is that we were going to be married but he died of 'flu.' The fact that it was Giles' baby I was carrying was a precious secret I was not prepared to share with anyone, least of all Lizzie.

'Well, well, so we're both in the same boat. No wonder you didn't hesitate when I asked you to come away with me. When's it due?'

'I'm not sure. Sometime early in August, I should think.'

'I think mine's due in late July.' She gave a wry smile. 'So we're really in this together, Alice, aren't we?' she said.

She was quiet for several minutes, deep in thought. 'I think you'd better start calling me Lizzie and drop the "Miss", Alice, because we shall have to pass ourselves off as widows whose husbands died in the war or in the 'flu epidemic,' she said at last. 'I don't think we can pretend to be sisters so we'd better just be friends.' She hesitated. 'We are friends now, aren't we, Alice?' she asked almost shyly.

'Yes, we're friends, M—Lizzie.' I leaned across and squeezed her hand to confirm it.

Twenty-One

'What's the matter?' I frowned at Lizzie. 'Why are you looking at me like that?'

She bit her lip. 'I don't want to offend you, Alice,' she said, obviously not wanting to say anything to upset our new-found and still fragile friendship. 'But your clothes...'

I looked down at myself. I was wearing my best coat and hat but I could see what she meant. I was dressed plainly and serviceably, like the servant I was. Or had been, till now. I shrugged. 'It's all I've got,' I said. 'What do you suggest?'

She smiled, a winning, slightly wicked smile. 'Wear some of mine. Then we'll both look the part.' She opened a portmanteau on the seat beside her and began flinging clothes out on to the seat. It was a good thing we were the sole occupants of the Ladies Only compartment because there were clothes all over the place. When she had found what she was looking for we pulled down the blinds and I changed into an ankle-length dark brown gabardine skirt and three-quarter length coat and a pink shantung blouse. She even found me a pair of artificial silk stockings – I would never have paid one and six a pair for such luxuries.

'There now,' she said, satisfied. 'I'm afraid your boots will have to do. My feet are smaller than yours. And your hat ... Oh, yes, I know what we can do. Wind this pretty scarf round it. That'll cheer it up.'

She looked me up and down. 'That's better. Now we look like equals.' She turned and gazed out of the window while I repacked the cases in which she had rummaged.

By the time we reached Norwich I had managed to persuade her that staying at a hotel was not a very good idea. I pointed out that it was not really a sensible way to spend money we might need in the future.

'At least let's go and see what we can find before we book into a hotel,' I suggested. 'We might even find ourselves suitable lodgings.'

'And we might not,' she replied rudely, annoyed at being thwarted in her plan.

'Well, we shan't know until we look.' I was determined not to let her rattle me. 'If we can't find anything we'll do as you say, and book a night at a hotel.'

Still slightly disgruntled, she agreed to us leaving our luggage at the station to be collected later, and we turned up our collars against a bitterly cold wind and went off to explore the city and see what we could find.

As we walked through the streets we were horrified to see the ravages not only of the war but also of the dreadful 'flu epidemic. It was everywhere we looked. Some shops were short-staffed, some were even boarded up with notices in the window, CLOSED UNTIL FURTHER NOTICE DUE TO INFLUENZA DEATHS. Most of the people we passed seemed to be in mourning. Those that could afford it were dressed completely in black, the less well-off wearing black armbands. Many of the windows of private houses were draped with black crepe or had a scrap of black ribbon tied to the door knocker. Spanish 'flu had been indiscriminate in its victims.

To add to these depressing sights, on almost every street corner there was an ex-soldier, often propped up on crutches, shivering with cold as he tried to earn a few coppers selling matches, song-sheets, papers of pins, or simply holding out a grubby cap. For my part, since I had never been in a city before, I had never before seen such dirty, ragged and under-nourished children playing in the gutter, never been jostled by so many uncaring people, never had my eyes and ears assaulted by so much traffic, both horse-drawn and motor. I found it all quite frightening and bewildering. If it had been left to me I think I would have handed out pennies indiscriminately to beggars, but in this instance Lizzie was less soft-hearted and more astute than me. No hard-luck tale prised money from her purse.

She did make one purchase. Or rather, two. We remembered, in the nick of time, that if we were to pass ourselves off as widows we needed wedding rings. Once they were on our fingers, after each spinning the same story to a different jeweller – of losing weight through 'flu and our wedding rings slipping off our finger and being lost as we pulled off a glove – we left the bustle of the city centre and managed to find furnished rooms in Bishop's Row, a quiet street in a quite respectable area of Norwich.

The rooms were on the first floor of a Georgian terraced house and consisted of two rooms, a large, high-ceilinged living room with a curtained-off kitchen area at the far end and the other one the same size but partitioned to make two bedrooms, each containing a single bed, a wardrobe and a chest of drawers. The living room was quite comfortably furnished, if a trifle old fashioned. There were two plush-covered armchairs with lace antimacassars either side of the black, wrought-iron fireplace and four solid-looking chairs, similarly plush covered, set round a rosewood pedestal table. A matching rosewood chiffonier stood against the wall opposite the fireplace and a walnut what-not in the corner held cheap china ornaments. An aspidistra stood on a tall, spindly table in the window. The kitchen area at the end of the room opposite the window consisted of a cupboard to hold china and saucepans, on top of which stood an enamel tray and a gas ring. A washing-up bowl stood on a shelf beside it with a bucket underneath. Water had to be carried up from the bathroom, which we were to share with Mrs Muir, our landlady. It was luxury to me although the kitchen was not quite what I was used to. Lizzie, of course, turned her nose up at everything till I nudged her and whispered that beggars couldn't be choosers. In fact, everything, including the rent, suited us very well.

We introduced ourselves as Mrs Buckram and Mrs Layton, names not too far distant from our real ones. Mrs Muir, our garrulous landlady, was sympathetic when we told the story we'd rehearsed about our husbands coming back from the war and subsequently dying in the 'flu epidemic. She told us that the reason she had been forced to rent out the room was because her husband had also died of influenza.

'There's no justice, is there?' she said sadly. 'We'd already lost both our sons at Gallipoli.' She shook her head. 'I don't think my husband ever really recovered from that. He just seemed to retreat into his shell. And then he got that dreadful Spanish 'flu ... Oh, he had a dreadful death...' She squared her shoulders. 'But life goes on, doesn't it? If you don't get what you like in this life you have to like what you get. I knew I had to go on living and I'd got no other income so I decided to let out these rooms – well, this is a big house and there's only me now so I don't need so many rooms, I'm quite cosy on the ground floor. I'm thinking of letting out the top floor too and perhaps the attics, and I could let out the basement if I was really pushed. Can you manage three months' rent in advance?'

She didn't mention anything about children, so neither did we. Unlike Lizzie, who fully intended to give her baby away and then go home, I was determined to keep mine. I couldn't bear the thought of handing over Giles' child to strangers. Of course I knew I would never be able to return to Rookhurst Hall, somehow I would have to find employment to keep us both, but that was a worry for the future.

The weeks wore on. We settled into our new home and by the time spring came both Lizzie and I were feeling much better. We both developed ravenous appetites, which I satisfied as best I could with tasty meals cooked on the gas ring in the tiny kitchen area. I was quite impressed with the way Lizzie handled her money. She allocated a set amount to be spent on rent and food each week and my task was to trawl the markets to find the best bargains. I soon got used to city ways and pushed and shoved my way around with the rest.

Needless to say, it was also left to me to keep the rooms clean and to manage the laundry, which had to be done in the basement scullery. Lizzie's idea of equality only extended so far.

Although we were both concealing them as best we could, I noticed Mrs Muir was beginning to look suspiciously at our growing figures. We were more than a little worried about this. After all, we hadn't told her we were both pregnant when we took the rooms and it was quite possible she would turn us out and we would have to look for fresh lodgings, which wouldn't be easy. But the weeks went on and she said nothing until one day, late in June, she was hovering in the hall as we went down the stairs for our afternoon walk.

'I hope you don't mind me mentioning it, ladies,' she said, looking slightly embarrassed, 'but I've noticed that you're both...' she cleared her throat delicately, 'in a certain condition.' Lizzie's pregnancy was more obvious than mine, although I had had to put gussets in both our dresses and we had taken to wearing either loose cloaks or shawls to conceal our condition as much as possible. 'When do you expect to...?'

'About the end of next month,' Lizzie said, looking anxious.

'Or the beginning of August,' I added, an uncomfortable feeling beginning to gnaw. Were our worst fears about to be realized?

They weren't. To our mutual relief a delighted smile spread across her face. 'Oh, how lovely. It will be so nice to have little ones about the place. And both to be born round about the same time! They'll be like twins, won't they? I've always wanted grandchildren, you know. But of course, with both my boys gone...' She spread her hands, then put her head on one side. 'You do realize I might have to put the rent up a little, though, don't you? Extra water for washing, extra heat, that kind of thing?' She didn't say by how much but we knew we would have to pay it.

That night Lizzie counted her money and laid out what was left of her jewellery on the table whilst I let out her dress yet again. Looking at my uneven stitches, I wished I had paid more attention when Aunt Maud tried to teach me sewing skills so I could have added to our income by taking in sewing.

She put her head on one side. 'I'll be sorry to see all this go.' She picked up several necklaces and let them fall through her fingers. Then she picked up a cameo brooch. 'I'll try not to part with this, though. It belonged to my grand-mother.' She put the rest of the items carefully back in their boxes ready to be sold when the time came. They were earmarked to pay the nurse Mrs Muir had recommended for our confinements.

I sighed. Things were moving inexorably on.

As we reached the last weeks of our preg-nancies the weather was so hot that neither of us felt like leaving the house. Everything we did was an effort – not that Lizzie did anything at all except get up in the morning and put on a wrap so that she could sit by the window all day to catch what little air there was. I managed to get to the market to buy fruit and vegetables but the effort of doing that exhausted me.

I tried to persuade Lizzie to take a little exercise. Although she was no taller than me, her baby looked to be a good deal bigger than mine and she herself had put on quite a lot of weight. I could go to the market with a loose shawl wrapped round me and not attract any notice even at eight months. Lizzie was so huge she could hardly manage to waddle down the stairs to the bathroom.

'Do you think I might be having twins?' she asked, frowning down at her enormous stomach.

'How should I know?' I was getting annoyed because she did nothing to help herself but expected me to wait on her hand and foot, ignoring the fact that I was just as pregnant as she was.

'Oh, well, we'll find out soon enough.' She bit into another apple.

Indeed, we found out sooner than either of us expected.

It was not many nights later that I woke to the sound of groaning from the next room. The partition between the rooms was so thin that every sound could be heard.

I crawled out of bed, annoyed because I had only just managed to get myself comfortable enough to sleep, and went through to Lizzie. She was kneeling by the bed holding her stomach. There was a pool of bloody water on the floor round her. She held out her hand to me.

'Thank goodness you've come.' Her face screwed up with pain. 'Oh, God. I believe the brat's on its way.' The brat was her way of describing her baby.

I went over to her and rubbed her back. 'I'd better go and fetch Mrs Brown. She only lives in the next street.'

'No. No. You can't leave me, Alice. I'm frightened. I don't know what's going to happen to me.'

'Well, I'll have to wake Mrs Muir, then. She'll go.'

'Help me on to the bed. Then you can go.' Suddenly, she screamed as a pain struck. 'No. No. Don't leave me,' she wailed.

'For goodness sake, don't make that awful noise, Lizzie.'

'Well, it hurts and I'm frightened.' She clutched my hand and wouldn't let go.

There was a tap on the door and Mrs Muir appeared, her hair shrouded in a bright pink hair net. She took one look at Lizzie. 'I'll get my clothes on and go for Mrs Brown,' was all she said.

My mind was numb with panic but suddenly I remembered how I had helped Agnes when Sheila's baby was born. I quickly gave Lizzie a handkerchief to stuff in her mouth to muffle her cries, then I released my hand so that I could tie a piece of cloth, I think it was one of her petticoats, to the foot of the bed for her to pull on. That done, and while she swore in words I had never heard before, I bathed her face with cold water and helplessly watched her struggle, knowing there was nothing more I could do. It was cold comfort to me to realize that it wouldn't be long before my turn came to go through the same agonies.

Mrs Brown arrived and took over with practised efficiency. After a few minutes she whispered to us over her shoulder, 'Someone had better fetch the doctor. This baby's much too big to be born to such a small frame.'

Once again Mrs Muir sped off. I held Lizzie and listened to her screams while Mrs Brown did what she could to help her. Then the doctor arrived, took one look at the situation and turned me out of the room, in spite of Lizzie screaming for me to stay.

'It looks to me as if it will be a case of saving either the mother or the child,' he said quietly at the door. He waited for me to answer but I couldn't bring myself to tell him what to do. Lizzie didn't want the baby, I knew that, but I still couldn't bring myself to sign its death warrant.

'Do what you think best, Doctor,' was all I could say before I went back to my room to cry and pray to a God I wasn't sure existed. Mrs Muir brought tea and we sat together listening to Lizzie's screams as the hours went by, but we didn't talk much. After what seemed an age the faint chemical aroma of chloroform percolated through the thin partition and Lizzie's yells subsided.

Suddenly we heard a baby cry. 'Thank God. It's born,' Mrs Muir breathed. A little while later Mrs Brown brought in the little bundle, wrapped in a blanket. 'A fine little girl,' she said, handing her to Mrs Muir. To me she said, 'Your friend wants to see you.'

'Is she...? Will she...?' I couldn't bring myself to say the words.

Mrs Brown didn't answer so I followed her into the next room. The doctor was rolling down his sleeves and bloody sheets were heaped on the floor. I went over to Lizzie. She was as white as the pillow, her dark hair matted.

'The brat knew I hated it,' she murmured, so low I could hardly hear her. 'So it got its own back. It put me through hell and now it's killed me.'

'No, Lizzie. Don't talk like that,' I said urgently.

'Why not? It's true.' She closed her eyes.

'Because you've got a beautiful little daughter. You'll love her when you see her. You'll want to live for her.'

Her lips curled in a ghost of a smile. 'You know that's not true, Alice,' she whispered. 'Anyway, I'm too tired. Just let me sleep.'

'You'd better go,' the doctor said quietly. He accompanied me to the door. 'I'll do what I can,' he whispered.

He could do nothing. Two hours later Lizzie died. I paid him out of her dwindling store of money and hoped I wouldn't need to call on him again.

Twenty-Two

Lucy handed the last page to Ben without a word. When he had read it he handed it back to her.

'Whew!' he said. 'Those girls really lived it up, didn't they? Both pregnant, running off to Ipswich in a stolen car...'

'That was Lizzie's doing. And after all that she died giving birth to the baby she'd never wanted in the first place. I think that's really sad.'

Lucy looked down at the sheaf of papers in her hand. 'Oh, isn't it infuriating that Granny stopped writing just there? After all, it could only have been a few days later that Mummy was born.'

'I expect she got writer's cramp. Or perhaps her Biro ran out. Would you rather have waited until she could send you the whole, finished story?'

'No, of course I wouldn't.'

Ben smiled. 'Then you'll just have to contain yourself in patience till the next bit arrives.'

She wiped a tear away. 'I'm sure you're right about Giles. I'm sure he intended to marry Alice and would have done if he hadn't died from that horrible 'flu. Oh, it's so sad that he died. They were very much in love, weren't they?'

He nodded. 'Oh, yes, there's no doubt about that.' His mouth twisted. 'It's ironic, isn't it, in spite of all Sir George's efforts to protect the inheritance by isolating the Hall, in the end both he and his eldest son died in the epidemic.'

'Alice was quite convinced it wasn't the inheritance he was worried about, it was his own skin.' She was quiet for several minutes, then added thoughtfully, 'It must have been dreadful for Lady Bucknell; to lose her eldest son and her twin daughters in the space of only a few weeks.'

'And her husband. He died too.'

Lucy made a face. 'I don't think she was too worried about him.' She paused. 'And then Lizzie disappeared. With Alice. I wonder what they all made of that.' She frowned. 'What are you looking at me like that for?'

Ben put his head on one side. 'I've just realized why you look like that girl in the photograph, Vonny or Vera, whichever one it was. She would have been your aunt, wouldn't she?'

Lucy thought for a minute. 'No, no, she would have been my great-aunt. Giles and Alice were my mother's parents so she would have been Mummy's aunt.'

'Ah, yes, that's right. I was missing a generation.'

'And Lizzie, the youngest girl in the photo-graph, she's the one who's just had the chauf-

238

feur's baby and died. She would have been Mummy's aunt, too, wouldn't she?' She smiled. 'She was a bit of a handful, by all accounts. And totally selfish. I'm surprised Alice didn't give her a slap.' She put her hand to her mouth. 'Oh, I shouldn't speak ill of the dead.'

They packed the wine glasses back in the picnic basket. Lucy sat back on her heels. 'Poor Lady Bucknell. Out of five children she's only got one left. Isn't that sad, Ben?'

He paused in the act of fastening the basket. 'Yes, but at least Peregrine hasn't gone waltzing off to the other side of the world. He and his wife are living in one of the wings of the house, the west wing, I believe.'

'So he's able to look after the estate.'

'Yes, I guess so.'

She got to her feet and folded up the blanket. 'Is it a very big estate?'

He gave her an odd look. 'I've really no idea. I daresay there's quite a bit of land attached to it. Alice talks about farms in the plural.'

'Ah, yes, so she does.' She stood hugging the blanket. 'Pity Perry hasn't got any children to hand it all on to. That must sadden Lady Bucknell.'

'Yes, I expect it does.'

They made their way back and stowed everything in the car.

'I wonder what happened to Lizzie's baby,' Lucy said suddenly as she got in beside him. 'I don't remember Mummy ever speaking about—'

'Oh, for goodness sake, don't start speculating,' Ben said a trifle impatiently, letting in the clutch. 'Just wait till you get the next bit of the story, then you'll find out.'

'You mean *we'll* find out. I've told you before I won't read it without you, Ben, it wouldn't be fair.'

'Oh, I wouldn't worry about that,' he said casually. 'I've told you, I'll be in London all next week.'

'Then I'll wait till you get back. I expect you'll be able to manage half an hour for a spot of supper with me.'

He didn't reply to that, but she realized it could have been because he was negotiating the car round a flock of sheep.

But she was surprised when he refused her invitation to come up to the flat for coffee when they got back, saying he had things to do before catching the train to London in the morning.

'Oh, will you be staying there, after all?' she asked.

'No, I don't think so. I haven't quite made up my mind.'

She hesitated. 'Are you still expecting me to come up to the fair with you next Thursday? You said I could come with you so that I could see what an antique dealers' fair is like.'

'Did I? Oh, yes, well, I expect that can be arranged.' He sounded quite offhand about it, which surprised her since it had been his idea in the first place.

'It doesn't matter. If it's not convenient, I

really don't mind,' she said, her voice puzzled.

'I said it could be arranged,' he said, drumming his fingers on the steering wheel as if he were impatient for her to get out.

He drove off and she went up the steps to her flat, puzzled as to what could have brought about such a sudden change in his mood. He'd been positively bad-tempered on the journey back, which wasn't like Ben at all.

Things were no better when he called in the next morning to look at the post. He dealt with it as quickly as he could and left, hardly speaking to her, and she didn't see him at all over the weekend. It occurred to her that if an antique fair put such a strain on a dealer it was hardly worth the trouble.

On Monday Alec came into the shop. Lucy was surprised to see he was not wearing his working clothes and big work apron. She thought he looked a bit tired.

'Ben's holding the fort up there this week and you're looking after things here, so I'm taking a couple of days off,' he told her, sitting down on the spare office chair. 'It's quite hard work, standing about all day in that hothouse atmosphere, you know, being polite to people who have no intention of buying anything.' He took out his pipe and filled it, tamping down the tobacco before putting a match to it. 'No, that's not fair, we're doing very well so far. I've sold quite a lot of stuff, including a nice set of chairs to an Italian count.'

'Oh, that sounds good,' she said.

'Yes, but he doesn't like the material I've covered them with so I've got to have them back in the workshop and do it all again.' He shook his head. 'Says he wants them for his wife's bedroom so they've got to be done in white.' He gave a little laugh. 'Would you believe he's going to have the material specially made! It's going to be done by a firm in Essex that special-izes in reproducing antique fabrics. They do a lot of work for stately home restora-tions.' He chuckled. 'I'll have to have a couple of stiff whiskies to give me Dutch courage before I take my shears to that!'

'I don't know about that,' Lucy said, laughing with him. 'I should think you'll need a clear head and a steady hand.'

'Yes, I guess you're right. Anyway, I've done enough of cutting into expensive material over the years not to let it worry me.'

She put her head on one side. 'You're very clever, Mr Manton. I wouldn't have known you'd made a new leg for the little escritoire if Ben hadn't told me. And the new foot you made for my bureau, after it had been propped up on books for as long as I can remember, I couldn't tell which one's the new one if I didn't already know.'

He puffed his pipe for a little while, then said, 'Well, I had a good teacher and he taught me all the tricks of the trade. You've got to remember I left school when I was fourteen and I was apprenticed to a man called George Hensman for the next seven years. Didn't earn much,

242

well, apprentices didn't in those days, but what he taught me was worth more than gold, I can tell you.' He jabbed his pipe in the direction of the showroom. 'We wouldn't have had all that if it hadn't been for what George taught me. Not only how to restore stuff but how to recognize the genuine article from the fake, and he gave me books to read so that I learned things like how to distinguish Hepplewhite from Sheraton, that kind of thing, and what designs were used in which period.' He shook his head. 'All very interesting.'

'And you've obviously passed that interest on to Ben,' she said.

'Yes. He's got a nose for it, too. He can spot a wrong 'un quicker than I can these days.'

She frowned. 'A wrong 'un?'

'A fake. You don't get many of those past the examiners at these London fairs, I can tell you. They examine every stand, every morning, they've got eyes like hawks and they know what they're looking for.'

'Do you enjoy going there, Mr Manton? Would you say it's worth going? Is it worth all the hard work you have to put in beforehand?' she asked, thinking of Ben's bad mood.

'Oh, yes, definitely. As I told you, we've sold quite a lot and made some new contacts. But more to the point, it advertises the name of Rosewood Antiques, gets us known over a wide area at home and abroad. We'll probably do quite a lot more business in the coming months through having been there, particularly with overseas customers.' He examined the bowl of his pipe, saw that it had gone out and put it back in his pocket. 'Ben enjoys it more than I do. I think he likes to socialize in the bar in the evenings before he comes home.' He grinned. 'Some of the big dealers like to have a pretty girl to grace their stand, so he never needs to be short of a bit of company.' He looked at his watch. 'Oh, lordy, I must go. I promised Martha I'd meet her for a spot of lunch at the Ivy Leaf so I mustn't be late. She was going to do a bit of shopping at the self-service shop in the square. She always complains that she comes out of that place with more than she went in for. But that's the idea, isn't it? They're on to a good thing, these self-service places. You go round the shelves looking for what you want and find you've put six other things that might come in handy in the basket while you were looking. They'll be putting the baskets on wheels next, then people will be tempted to buy even more.' He got to his feet. 'Everything all right here?' he added as an afterthought, giving a cursory glance around.

'Yes, everything's fine.'

When Alec had gone Lucy wound a sheet of paper into her typewriter and sat staring at it, her mind miles away. She wished now she hadn't reminded Ben of the day he had promised her in London, although from the things his father had been telling her she would dearly love to go and see it all for herself. But Ben clearly didn't want her there. In fact, he had made it quite plain that he didn't want her at all.

She frowned, trying to fathom what had caused such a sudden change in his attitude towards her the previous Sunday. They had been so happy and carefree on the beach, paddling in the sea like a couple of children, picking up shells and chasing each other with bits of seaweed. He had put his arm round her and held her close as they wandered back up the beach and they had talked and laughed easily together as they shared the picnic.

Remembering all this, had she been mistaken in thinking that he enjoyed her company as much as she enjoyed his? Had it been nothing more than wishful hoping on her part? Had it just been her imagination running riot, thinking that he was beginning to fall in love with her?

She closed her eyes and put her head down on her typewriter, curling up inside with shame at the sudden thought that he might have felt she was throwing herself at him when she insisted that she wouldn't read the next part of Alice's story until he was there with her. And yet he had insisted right at the beginning that he wanted to 'be in on the happy-ever-after bit'.

But something had brought about a sudden change of heart in him. She only wished she knew what it was, because without him by her side she couldn't see that there was ever going to be a 'happy-ever-after bit' for him to be in on.

Alec was back at his bench on Wednesday but he wandered through to the shop when he thought it was time for Lucy to put the kettle on.

'You know, you're a real asset to this place, Lucy,' he remarked as she spooned coffee into the matching set of china mugs she had bought to replace the old pottery ones. 'Matching mugs, a new kettle, fresh flowers in the show-room. And this office...'He gazed round and shook his head. 'It's a marvel to me you can find anything, it's all so neat and tidy.'

Lucy laughed. 'I thought it was a marvel you could find anything before I sorted it all out,' she said. 'Everything was in heaps and covered in dust.'

'Yes, well, I'm not much of a one for office work and Ben's always too busy, although he used to have a purge every now and then. It's much better now you're here. Which reminds me, did you order those brass claw casters for me? I need them for the feet of the Pembroke pedestal breakfast table I'm working on.'

'Yes, they should be here by tomorrow. You'll have to watch out for them because it's possible I may not be here.' Although since she hadn't heard anything from Ben since Sunday and he had sounded less than enthusiastic about her trip to London with him, she wasn't at all sure she would be going.

'Ah, yes. That's right. You're going up to the fair with Ben. I'm glad you reminded me.' Alec sounded a good deal more confident than she felt. 'Ben asked me to tell you he'll pick you up at half past seven tomorrow morning to drive to

Ipswich to catch the London train. And you don't need to worry about things here. Mrs Wills is coming to do the cleaning tomorrow so she'll mind the shop and I'll be on hand if she needs me. Is that OK? Half seven not too early for you?' He looked at her uncertainly.

She shook her head. 'No, no, that's fine.' She didn't know whether she was pleased or sorry that Ben hadn't changed his mind. She spent the rest of the day agonizing over what to wear, although in the end the choice was obvious. When she had been shopping with her mother for wedding clothes Lucy had chosen a very smart, expensively tailored grey suit, which Margaret had dismissed as quite unsuitable for a wedding, insisting instead on buying her a long silk dress and a fur stole. But when the parcels were delivered from the shop it was typical of Margaret's generosity that the suit had been among them.

'Well,' her mother had said with a shrug, when Lucy thanked her. 'I knew you liked it. But you're not to wear it to the wedding. It's much too austere.'

But it wasn't too austere for the trip to London. Softening it with a cerise blouse with a floppy bow at the neck, she wore it with black patent court shoes that emphasized her shapely legs in their sheer nylon stockings and carried a matching black patent handbag. With her hair tamed into a smooth bob that curled round her ears, she knew that she had achieved the cool, businesslike image she wanted to project, even if she didn't feel either cool or businesslike inside.

In fact, she had seriously considered pleading a migraine and calling the whole trip off. But that would have been the coward's way out, and anyway she was curious to discover the end result of all the hard work over the past months.

Twenty-Three

Lucy didn't sleep much. She was too worried about spending the day with a man who for some reason had suddenly seemed to find her presence irritating. In the end, she decided that the best thing was to be as professional and businesslike as she appeared, to dispel any fear he might have had that she might be falling in love with him.

That decided, she was ready and waiting outside the shop when Ben drove up in his car.

'I didn't want to keep you waiting,' she said crisply when he expressed surprise at seeing her standing on the pavement. 'I wouldn't want you to miss the train on my account.'

'Oh, there's no danger of that,' he said, holding open the door for her.

She got in, smoothed down her skirt and rested her handbag primly on her lap.

'My word, you're looking very chic today,

Lucy,' he said admiringly.

'Thank you. I thought a suit was appropriate,' she replied coolly. She didn't feel cool inside, though. The sight of Ben in a dark blue single-breasted suit with a very fine stripe, a snowy white shirt and a maroon tie, had made her heart skip several beats and her determination to maintain a cold, off-hand attitude towards him was beginning to waver.

'Yes, I'm afraid it is a bit of a formal day,' he agreed. He hesitated. 'I don't exactly want to throw you in at the deep end but I have to warn you. Will you be happy to look after the stand for part of the time while I go and do a bit of business with other dealers?'

'Of course,' she said. 'It won't be that much different to looking after the shop, will it? In any case, isn't that why you've asked me to come?'

He gave her a puzzled glance. 'No, of course not. At least, not entirely. I thought you'd like to see what goes on at these fairs and I've done what I said I'd do and booked dinner for this evening. I'd hoped there would be time to take in a show as well but I'm afraid that was a bit over-optimistic. And anyway, *The Mousetrap* was fully booked. Perhaps another time.' He frowned as he glanced again at her unsmiling face. 'Unless, of course, you'd rather not...?'

'Thank you. It's very kind of you. I shall look forward to it,' she said primly.

He obviously sensed her mood because walking from the station car park to the train he stopped and turned to her. 'Lucy, before we go any further, I have an apology to make. I'm sorry if you thought I was in a bad mood Sunday. It wasn't that ... I wouldn't want you to think—'

She cut across his words. 'No, of course not. It's perfectly all right, Ben. I understand, really I do. There's no need to apologize.' She looked up at him and smiled, a little too brightly. 'Now, would you like me to call you Mr Manton today, as it's a formal occasion?'

He shook his head. 'Oh, don't be silly. Ben will be fine,' he replied, slightly irritated.

They spoke very little on the journey. He was immersed in the papers from his briefcase, while she attempted to read the newspaper he bought for her. But the print kept blurring as she faced the indisputable fact that she had been stupid enough to read far too much into their relationship. She hadn't been able to let him finish his sentence just now because she couldn't have borne the humiliation of hearing him say the words – 'I wouldn't want you to think I regard you as anything other than a friend.' Or at worst, 'As anything other than a secretary and shop assistant.' She had been a fool to think otherwise, she realized that now, but she was determined never to let him know that she had been stupid enough to step into the age-old trap of falling in love with the boss.

She laid the newspaper down on the table between them, deliberately opened at the jobs section, and began to scan it.

He looked down at the page she was reading and frowned. 'Surely, you're not...' he began.

'Not what?' she asked, raising her eyebrows.

'Nothing.' He went back to the papers he was studying and she bent her head again to the newspaper, although she had no idea what she was looking at.

They reached Liverpool Street station and he took her arm to guide her through the morning crowds to the tube, which she had always hated. It was worse than ever today, crushed as they were against bodies that reeked of anything from cheap aftershave to sweat with the occasional waft of Chanel. She was glad to see daylight again.

A large sign outside the huge town hall announced the antique dealers' fair. Inside the foyer there was an air of what Lucy could only describe as discreet bustle as porters carried furniture through to the stands in the enormous ballroom or in other, smaller rooms off to the side. Dealers, already looking somewhat flustered, were directing them, impatient to make sure their stands were ready before the ten o'clock opening, and to add to the confusion florists in green aprons were going round checking displays, watering plants and re-placing jaded blooms. One or two dealers were carefully polishing off specks of dust and straightening pictures, or discreetly checking their appearance in a mirror if there was one handy.

Ben greeted several people as they made their

way through to one of the smaller stands, where a highly polished piece of rosewood bearing the carved and gilded words *ROSEWOOD ANTIQUES*, and in smaller letters, *Manton & Son, The Square, Laxhall St Mary's, Suffolk*, stood prominently placed on the corner of a small bow-front chest of drawers.

'As you can see, we don't go for the ostentatious,' Ben explained, nodding towards a large banner further down the hall proclaiming a firm of antique dealers whose name Lucy recognized from large advertisements in the *Antique Dealer and Collectors Guide*. 'We prefer to let the quality of the goods speak for themselves.' He looked round the stand. 'Let me see, the set of chairs has gone and so has the French commode, the Chippendale mirror and the little bronze Cupid.' He nodded. 'I'll just go and tell the porters what I need them to bring to replace all that. I think we've got a little oak blanket chest that will sit very well in that space. I shan't be long.'

While he was gone, Lucy surveyed Rosewood Antiques' stand. It was small compared with some, but it was set out with flair, concentrating on showing off some well-chosen pieces to the best advantage, not trying to crowd too much into the small space as some of the others had done, or to have too many floral displays and pot plants. A fan of catalogues, which Lucy recognized because she had typed them ready for the printer, were laid out on a small Chippendale tea table at one side. She also recognized the china displayed in the pine corner cupboard, recalling how she and Ben had washed and packed it not all that many days ago. The brass jardinière she had polished now held the only flower arrangement, of yellow and bronze mop-head chrysanthemums. They were similar to the ones Ben had brought her the evening he came to tell her he had discovered where her grandmother lived. That seemed a very long time ago although it was only a matter of weeks.

When Ben came back with two porters in tow he suggested that it would be a good time for her to take a look round the other stands before the doors were opened to the public. The ballroom was enormous, with four huge cut-glass chandeliers hanging from a ceiling decorated in Adam-style plasterwork. There were stands, like three-sided rooms, down the length of the hall and either side of the big double doorways at each end, and two more rows standing back-to-back down the centre, yet there was still plenty of room for a wide, carpeted aisle where people could walk. There were also displays in other, smaller rooms off the main hall. Lucy realized she was prejudiced but she didn't see any that were set out more tastefully than Rosewood Antiques. As she walked round she tried to identify some of the items on display and was amazed at the number to which she could both put a name and date the period – William and Mary, Georgian, Regency – in which they were made.

She got back to the Rosewood Antiques stand just as the doors were opened. Ben was deep in conversation with a tall, striking-looking woman in a flowing red ankle-length dress and jacket. She had a long scarf tied round her hair, the ends trailing over her shoulder.

The woman turned as Lucy arrived. 'Oh, here's your little helpmate, Ben, darling, so we can go and have that cup of coffee together after all.' She smiled a trifle condescendingly at Lucy. 'You can hold the fort for half an hour, can't you, sweetie? And would you mind keeping an eye on my stand? It's the one opposite. Everything's priced and there are positively no discounts, so don't let them try and beat you down.' She linked her arm through Ben's, who skilfully extricated it as he turned to Lucy.

'You'll be OK here for fifteen minutes?' he asked, adding under his breath, 'I'll be as quick as I can.'

'Of course, take as long as you like, there's no hurry,' she replied coolly.

She sat down on a Chippendale elbow chair and pretended to study a catalogue, glancing up every now and again as people stopped and looked at the stall opposite. It was decked out with Chinese lacquered furniture; obviously this was what Samantha Crickett-Thompson – the name was prominently displayed on a particularly garish red lacquered chest – specialized in. Lucy decided she definitely didn't care for lacquered furniture, particularly red and green, and didn't much like the black, either.

She wasn't surprised that she didn't make a sale from Samantha Crickett-Thompson's stand, although it arrested a good many people's attention.

Ben was back in less than ten minutes. 'That's that duty done,' he said under his breath. He smiled at her. 'Are you OK here for another ten minutes? I've just seen a chap I sometimes do business with. I ought to go and have a word with him.'

'Yes, I'm fine. I haven't made a sale yet, though,' she said, letting her guard drop and smiling back at him.

He squeezed her arm. 'You will. You're a real asset to the stand.'

He was right. By the time he returned, over an hour later, she had sold the oak blanket chest that had only been brought to the stand that morning.

In spite of her determination to keep her relationship with Ben on a cool, formal footing, the buzz that the atmosphere generated, her excitement at having made a sale and her keen interest in everything that was going on meant that as the day progressed Lucy's guard relaxed. She found she was enjoying herself far more than she had expected – or intended – to, and was amazed when he told her to go and grab herself a sandwich in the restaurant.

'But don't eat too much. Remember we're going out for dinner tonight,' he reminded her. 'And don't be too long, because I haven't had mine yet.'

She was longer than she intended because a pleasant young dealer came up and joined her while she was eating her prawn sandwich.

'He was very nice,' she explained as she apologized to Ben for being late back. 'I think he was Scottish. His name was Ben, too.'

Ben nodded. 'I know who you mean. He belongs to one of the biggest dealers in Scotland.' He raised his eyebrows. 'Was he trying to poach you?'

'What do you mean?'

'Did he try to persuade you to go and work for him?'

She frowned. 'No, of course he didn't. He was just telling me what a beautiful place Scotland was, that's all.'

'You need to watch him, then. It's the classic beginning.' He paused. 'Unless you fancy working in Scotland, of course.' He went off before she could answer.

The day was so busy and so interesting that Lucy was amazed when the fair closed and it was time to go. She couldn't believe how tired she was and she was glad that the restaurant Ben had chosen was not far away.

'How about stuffed avocado followed by lamb cutlets with rosemary?' he suggested as they studied the menu.

'That sounds lovely. If there was horse on the menu I think I could eat it, I'm starving,' she said.

'Have you had a good day, Lucy?' he asked, over the lamb cutlets.

'Oh, yes,' she replied warmly. 'I've really enjoyed it. And I've met a lot of interesting people, too.' She laughed. 'And you were right about that young Scottish man. He came back while you were off the stand and offered me a job.'

'Cheeky beggar.' He cocked an eyebrow. 'Did you take him up on it?'

'No, I didn't.'

'You missed an opportunity then, didn't you?' he said lightly. 'But no doubt you told him you had other fish to fry.'

'Something like that. I told him I have ties in Suffolk so I don't want to move away. Especially to the north of Scotland.'

'You have ties. Yes, of course, you have.' He busied himself refilling her wine glass and his own, his expression unreadable.

She leaned forward. 'I've only just found my grandmother, Ben. I'm still learning my family history. I'm not likely to walk away from that, am I?'

He shook his head. 'Indeed, no, I'm sure you'll never do that,' he said enigmatically.

They finished the meal and caught the train back to Ipswich, but the easy companionship they had shared during the day had gone and Ben was very quiet. Taking her cue from him Lucy said little, but spent the journey wondering what she had said during the meal that had caused the change in him. She could only suspect that he regretted his earlier friendly behaviour. Stealing a glance at him as

he sat opposite her, she saw how tired he looked and she longed to lean across and stroke
back the stray strand of hair that had fallen
across his forehead. As if he sensed her gaze
he opened his eyes, brushed his hair back
and smiled briefly. She looked away, embarrassed.

Some half an hour later, after leaving the train
and driving back to Laxhall St Mary's, Ben
pulled up outside the antique shop and turned
the car engine off.

'I just need to fetch some papers from the
shop before I go home,' he said in explanation
as he opened the car door for her.

She hesitated. 'Would you like some coffee?
I'm sure you must be tired and it'll save you
having to make it yourself when you get back to
your flat.'

'Thank you. That's very kind.' His tone was
as stilted as hers. 'I'll just pick up the papers I
need then I'll be along.'

Five minutes later he knocked on the door. He
had a flat package in his hand. 'This was
delivered to the shop today,' he said, handing it
to her.

Her eyes lit up. 'Oh, it must be more of
Granny's life story,' she said, recognizing the
writing on the label. 'Shall we...? I mean, have
you got time?' She hesitated. 'Or perhaps I
should say, are you still interested?'

'Oh, yes, I'm still interested,' he said quietly.
'Although I rather think I may have guessed the
end of the story.'

'Have you? Well then, you'd better sit down and read it while you drink your coffee and see if you've guessed right.'

Twenty-Four

Lizzie was dead but I had little time to grieve over her because I had her baby to tend. She was a beautiful baby, with thick black hair and beautiful blue eyes. She was a hungry baby and at first I fed her from a rag dipped in milk until Mrs Muir went out and bought a bottle for her. As I gazed down at her in my arms I couldn't help wondering whether, if Lizzie had been able to hold her as I was doing, she would still have been hard-hearted enough to put her up for adoption or, worse, send her to an orphanage. It was something I would never know. But what I did know was that I never could. She was not my child but she would be brought up with my baby. They would be as good as twins, because I knew it wouldn't be many days before my own baby would be born. How on earth I was going to manage on my own with two babies I couldn't begin to imagine, but I was sure I would find a way.

In spite of my own imminent confinement I managed to make arrangements for Lizzie's burial and to attend the funeral. She had not been an easy woman to live with, she had been petulant and demanding, and quite unsympathetic to the fact that I was pregnant as well as she was. But we had been through a lot together and towards the end she had treated me very much as her equal. She still expected me to wait on her, but we had been good friends and I was going to miss her terribly.

I agonized over whether or not to contact M'Lady to tell her of Lizzie's death. In the end I decided that it was kinder to do nothing. Better to let her mother grieve over her disappearance than to taint her memory of her daughter with the knowledge that she had died giving birth to the illegitimate child of her father's chauffeur. I still don't know if I did the right thing. But I had her real name, Eliza Mary Bucknell, put on her death certificate and inscribed on her tombstone. I thought it only right that she should die with her proper name.

It was only three days after I'd laid Lizzie to rest that I went into labour myself, and all thoughts of whether or not I should have contacted Lady Bucknell left me. Unlike Lizzie's my confinement was quick and easy, so quick, in fact, that my little son was born almost before Mrs Muir could get back with the midwife. Also unlike Lizzie, I was the one who lived. My precious, tiny little son died less than a day after he was born.

I could not believe that this tiny being I had treasured under my heart for nine long months was dead and I held his lifeless little body in my arms and wept bitter tears. I had made such plans for Giles' son – I had been quite sure all along that it was his son that I was carrying. Of course I had known life as a single mother with a child wouldn't be easy, but I had been prepared to work my fingers to the bone to give him a good life, to make him into a son his father would have been proud of. But I wasn't going to have the chance to do that. My darling boy only lived long enough for the vicar to come and baptize him before he died in my arms.

I wanted to die, too, but that was not an option because I still had little Margaret to tend. I wept as I nursed her, now feeding her the milk that my body had prepared for my baby son instead of giving her prepared bottles. But she wasn't my son, she was Lizzie's daughter. It was not her fault that she had killed her mother, nor that she had lived when my little boy had died. So I smothered my resentment and dropped a kiss on her forehead, already damp with the tears I had shed.

'At least we've got each other, Margaret,' I whispered when I returned from burying my little boy in a tiny grave next to Eliza Mary Bucknell, his aunt. I had named him Alfie, knowing that Alfred was his father's second name.

Eventually, I poured all the love I would have given Alfie on to Margaret. She was all I had now and I cared for her as if she were my own daughter. Indeed, she *was* my daughter now. But I have to admit she was not an easy child. As a baby she was fractious and demanding, she always seemed to be crying. And it didn't help that I was beginning to get worried over money. Two funerals and two confinements had made a big hole in my finances, there wasn't much of Lizzie's jewellery left to sell and I wasn't in a position to go out and find work with such a young, difficult baby. I ate very little to conserve what money I had, but that meant my milk was in danger of drying up leaving Margaret hungry and even more fractious. So I had to scavenge the market for vegetables to make myself nourishing soup, which in turn helped to nourish her.

Mrs Muir was very understanding and would sometimes give me half a loaf of bread. Then one day she came to me with a suggestion.

'Forgive me, Mrs Layton,' she began, using the name I had adopted when Lizzie and I moved in. 'But I realize how difficult things are for you at the moment and I do sympathize.' Fear clutched at my heart as I waited for her next words. My worst nightmare was that she might be going to turn me out on to the street. But then she smiled. 'Don't worry, my dear, I'm not going to turn you out,' she said, reading my thoughts. 'I was simply wondering if you might like to change rooms and move downstairs to the basement. You see, I could charge you considerably less rent if you lived down there, because these rooms...' she glanced round the living room, which I had always been very careful to keep spotless, 'these two rooms are, of course, my prime rooms.' Her inference was that she could charge new tenants a higher rent than I was paying. She laid a hand on my arm. 'I admit it wouldn't be quite so big and airy but the room next to the scullery is quite large and I would make it nice and comfortable for you, if you're agreeable.'

I could hardly refuse. I really couldn't afford the rent I was paying at present, let alone if she increased it, and even with the baby I could easily manage in one room. I knew, too, that she was naturally anxious that the baby shouldn't disturb the new tenants on the second floor. I didn't blame her for that, sometimes Margaret's crying got on my nerves. In fact, her suggestion suited us both – my rent would be more than halved and she could let out the first floor to new tenants at a higher rent. Mrs Muir was becoming an astute businesswoman.

Actually, apart from the fact that I had to drag the second-hand pram I had bought up the area steps each time I went out, it suited me very well to move downstairs. To her credit Mrs Muir had whitewashed the brick walls and put linoleum on the stone floor. And there was even an old kitchen range which, once the chimney was swept and it was given a good polish, gave out plenty of heat and had an oven that cooked well. In that respect I was better off in the cellar than I had been upstairs with only a gas ring to cook on.

She had furnished it, too. A single bed in the corner, an armchair and a sofa, plus a folding table and two chairs was perfectly adequate for my needs. There was already a built-in cupboard beside the fireplace.

Even so, for one large room that was inclined to be damp if the fire wasn't lit, with a scullery next to it where everyone did their laundry, I still found it difficult to pay the rent and manage to feed and clothe us both adequately. And whatever else went by the board the rent had to be paid, every Friday, without fail. I couldn't face the risk of losing the roof over our heads.

Now that she had found it was a profitable business to let rooms, Mrs Muir even turned the attics into single rooms to be let out to gentlemen – they were always 'gentlemen', never just 'men'. These were always completely respectable men, usually commercial travellers or businessmen on trips for their firms who simply wanted an overnight stay, with breakfast if they were prepared to pay for it.

By this time I was getting desperate to earn money from somewhere so I saw this as an opportunity. I asked Mrs Muir if she would like to pay me to clean the rooms and take care of the laundry between these short-term tenants. I knew these were tasks she didn't like, tasks she rather felt were beneath her dignity. She was very happy with this arrangement and it suited me too because I'd be able to earn money without leaving the house. I could leave Margaret asleep in her cradle, or outside in the garden in her pram – Mrs Muir had given me permission for that – where I could hear if she cried. But it was hard work. Even if the bedding had only been on for one night it still had to be washed and dried, ironed and aired. Easy enough in the summer, when it could all be hung outside in the sunshine, not so easy in the winter. However, I was being paid to do it, so I couldn't complain.

Before long I was doing more and more for Mrs Muir. Now that she had more tenants and was able to collect higher and higher rents from them, she began to feel that it was beneath her dignity to be seen doing menial tasks like polishing doorknobs or keeping the hall and stairways swept and clean. So she asked, as if she were doing me a favour, if I might like to take on these jobs, 'Instead of me putting up your rent, love.' Naturally I agreed, what else could I do?

I was already being paid by the other, long-term tenants to do their cleaning and laundry, often ironing late into the night after Margaret was asleep, so I was managing quite well to keep our heads above water. Of course, as she got older I had to take her with me when I did the cleaning and she had her own little dustpan and brush and her own duster. Not that she ever used them. She used to sit and play with her rag doll, or pretend to be a 'lady' as she called it, hitching herself up on to the settee and spreading her skirts as she smoked a make-believe cigarette in a long holder.

'Why can't we have a nice place like this, Mummy?' she would ask, gazing round at the expensively furnished flat (the rooms had been refurbished and turned into 'flats' now, because they could be let unfurnished at a higher rate).

I would look up from my polishing. 'Because we can't afford it, dear,' I would tell her cheerfully. 'Don't you like our home?'

'No. It's got a funny smell and the sofa is all saggy and the chairs don't match. I like *nice* things.' She would lift her chin and puff on her imaginary cigarette.

I was a bit hurt at that. I had done what I could to make our little home as bright as I could, with brightly coloured rag rugs that I had made from old coats and dresses the other tenants in the flats had discarded. I had also bought a truckle bed for Margaret, now that she was too big to sleep in her pram. The pram had been taken by the second-hand dealer in part exchange for the bed, a transaction that had suited us both very well. Recently, I had covered both her bed and mine with patchwork quilts, which again brightened the place. Heaven knows where I found the time to do all these things. But I never stopped working, I suppose that was the answer.

But Margaret didn't know that. She wasn't old enough to understand, so I would simply smile and answer, 'I like nice things, too, dear, but beggars can't be choosers.'

'Oh, Mummy, don't say that! We're not *beggars*, are we?' she would protest, horrified.

266

'No, dear, of course we're not.' I would ruffle her curls and be rewarded by her impish smile. She was a lovely child. I loved her very much, although a corner of my heart would always be kept for my little Alfie. Sometimes, before I fell asleep at night, I would take out the memory of holding his lifeless but perfect little body in my arms and try to imagine what he would be like now, had he lived. Then I would sleep and when I woke my pillow would be wet with tears.

Twenty-Five

Things began to get easier when Margaret started school because it meant that I could work for people other than Mrs Muir. One of the ladies I worked for lived quite near to the school so Margaret could come and find me there when she had finished lessons for the day.

'Oh, not *still* scrubbing, Mummy!' she would say exasperatedly if I was just finishing off the front step when she arrived.

'Yes, I've nearly done. Then we'll go home through the market and I'll buy you a hair ribbon.'

'And a lolly?'

'If you're good and sit quietly with your book till I've finished.'

The hair ribbon and the lolly were bribes, of course. I still trawled the market at the end of the day because that was when the best bargains were to be had. There were oranges that had rolled off the stall, the odd cabbage where the outside leaves had withered, potatoes in the gutter where the sack had split, it was surprising what could be picked up. And I wasn't the only one looking for bargains, quite a number of people came regularly to see what they could find after the stall holders had packed up and gone.

But Margaret hated me doing this and she would never help, even though it sometimes resulted in her favourite carrot and orange soup. In fact, she would go and stand looking in nearby shop windows so that she could pretend that I was nothing to do with her, following me home at a distance when I had finished. It didn't occur to her that I might hate having to do it.

It got even harder as she got older. To my pride and delight she won a scholarship to the high school and I made sure she had exactly the right uniform, from the most expensive outfitters in the city and not a cheap copy from the Co-op, even though it meant taking on more and more work. I was constantly tired and my hands were red and raw from being in water so much. But I didn't mind. Margaret was everything to me. She was a clever girl and I was proud of her and anxious not to let her down.

'Why do we have to live in this dreadful place, Mummy?' she asked one day when she was about fourteen, flinging the new leather satchel I had recently bought her on to the settee. 'I hate living in a basement where you can't see the sun. When you look out of the window all you can see is feet walking along the pavement.'

'Where would you like to move to, dear?' I asked, humouring her as I ironed yet another sheet.

'Oh, I like the address well enough. It impresses people when I say I live in Bishop's Row. I just don't like living in a hole in the ground with the ever-present smell of wet laundry.' She bit into an apple. 'It would be nice to have a room of my own, too. The other girls all have their own rooms and they sound *fantastic*. Not that I tell them I live in a hole in the ground.' She rolled her eyes up. 'I'd be *mortified* if they ever found that out. Absolutely *mortified*. So I pretend I've got this wonderful room with a marvellous view.' She took another bite of apple. 'They're quite impressed.'

'Has it ever occurred to you that they might be lying too?' I asked, trying not to smile as I selected another sheet to iron.

She sat bolt upright. 'What do you mean, lying too?'

'Well, they might not actually live in such marvellous surroundings as they make out, any more than you do. It seems to me you're all vying with one another to make up the most colourful stories.'

'Rubbish. Rachel's even got a pony called

Hoppit. She wouldn't have made that up now, would she?' She picked up her new copy of *Girls' Own Paper* and buried her nose in it.

Nevertheless, I had to admit that she had a point. It was very difficult to get away from the steam when clothes were being boiled in the brick copper in the scullery next door. And when it was raining all the wet washing had to be strung on lines across the room. It is a strange fact that even though it is quite clean, wet washing has an unpleasant pungent smell that percolates even through closed doors.

So I counted up my earnings. Things were becoming a little easier now that I could work longer hours, I was even managing to save a few coppers each week. And I had to agree with Margaret, it would be nice not to live in a hole in the ground. I did my sums again. Yes, I was sure I would be able to manage the rent. So when the people moved out of the second floor flat I took the opportunity to approach Mrs Muir.

'I really think it's time Margaret had her own bedroom,' I explained when I suggested we might move out of the basement to the flat upstairs.

She shook her head. 'You really spoil that girl, Alice,' she said with a smile, 'but I can't say I blame you for wanting to get out of the cellar, if you're sure you can afford it.'

'Yes, I'm quite sure I can manage it,' I said, crossing my fingers behind my back that she wouldn't put the rent up as she usually did when a new tenant moved in.

To her credit and my relief she didn't.

Naturally, Margaret was ecstatic at having her own room, it was a joy to see her deciding where everything should go and putting her things away. I have to admit I was equally ecstatic because this flat had a proper, separate kitchen with even a small gas cooker, which was one up on the old range downstairs, so at least I didn't have to light a fire in the middle of summer to cook a meal now. Mrs Muir had made great changes since I first rented a room from her! Of course I had to work very hard to pay the rent and also to keep Margaret's needs supplied, but all in all they were good years.

I went to all her sports days ('For goodness sake wear gloves, Mummy, and don't take them off. I'd be *mortified* if my friends saw your red hands') and to the concerts where she sang in the choir. My heart swelled with pride when she actually sang a solo.

Looking round at the audience I noticed with interest that several other parents were struggling just as much as I was to keep up their daughters' appearances. It was the beginning of the depression and there were quite a number of slightly down-at-heel shoes and coats that had seen better days, and I recognized the same hats appearing time after time. I have to admit I wore the same hat, too, but each time I trimmed it with a different ribbon or put a sprig of artificial flowers on the brim, anything to make it look less recognizable. Naturally, I didn't point any of this out to Margaret, who was still convinced that everyone else was better off than we were. I simply took on extra work so that she could have a new tennis racquet and hockey stick.

And of course, it was all worth it when she flung her arms round my neck and said, 'Oh, thank you, Mum, I do love you.'

There were worrying trends, though. Many people were out of work and there were long queues at the labour exchange. Awful tales began to circulate of the indignities men who were desperate for work had to suffer, like being told to go and sell rock on the beach at Great Yarmouth. (Where they would get the rock from and how they could afford to buy it was never specified. Nor whom they would sell it to.) There were other tales, too, just as heart-less. It was humiliating enough for these skilled craftsmen to have to beg for work without those added insults.

But what affected me more was that even the better-off people were beginning to feel the pinch, because one of their first economies was always to dispense with the services of the char-lady, which in several instances was me. Luckily, I was beginning to earn a bit of money dressmaking – after Margaret's outburst at the state of my raw hands I always made sure to wear rubber gloves for rough work and I rubbed olive oil and sugar into my hands every night so they were soft and didn't snag the material. I also treated myself to a second-hand sewing machine. This really was a treat. Buying something for myself was a rare occurrence, I didn't usually spend more than a minimal amount on my needs.

As I practised sewing straight seams and making buttonholes I realized what a debt of gratitude I owed Aunt Maud. Although I hadn't been very attentive as a young girl when she had tried so hard to teach me her dressmaking skills, her words had obviously become ingrained in my mind. I realized that even after all these years I knew exactly what I had to do, all I lacked was patience and practice. In time I found that I actually possessed the skills I had never had the patience to develop as a girl and they certainly began to come in handy. Ladies who would have thrown away dresses (or given them to me to make over for myself) now came and asked me to alter them and make them more up-to-date so that they could continue to wear them. Skirts were shorter now, some of the younger ladies were even showing their knees, and styles were fairly straight and low waisted. So I had no difficulty doing what they wanted, even when I was asked to make new dresses. I found I enjoyed using my new-found skills and gradually my dressmaking took over from the cleaning work. For one thing it was easier on the knees and for another it meant that I was always at home with a meal ready for Margaret when she came home from school.

In 1935, when she was sixteen, Margaret left school with really good exam results. I was truly proud of her. The depression was showing signs of easing at last, the queues at the labour exchange were not quite so long and the children playing in the gutter looked slightly better fed. Some of them even had shoes, though they were often several sizes too big.

Margaret was lucky enough to find work in the office of a small factory on the outskirts of Norwich. This little factory had something to do with the aircraft industry, I was never quite sure what, but they seemed to have plenty of work and she was very happy there.

But in the wider world things were not looking very good. The name of Adolf Hitler, the German Fuehrer, seemed to be a lot in the news. He was making very war-like noises all over Europe, which was very worrying. It was less than twenty years since the end of one terrible war. The thought that there could be another one, that the whole thing could start all over again, was just too awful to contemplate.

I kept my fears and worries to myself. Margaret was really enjoying life. She was earning good money and she was learning shorthand and typing at night school three times a week. As well as that she usually went to the pictures twice a week with girl friends from her office – Fred Astaire and Ginger Rogers were their idols – and on Saturday evenings they all went dancing. I was very flattered when she asked me to make her an evening dress for a special midsummer dance. The dress, in pink shot silk, had a cross-over bodice into a tight waistband from which fell a full floor-length skirt. I had modelled it on one that Ginger Rogers had been wearing in one of her films, it could have been *Top Hat*, I don't really remember. It was very much admired, much to Margaret's delight, and resulted in orders for me to make several more. It had happened very gradually but I began to realize that I was making a name for myself as a dressmaker of quality. I was quite surprised. But I knew it was all thanks to my dear old Aunt Maud.

Inevitably, our fears over another war were justified. Despite the best efforts of Mr Chamberlain, the Prime Minister, to secure lasting peace Adolf Hitler just got more and more greedy and when he invaded Poland Britain declared war on Germany. It was September 3rd 1939.

Margaret, who of course had no conception of the horrors of war, was quite excited and was all set to join the ATS. But the factory, where she had risen to be the managing director's private secretary, had grown considerably since she had begun work there and was now doing important war work. To her disappointment and my relief her boss would not release her; he told her the importance of her work made her exempt from joining the forces and she would be helping the war effort far more by staying where she was. This didn't please her at all, but there was nothing she could do about it except revel in telling people she was engaged in vital war work.

In any case, she really loved her job, she knew

she was good at it and it was flattering to know how much her employer depended on her. And what was more to the point, even though most of the able-bodied men from the district were being called up, there was an RAF camp nearby so there was no shortage of dance partners.

I went to work in the canteen of a nearby munitions factory. I enjoyed this work very much and it was nice to have a regular wage. Also, for the first time since I had left Rookhurst Hall I was working with, rather than for, other people, which helped to increase my rather battered self-esteem. Of course food was once again rationed, but it was surprising the tasty meals we cooks managed to devise in spite of the shortages. Spam fritters, corned beef shepherd's pie, sausages that contained so little meat that they were known as 'bread in battledress' were usually on the menu, as were vegetable pasties and stews. Cooking up something different every day tested our ingenuity and there was always plenty of banter from the workers as they queued up for their meals.

Naturally, at the back of my mind was always anxiety about Margaret. She was a very pretty girl with her dark curls and blue eyes and curvaceous figure. In my imagination there was always some shady figure lurking round the next dark corner ready to subject her to unspeakable things. But she only laughed at my anxiety.

'Oh, you don't need to worry about me, Mum. I can take care of myself. Don't forget, I've worked in an aircraft factory full of men for the past four years,' she would say.

Coming home in the blackout didn't seem to bother her either, although she usually made sure to walk with a friend and always carried a large torch – not to light her way, that wasn't allowed in the blackout, but as a weapon. An added hazard on nights when there was no moon was that it really was pitch black because there were no street lights and no lights in houses or shops. There was always the danger of walking into a lamp post in the darkness or slipping off the edge of the pavement. She sprained her ankle doing just that one dark night, but apart from curtailing her dancing for a few nights no lasting damage was done.

As time went on most of the young men from the factory, as well as from other walks of life, disappeared into the forces, to be replaced in their jobs by women who, the authorities were surprised to find, did the work just as quickly and efficiently.

But, as I said before, Margaret was never lacking in men friends. There were always young airmen from the RAF station nearby queuing up to make a date with her, to take her to the cinema or out dancing. I knew she was a bit of a flirt and usually one of them, rarely the same one twice, would bring her home from a dance or the cinema and she would ask him in for a mug of cocoa. They were all lovely lads, most of them very young, too young in my opinion to be in training to be fighter pilots.

Some of them were even younger than Margaret, yet they were all full of beans and excited at the prospect of 'having a go' at the Hun. They seemed to regard it all as something of a game. Perhaps it was as well. I knew they would find out soon enough that war was no game.

It wasn't long before I began to notice that one young budding pilot was coming home with her more and more often. He was a pleasant enough young man, about Margaret's age. His name was Roddy Armitage. He didn't tell us very much about himself except that his parents lived somewhere in the north of England. It soon became quite clear that he idolized Margaret and she seemed equally keen on him. But Margaret was fickle, I had seen her in love many times and it never lasted. I just hoped she wouldn't break this young man's heart because he was such a nice lad. I needn't have worried on that score, although I have to admit I was a little surprised at how little time they had wasted when she came home one evening wearing an expensive diamond engagement ring.

Twenty-Six

'Of course I'm happy for you, darling,' I said, hiding my dismay, when she showed me her engagement ring. 'But isn't it a bit soon? After all, you've only known each other a matter of weeks.'

She kissed me. 'Haven't you ever heard of love at first sight, Mummy? I knew the first time I saw him that Roddy was the only man in the world for me.'

I couldn't argue with that. I knew all about love at first sight. Hadn't I fallen in love with Giles the first time I saw him?

So when Roddy next came round we had a celebration tea, a tin of salmon I'd been hoarding for Christmas and a cake that I made from rations I had been saving to make a Christmas pudding. Roddy's contribution was a tin of peaches, the like of which we hadn't seen since war began. He didn't say where it came from and I didn't ask. Sometimes it's best not to know these things.

After we'd eaten we drank a toast, to them, to me, to the end of the war, to England, to anything else we could think of (we emptied the bottle), in sherry Roddy had bought from the mess. Then they dropped their bombshell. Sitting side by side on the settee and holding hands, they announced that they planned to get married, by special licence.

'Before Roddy finishes his training,' Margaret said eagerly.

'Yes. Because I guess I'll be posted to the south of England,' he added.

'Well, here's to you both, then,' I said, draining my already empty glass and then upending it with a laugh to hide my surprise. Shock might have been a better word.

There wasn't much time but we pooled our clothing coupons to buy a length of soft woollen material and I made her wedding outfit, a smart blue dress and jacket that would be serviceable enough to wear later and a little matching hat trimmed with forget-me-nots and a wisp of veil. She wore it tilted cheekily over one eye and looked quite enchanting. Not having a traditional white wedding didn't worry her; in those austere days white weddings were a rarity.

They were married on New Year's Day 1940 and after a three-day honeymoon at a country pub somewhere in the West Country, Roddy got his posting to the south of England.

After those few hectic weeks life resumed much of its usual pattern, except that instead of going dancing every night Margaret now spent her time writing to Roddy or telephoning him from the phone box on the corner of the street. She always came back from making these calls looking worried and saying he was tired and flying too many 'ops'. Once or twice she travelled down south to spend the weekend with him but that was a rare occurrence. For one thing, he didn't get many weekends free and for another, she hated the journey, complaining that the trains were dirty and overcrowded, mostly with members of the forces, and that they never ran to time. She found crossing London in the blackout a nightmare, too, with tube stations being used as air raid shelters, the platforms crowded with families who would spend the night there to escape the fear of bombing, huddled under blankets. Desperate though she was to see her beloved Roddy, Margaret was always pleased to get home again.

She found it even more difficult once she discovered she was pregnant.

Margaret didn't like being pregnant. It was not at all what she and Roddy had intended so soon after being married and she hated the thought of losing her once perfect figure. It didn't help that she felt permanently sick, a feeling made worse by the fact that she had to hide how awful she was feeling from her employer, because he regarded pregnancy in his female staff as an irresponsible annoyance. She crept about feeling sick and miserable, bad-tempered with everybody, especially me. I did what I could for her, making her chamomile tea, which she hated, and raspberry leaf tea, which she didn't like much better.

Then she received a letter from Roddy

announcing that he had found a cottage to rent not far from the airbase. Suddenly, her mood changed and she was ecstatic. She gave in her notice, which her employer accepted without argument when she told him she was pregnant, packed her bags and went to live in Kent. It all seemed to happen in a matter of days. One day she was there, the next she was gone.

Of course I missed her dreadfully. I had loved and cared for her for the past twenty years and her departure left a gap in my life that was impossible to fill. But that was my secret, I still enjoyed my work in the canteen and I wrote her happy and chatty letters every weekend. In my spare time I worked at my sewing machine or knitted tiny garments, which I posted to her at regular intervals. She wrote back, often complaining of backache and indigestion and saying how tired Roddy was becoming with all the flying he had to do. She often said she was lonely when Roddy was on duty and hinted that it might be nice if I were to sell up and go and live in Kent with them, saying that the cottage was plenty big enough for me to have my own quarters.

I didn't take the hint, much as I would have liked to. I had carved out a life for myself with my work at the canteen and my dressmaking. I was able to earn quite a lot with my sewing now, because with the slogan 'make do and mend' on every billboard, people were always asking me to restyle old dresses or make one new one out of two old ones. It's surprising what you can do with a little imagination and ingenuity and I got quite a name for it in the area, so I was better off financially than I had ever been.

But then, in the fifth month of her pregnancy, Margaret wrote and said she'd been ordered to rest in bed for a few weeks. Could I go and look after her? She finished up, 'It would be lovely to see you, Mummy. I do miss you.'

How could I refuse?

I packed up my bags, said goodbye to Lily Muir, who made me promise I would come back, and went off to Kent.

Now it was my turn to experience the nightmare of the train journey. It was the beginning of June, and the seats in the carriage were all taken. I had to stand in the stifling, crowded corridor for most of the journey jammed between two airmen, one of whom was kind enough to give me his kitbag to sit on when there was enough space for it. All around me the talk was mostly about the evacuation of Dunkirk and the flotilla of heroic little boats that had gone over to help with the rescue. And when I reached Liverpool Street station I saw some of the effects of it – the platforms were crowded with hundreds of soldiers in filthy, tattered uniforms, their grimy faces grey and lined with tiredness and horror at what they had just experienced. Yet those who had the strength helped those who were wounded, and a space was kept clear for stretchers to be carried to the queue of waiting ambulances, whilst women from the WVS joked with the survivors as they handed out endless mugs of tea and cigarettes. It was chaotic and a sight I shall never forget.

The tube stations were equally crowded, this time with the people who spent their nights there to escape the air raids. They came armed with thermos flasks and blankets, the lucky ones finding a bed on the hastily built wooden bunks that lined the stations, the others finding a space to roll out sleeping bags or eiderdowns on the hard platforms. They were all amazingly cheerful, cracking jokes and repeating catch phrases from *ITMA*, Tommy Handley's popular comedy programme on the wireless.

It was ten o'clock at night before I finally reached my destination, Stelling Green, exhausted and shattered by what I'd seen. It was a journey I'd begun at nine that morning.

Roddy was on the platform to meet me. He told me he'd met every train since three o'clock in the afternoon, grinning as he admitted that that didn't amount to much since there had only been two before I arrived. He carried my case and we walked the short distance to the cottage.

It was not until the next day, when I saw it in daylight, that I realized Margaret hadn't exaggerated. The cottage was large, thatched and standing in its own grounds. It was so pretty it wouldn't have looked out of place on the lid of a chocolate box or as a jigsaw puzzle. It even had roses growing round the door. Inside, it was all low ceilings and beams but it also had bathrooms tucked in odd corners and every modern convenience. Margaret didn't tell me what the rent for the cottage was and I didn't ask, but I guessed it was expensive.

Roddy took me to a large room on the ground floor at the side, with French doors that overlooked the garden, and told me it would be mine if I sold up in Norwich and came to live with them permanently.

'I know Margaret would like that,' he said, smiling at me. 'And so would I.' He looked older than when I had last seen him and there were lines of strain round his eyes. There was a weariness about him, too. It was difficult to remember that he was still only twenty-one.

Margaret was lying in bed, bored and petulant despite the books and magazines surrounding her. But she brightened when she saw me.

'Oh, Mummy, you're here at last!' she cried as I sat on the bed and hugged her. 'I get so fed up here all day on my own when Roddy's off on ops,' she sighed, 'which is most of the time, these days.'

He looked at his watch. 'Yes, and I'd better be getting back now. I'm on early call tomorrow so I'll sleep at the base.' He dropped a kiss on Margaret's head. 'You'll be OK now your mother's here, darling. She'll look after you till you're up and about again.'

'And how long is that likely to be?' I asked.

'Three weeks, the doctor said.' Margaret yawned. 'The worst of it is, I'm missing all the nice sunshine, stuck upstairs in bed. And what's even more annoying, I feel as fit as a flea now. Not like I did for the first few months, when I didn't know how to crawl about.' She put out her hand to me. 'You will stay, Mummy, won't you?'

I smiled at her and nodded. 'Of course. For the time being.'

I wouldn't, I couldn't, commit myself. After all, my life was in Norwich, I had work and friends there, especially Lily Muir, who had been such a support to me when times were bad. We were good friends now, we swapped wartime recipes, went window shopping together and regularly went to the pictures every Friday night. We had queued for hours to see *Gone with the Wind*, drooling over Leslie Howard and Clark Gable. So I was reluctant to leave all that to come and live not far from the south coast, near a noisy airbase, with air raid sirens going off at frequent intervals and the threat of invasion a constant fear. Here, the enemy was poised only a few miles away across the Channel and we could sometimes even hear their guns pounding Dover. At least I would feel a bit safer a hundred or so miles away in Norwich.

Margaret soon recovered and although I often spoke of going home, somehow there was always something that delayed my departure. Roddy was flying more and more operations and he said what a relief it was to know that I was there, looking after Margaret, keeping her company while he was away. She had been terrified of being alone at night and during air raids, hearing the enemy planes droning over, never knowing where the next bomb would fall. But now I was with her she insisted that we should stand in the garden to watch the daylight dog-fights in the sky over the Channel as the Spitfires and Hurricanes battled it out with the German bombers and fighters. We were both terrified at what we were watching, yet the sight mesmerized us and we were unable to turn away.

'Oh, please God, don't let that be Roddy,' she breathed as a blazing plane spiralled into the sea.

'No, I'm sure it wasn't one of ours, it was one of theirs,' I told her, although in truth they were all too far away for me to tell.

Day after day it went on. They called it the Battle of Britain and Winston Churchill, now Prime Minister, gave a speech in which he said, 'Never in the field of human conflict was so much owed by so many to so few.'

Roddy was one of those few. And if he'd lived my little Alfie would probably have been another, I realized sadly.

On the rare occasions that we saw Roddy now he looked twenty years older, and although he tried to keep up his old, jaunty appearance it was often too much of an effort. All he really wanted to do was to fall into Margaret's arms and sleep.

One day he spoke to me when I was sitting in the garden on my own while Margaret had gone upstairs for her afternoon nap. He came and sat in the vacant chair beside me.

'I know you'll take care of Margaret if you get news that I've bought it, Alice,' he said quietly. I knew what he meant. 'Bought it' was the pilots' euphemism for being shot down and killed, words they would never use. He went on, jiggling his knee in the nervous gesture he had adopted recently. 'I've made sure she'll never be short of money. There's an annuity from an inheritance from my godmother. I've put it in her name, so there'll be plenty to look after her needs – and the baby's, of course.' He ran his hands through his Brylcreemed hair and stared into the distance, sitting quite still apart from the tell-tale jiggling knee. 'I wonder if it'll be a boy or a girl. If it's a girl, will you tell Margaret I'd like her to be called Lucy, after my godmother...'

'You'll be able to tell her yourself in a couple of months,' I said briskly, anxious to put an end to his train of thought. I knew they had agreed that it would be 'unlucky' to discuss names before the birth, a superstition I had never come across before, but nowadays life was riddled with superstitions, especially among the young pilots.

He gave me a twisted smile. 'Yes, of course I will, Alice. It's just...'

'I know, dear.' I put my hand on his arm. 'Don't worry about Margaret. Just concentrate on looking after yourself.'

He nodded and got to his feet. 'I have to get

back. I'll just go and say cheerio to Margaret.' He never, ever, said 'goodbye', it was too final.

I stood up too. 'Take care, Roddy.' I reached up and kissed him and for a moment we clung together. Then I watched him walk across the garden and into the house. I think I knew then that I would never see him again. I think he must have known it, too, because when he reached the French doors he turned and blew me a kiss.

He was shot down off the Kent coast that night, one of the flight of fighter planes sent up to intercept German bombers heading towards the East End of London.

Twenty-Seven

Margaret was inconsolable. I knew exactly how she felt because I'd been through it all myself. I could only hold her in my arms, let her weep and urge her to think, as I had done, of the child she carried – Roddy's child.

Helping her to come to terms with her grief – as if anyone ever 'comes to terms' with such a loss – brought back my own grief when Giles died. The difference was, of course, that mine had had to be hidden. Whereas Margaret could subside into floods of tears, knowing she had a comforting shoulder to cry on, I'd had to carry on as if my life hadn't fallen apart. There had been nobody to care how I felt because nobody had any idea that my heart was broken. Holding Margaret as she wept I realized that now was not the time to tell her that the pain, the sense of loss, never goes away, you just get used to bearing it.

'Odd, isn't it? My father never saw me, just as Roddy will never see our baby,' she mused one day, when she was again able to think and speak rationally. 'What was my father like, Mummy?'

Strange she had never asked the question before. Nervously, I fingered the wedding ring I was not entitled to but had never removed. 'He was at Rookhurst Hall, where I worked. He died in the terrible 'flu epidemic of 1918,' I answered, being truthful but at the same time evasive.

'Oh, Mummy, 'flu's not that bad. It's not usually anything people die of.'

'They called this Spanish 'flu and millions of people did die.' I told her a bit about the terrible scourge and the moment passed. She didn't mention her father again.

Of course, there was now no question of me leaving her, she was still hardly in a fit state to look after herself, let alone tend to the baby as well. But I felt it was important that we should get away from the cottage at Stelling Green and make a fresh start, somewhere where she wouldn't be constantly reminded of the bliss she had shared with Roddy, somewhere where there wasn't the constant drone of aircraft overhead, somewhere where every other person you met, both male and female, wouldn't be wearing air force blue.

'But I've got everything in place to have the baby here,' she protested when I suggested it. 'Roddy and I planned to—' She stopped and tears welled again. 'Well, anyway, I've only got a few weeks to go. I couldn't possibly move before the baby's born. Then we'll think about moving back to Norfolk. But not Norwich. I don't want to go back there.' She was adamant about that.

Margaret's daughter was born on the third of October. It was a quick and easy birth. I told Margaret about the afternoon Roddy had told me his wish that his daughter should be named Lucy and we both wept afresh that his young life had been cut short so tragically.

'He knew he was going to die, didn't he?' she said, weeping.

'Yes, I think he did,' I agreed. 'But he's given you a lovely little daughter to remember him by.'

'Like my father left me for you,' she said, managing to smile through her tears.

I swallowed hard as I remembered holding my precious little son in my arms for those few hours before he died, something I had schooled myself to do only rarely over the years. I smiled back at her. 'That's right.'

Lucy was a lovely child, as fair as her mother was dark, as placid as her mother had been fractious. But when I spoke to Margaret about taking the baby to visit Roddy's parents in Yorkshire she shook her head. It was out of the question, she told me. Roddy had hardly ever spoken about them, she didn't even know where they lived. It seemed he had cut himself off or been cut off from his family when he left school and had gone to live with his godmother, quite a wealthy woman who had since died, leaving him as her heir.

'So at least you'll never be short of money,' I remarked.

'Thank God for that!' She shuddered. 'I wouldn't want to go back to the days of my childhood. I'll never forget how humiliating it was to be so poor.' She leaned over the pram, a very smart coach-built job with huge wheels. 'At least you'll never have to suffer like I did, Lucy,' she crooned. 'Your mummy will see to it that you always have the best of everything.'

I said nothing, but her words stung.

We moved house just before Christmas. The Battle of Britain was over but the war still raged and everything was either rationed or in short supply. Leaving me to look after Lucy – of course the baby was bottle-fed, Margaret would have no truck with breast-feeding – she wrapped herself in the fur coat that Roddy had bought her as a wedding present and travelled to Norfolk to look for a house to rent. I think she had the idea that the shortages and rationing wouldn't be as acute there, which of course was nonsense.

Now that I had done it myself, of course I worried even more about her going through London. The Blitz was at its height, with bombs dropping on the city night after night, and I could just imagine the nightmare of a journey she would be having.

But although the anxiety was always at the back of my mind, I was kept busy with looking after Lucy and taking her to the local clinic to have her weighed and to collect her ration of dried milk and rose hip syrup. This was always my task, even when Margaret was there. She didn't like being told how to care for her own baby.

She was away for just over a week. When she came back she was euphoric with the news that she had bought, not rented, a house on the western outskirts of Norwich.

'But I thought you didn't want to go back to Norwich,' I said, flabbergasted at her news.

'No, I didn't. But houses there are going for peanuts now because everybody's afraid to put their money into property in case it gets bombed.' She shrugged off her fur coat and flopped down on the settee. 'Just the time to buy, I said to the estate agent, and he agreed with me.' She flung out her arms. 'So I bought. It's a really nice house, it stands in its own grounds, double-fronted, a good size but not big enough to have been requisitioned by the Ministry of Defence. We can move in any time we like.' She smiled widely. 'I thought it would be nice if we were settled in by Christmas.'

'That's less than a month away,' I said, horrified.

She smiled again. It was good to see the old bright-eyed, enthusiastic Margaret back after all those weeks of grieving apathy. 'We'll have to get our skates on, then, won't we?'

Of course, Margaret got her own way and we moved into Benfleet House two days before Christmas.

It was a marvel to me how Margaret always managed to fall on her feet. Benfleet House was full of character, late Victorian, red brick, with a pillared portico and a massive black-painted front door. In fact, it looked larger on the outside than it was on the inside because although the hall was spacious, with a wide, curving staircase, the rooms were small enough to feel homely. I judged that it was a house built by a man who wasn't quite as wealthy as he would have liked people to think and managed to keep his economies out of sight. I loved it and it had the added advantage that it was sold partly furnished. In those days of dockets and coupons this was invaluable, especially as 'utility' furniture, as it was known, had little to recommend it, being as its name implied utilitarian and plain as well as difficult to get.

'No, we don't want any of that old utility stuff, it's mostly made of compressed cardboard, anyway,' she said airily. 'We'll have a poke around the second-hand shops and see what we can find. It'll be fun.'

It was fun, too, hunting round dusty old shops

that sold everything from massive wardrobes to paraffin stoves, from chamber pots to horsehair sofas. Margaret bought whatever she fancied, in fact there were times when I wondered how she would fit everything in. She bought a large drop-leaf table because she didn't like the one that was in the house and when she found there were six matching chairs she bought those as well. Money, it seemed, was no object.

The one thing I really liked as we trawled the antique shops was an old oak bureau tucked away in a corner. It had three drawers with brass handles and the flap – the man in the shop called it a 'fall' – dropped down to reveal a writing desk and lots of little carved and fretted compartments to hold letters and documents. It was far too expensive for my pocket. Nevertheless, I felt drawn to it and went back several times, searching for secret compartments, pulling out the drawers to see if they ran easily, running my hand over the smooth wood, admiring the elaborate brass escutcheons.

'You really like that, don't you, Mummy?' Margaret said, smiling, as I went over to it yet again when we revisited the shop where it was displayed.

'I just feel drawn to it. I don't know why,' I said, feeling a bit silly. 'I think it must have had an interesting past.'

'Well, maybe it'll have an interesting future, too,' she said with a laugh. 'Come on, we've spent enough for one day. Let's go home.'

Three days later, a van drew up outside the

house and the bureau, my bureau, was delivered. I hadn't seen her buy it.

'Well,' she said, giving me a kiss, 'I knew you liked it so I thought you should have it.' She became serious. 'You know, I do appreciate what you do – what you've always done for me, Mummy.' She put her arm round my shoulders and gave me a squeeze. 'You're not a bad old stick, are you?' She gave me another kiss.

Margaret was not a girl to pay compliments so I knew she meant it. Naturally, the bureau took pride of place in my room.

Gradually, our lives settled into a pattern. I ran the house while Margaret looked after the baby, bathing her, feeding her, taking her for walks. But Margaret was never the domesticated kind and she soon got bored with doing nothing but look after Lucy. She would bath her and play with her for half an hour but she got irritated with her if she cried and would hand her over to me to placate. After a few months, during which she became increasingly bored and listless, she decided that perhaps she ought to do some war work.

'You don't have to,' I pointed out. 'Women with young children are exempt from war work. It's only single women that can be directed to work wherever the need is.'

'Well, I might be able to find something locally. I certainly wouldn't want to be sent somewhere like Sheffield.' She made a face.

But as usual, luck was with her. She even managed to get her old job back as secretary to the managing director of the firm making aircraft engine parts. Before long I was glad to see her blossoming into her old self again. She loved being out at work and was also out nearly every night dancing and socializing, saying half-apologetically that it was better than sitting at home every night grieving for Roddy.

'Although I shall never, ever forget him, Mummy, you realize that, don't you? He was the love of my life,' she would tell me as she cleverly rolled her dark hair over an old silk stocking into a thick roll round her head in the fashion of the day and applied rather more lipstick than I thought necessary before going out on another 'date'.

I knew this was true and I worried that she might be flinging herself into frantic love affairs in an effort to hide the ache in her heart. I could have told her from bitter experience that nothing could even begin to cure that ache except time. But I knew there was nothing I could do or say. Margaret had always been headstrong, she wasn't likely to listen to me.

So I contented myself with running the house and looking after Lucy, which left me no time for much else. In truth, I think it was probably one of the happiest times of my life because Lucy was a delightful child, always happy and smiling. I would take her for walks to feed the ducks or sit with her on my lap and sing nursery rhymes with her, which she loved. I was there when she took her first steps and I was the one who taught her to say her first words.

When she began to talk she would try to tell Margaret where she had been and what we had been doing. But Margaret was always either going out or coming in, always busy and preoccupied with her own affairs.

'Later, darling. Mummy's tired now and wants to put her feet up,' she would say. Or, 'When I come back I'll hear all about it, darling.'

'But I'll be in bed when you come back, Mummy,' Lucy would reply, disappointed.

'I'll come and kiss you goodnight, darling. I always do.'

'But I'll be asleep so I won't be able to talk.'

'Then I'll hear about it tomorrow.'

'I don't s'pose I'll memember by then.'

'Don't be tiresome, darling.' Margaret would drop a kiss on top of Lucy's head, at the same time rolling her eyes up at me.

It was hardly surprising that it was always me that Lucy ran to when she wanted a cuddle or to have a grazed knee kissed better.

Of course, I might have known it couldn't last. It was when Lucy was nearly three years old that my life changed.

Completely.

Twenty-Eight

I'll never forget the day my life fell apart, it was just a few days before Lucy's third birthday. I was upstairs reading Lucy her favourite bedtime story, 'The Three Billy Goats Gruff', when Margaret called up the stairs, 'Mummy, I can't find my cheque book. Have you seen it? I need it, I'm going out in a minute.'

I had been tidying up that day. Margaret was the world's worst for leaving things about, I was always clearing up after her, but I didn't remember coming across her cheque book.

I thought for a moment, then I called back. 'Look in the drawer of the sideboard. If it isn't there, see if I put it in my bureau with some other papers by mistake.'

'Oh, Mummy, you really are the limit,' she complained impatiently.

I thought no more about it. I finished reading the story, settled Lucy with her teddy and kissed her goodnight and went downstairs.

Margaret was sitting at the table, a flimsy-looking piece of paper in her hand.

'I've just found this in your bureau,' she said in a rather clipped voice. 'Do you know anything about it?'

I frowned. 'How did you find it?'

'Oh.' She made an impatient gesture. 'Does it matter? I was rummaging about, looking for my cheque book. I suppose I must have touched something, some spring or other and a little door flew open and it just fell out.' She looked up, a strange, hard expression on her face. 'It's my birth certificate, isn't it?'

I nodded, my mouth dry. 'That's right.' This was the moment I'd been dreading, but the moment I could no longer avoid. The time had come to tell Margaret the truth. I could only pray she would understand that I had acted for the best. I took a deep breath.

'Yes, it is your birth certificate, dear,' I said, watching anxiously for her reaction. 'Eliza Bucknell was your mother. Lizzie died giving birth to you.'

Her jaw dropped and she just stared at me. 'Why didn't you tell me this before? Why have you let me go on thinking you were my mother all these years? For God's sake, who are you? Who was she?' She tapped the certificate. 'Oh, my God,' her voice rose wildly. 'Who am I?'

'You're the same person you've always been,' I said, managing to sound a great deal calmer than I was feeling inside. 'Eliza Mary Bucknell gave birth to you, but Lizzie died when you were born so I became your mother.'

She stared at me, her face white. 'No, you're not my mother. According to this Eliza Bucknell is, or was, my mother.' She tapped the birth certificate with her pen. 'But who is this Eliza

Bucknell? You must have known her. In fact you must have known her well, since you called her Lizzie.'

'Oh, yes, I knew her very well. She was my...' I hesitated, 'she was my ... friend.' I paused, then went on, 'You see, Lizzie and I were both pregnant at the same time. As I've told you, she died giving birth to you and my baby was born less than a fortnight later. But he only lived a few hours, bless him. So, since you were motherless and I had lost my child it seemed only natural that I should take you and bring you up as my own.' I knew I was speaking jerkily, but the words felt as if they were being wrung out of me. 'Not that I wouldn't have done the same if my Alfie had lived. Of course I would. As soon as Lizzie died I knew I was going to keep you and bring you up with my baby. It would almost have been like having twins. But it was not to be, because my little boy didn't live.' I couldn't help a catch in my voice even after all this time.

Her lip curled derisively. 'So what were you, two old whores together who got landed in the family way?'

I was shocked. I really hadn't expected that! I felt as if she'd smacked me in the teeth. I got to my feet and gripped the back of my chair till my knuckles showed white. 'No, Margaret. Indeed, we were *not*,' I spat. 'Far from it, in fact. If you want the truth your mother was the daughter of Sir George and Lady Bucknell who lived at a place called Rookhurst Hall in Suffolk. I was housemaid there.'

Her mouth dropped open and her eyes narrowed. 'My mother was the daughter of Sir George and Lady Bucknell, whoever they are? You're telling me I'm rightfully the grand-daughter of titled people who live in some grand house not a million miles away from here?' she said furiously. 'Yet you had the effrontery to keep me from them and bring me up as your own child, living in a cellar in abject squalor. How could you do such a thing? How dare you deprive me of my birthright like that? You're an evil, wicked woman.'

'Am I? Am I so very wicked, Margaret? What do you think I should have done, then?' I was just as furious as she was now at her totally unjust accusation. 'Should I have taken you back to Rookhurst Hall and presented your grandmother with the product of her daughter's sordid little affair with the chauffeur, a married man whose wife was pregnant at the time? Do you think she would have welcomed you with open arms? I can tell you that if that's what you think you're deluding yourself. Particularly since Lizzie had been forced to steal away in shame when she found she was pregnant, because she knew that if she didn't go of her own accord she would be turned out by her mother. God knows, M'Lady had suffered enough in the dreadful 'flu epidemic. First she lost her twin daughters, then her husband and then her eldest son. I think it would have sent her insane to discover her remaining daughter had played fast and loose and given birth to an illegitimate child fathered by one of the servants. If indeed she could bring herself to believe what I had to tell her. She could have simply called me a liar and sent me packing.'

'And are you?'

'Am I what?' I looked at her blankly.

'Are you lying?' Margaret's tone was scathing.

'Of course I'm not lying. You should know me well enough to know I never lie.'

'Know you? I don't know you at all, do I? I thought you were my mother.' Her voice was like granite. 'And what about this child you say you had? Was his father the chauffeur, too?' she sneered.

'No,' I said quietly, refusing to rise to her bait. Laying bare my memories to this unyielding woman was the most painful thing I had ever done. 'My baby's father was your mother's elder brother. We would have been married if he hadn't died in the dreadful 'flu epidemic of nineteen eighteen.' I saw the look of scorn on her face. 'And please don't make sarcastic remarks about the son of the house and the dolly mop housemaid because you didn't know Giles and nothing could be further from the truth,' I said wearily. I waved my hand, dashing a tear away as I did so. 'But this is not about my past. My past is my business and nobody else's. As far as you're concerned I did what I thought was right. I loved you and brought you up as if you were my own child. Whatever you may think, I always did the best I could for you.'

'And you call scavenging for vegetables at the market the best you could do? You call having to watch you scrubbing other people's front steps and being mortified in case any of my friends recognized us "doing your best"? Living in a damp cellar? Never having any money? Was that "doing your best"? God, what sort of a life was that!'

I hesitated, remembering the hard, long hours I had worked in order to give her the best in life that I could. I didn't want her to be grateful, for heaven's sake gratitude was the last thing I was looking for, but I had hoped that she might have recognized that my life hadn't been easy either, that I had been forced to make sacrifices in order to keep a roof over our heads and support us both on what little I could earn. Instead of which, all she could do was to fling back in my face all the things I had done to try and give her a better life.

I was stung into telling her the whole truth, something I had vowed I would never, ever do.

'Let me tell you, your life would have been much worse if your mother had lived,' I said, my voice low with fury. 'You would never have been taken to live a life of luxury at Rookhurst Hall, if that's what you're imagining. Oh, Lizzie intended to go back there, of course she did, but not until she'd got rid of you. She never intended to take you with her. Her plan was either to put you up for adoption or if that failed she was going to put you in an orphanage. She didn't really care which, as long as she could be rid of you,' I said, realizing I was being brutal. 'What sort of a life do you think you would have had living in an orphanage? Would it have been better than the life you had with me?'

'You're lying,' she said again, this time through white lips. But she knew it was no lie.

I shook my head. 'No, it's the truth I'm telling you. It's what she always said she would do. She didn't want you and never intended to keep you.' Even now I couldn't bring myself to tell her that Lizzie had always called her 'the brat', that would have been too cruel. Instead, I tried to soften the blow by adding, 'Although I like to think that if she had held you in her arms she might have changed her mind and not wanted to ever let you go.'

'But she didn't?'

I shook my head again. 'I'm not sure she ever laid eyes on you. There wasn't time. She didn't live long enough.'

She was quiet for a long time, her elbow on the table, leaning her head on her hand. I sat down again opposite her, my hands folded in my lap, waiting. There was nothing more I could say.

Finally she lifted her head, her face ravaged.

'Why have you never told me all this before?' she asked, her voice hard. 'Why have you allowed me to live this lie for so long?'

I spread my hands. 'I don't really know. I used to think about it a lot when you were small. I used to agonize about when would be the best time to tell you, how long I should wait.' I shrugged. 'Somehow, the time never seemed right. There was always some reason why it would be better to wait a bit longer. Then...' I looked straight at her. 'You probably won't believe this, but quite honestly I was so busy trying to give you the best life I could that I forgot all about it. In any case, it didn't really seem to matter any more. After all, I'd been your mother ever since you were born, I'd fed you at my breast, I'd cared for you all your life. You *were* my daughter.' I pointed towards the birth certificate lying between us. 'In everything but that.' I gave a twisted smile. 'Has it been such a terrible thing having me for your mother, Margaret?' I asked. 'I've always done the best I could for you, even if it was never as much as you would have liked or felt you were entitled to. But I can tell you this, I've loved you and cared for you far more than your real mother would ever have done.'

She didn't answer that. She just looked at me, her expression as cold as a hoar frost, and said, 'But that's just the point. You're not my mother, are you? All these years you've lived a lie, pretending to be something you're not. You deliberately deceived me into believing you were my mother, when in reality my mother was the daughter of a titled lady. I shall never forgive you for that. I think it was a despicable thing to do and of course I know I can never trust you again, particularly with my daughter. God knows what lies you've been feeding her.'

I gasped. 'Margaret! How dare you say that? You know I would never—'

She cut across my words. 'I want you out of my house. Now. Tonight. Just pack your bags and leave. I never want to see you again.'

My head was reeling with the shock of her words. I simply couldn't believe that my Margaret could be so callous and cruel. A horrible cold hand clutched my stomach. 'Don't be silly. You can't mean that, Margaret,' I said, horrified. 'What about Lucy? Who'll care for Lucy?'

'That's my business. My daughter is no longer any concern of yours. Do you think I want her associating with a woman I can no longer trust?' She got to her feet before I could open my mouth to reply and said, 'While you pack your things I'll book you into a hotel and you can stay there at my expense until you find yourself somewhere to live.'

I swallowed my pride and pleaded with her, but only for Lucy's sake. 'Don't you think perhaps we should both sleep on this, Margaret?' I said, forcing myself to speak quietly. 'I know all this has been a terrible shock to you but things may look different in the morning.' I was trying to be reasonable, trying to hide the dreadful hurt. 'After all, nothing's really changed—'

'Don't be so ridiculous. Everything's changed,' she snapped as she went over to the telephone. 'I've discovered you're not my mother. I've discovered you're nothing but a lying, scheming—'

I got to my feet, holding up my hand to

silence this cold stranger who had been my beloved daughter until half an hour ago. 'None of that is true and you know it,' I said sharply. I lifted my chin and walked to the door. 'But if that's the way you choose to regard me there's nothing I can do about it. And you can put the phone down. I don't need you to book me into a hotel, I'm perfectly capable of making my own arrangements, thank you. I don't need your charity.' I turned to her. She was staring at the wall and wouldn't even look at me. I shook my head sadly and said quietly, 'Goodbye, Margaret. Perhaps you'll be good enough to send on my things when I let you know where I'm living.'

I put on my coat and hat, picked up my handbag and walked out of the house. I hadn't dared to look in at Lucy, sleeping upstairs in her little bed, peacefully unaware of the drama unfolding downstairs, because I knew my pride would have broken and I would have gone down on my knees and begged Margaret to let me stay. Not that she would have listened.

I must have walked for hours in the gathering early autumn darkness, reliving over and over again that dreadful conversation. I simply couldn't believe that Margaret had turned on me in that way. She had been everything to me for the past twenty-four years, everything I had done, every penny I had earned had been to make a better life for her. I had always thought she loved me in return. I had clearly been quite wrong.

I walked on for what might have been hours, half blinded by tears, not thinking, not caring where I went. It must have been instinct that led me back to Bishop's Row, where Margaret and I had lived for so many years. I rang the doorbell of number fifty-one and when Lily Muir answered it I fell sobbing into her arms.

If Lily hadn't taken me in that night I think I might have thrown myself under a bus. She listened as I poured out my story, plying me with endless cups of tea before making me up a bed on her sofa.

She never passed judgement, never once said I'd spoiled Margaret – which of course I had, never once said Margaret was unkind and ungrateful for the sacrifices I had made for her. Because nobody knew better than Lily how I had struggled to make a good life for Margaret, a child she knew was not my own.

That night a friendship was forged that lasted until her death.

Twenty-Nine

The next day Lily offered me a room on the top floor of her house – one of the rooms I used to keep clean for her 'gentlemen', the commercial travellers who only stayed a night at a time. But now, of course, it was wartime. Those same men were now either in the forces or doing war work in some distant bomb-blasted city. Nowadays the rooms were only used occasionally by the wives or sweethearts of men from the RAF station sharing a few precious days of leave.

I stayed with Lily till the end of the war. I bought myself another sewing machine because when I sent for my things Margaret simply bundled up my clothes and shoved them (there's no other word for it) into a couple of suitcases. She forgot, or didn't bother, to send quite a lot of my other possessions, including my sewing machine. She didn't send my oak bureau, either, which rather upset me. But I could hardly complain about that since she had bought it for me in the first place. I wondered if she had kept it as an act of revenge, I knew she didn't much like it.

With my savings and the money I could earn with my dressmaking I managed to pay my way quite well living in Lily's house. We found we had a lot in common. We would sometimes pool our rations and have a meal together or go down to the café near the castle for bangers and mash. Every week we went to the cinema at least twice and came home humming the latest songs, which we sang when we had to go into the Anderson shelter during the air raids, to drown the sounds of the planes going over and the bombs dropping. We also formed the habit of going to church every Sunday, where we prayed for an end to this horrible war that was dragging on and demoralizing us all.

But almost every afternoon I went for a walk on my own and my steps always took me to the park where I used to take Lucy to feed the ducks.

I was lucky enough to catch sight of her quite often although I was always careful that she never saw me. All I wanted was to know that she was happy, that she wasn't pining for me, although I was human enough to hope that she was missing me a little. It rather upset me to see a succession of nursemaids accompanying her, it was rarely the same one for more than a month at a time, but she appeared happy and well cared for so presumably this didn't worry her. In any case, there was nothing I could do about it. I never once saw her with Margaret.

'I think you're silly, torturing yourself by going to that park every day, Alice,' Lily said one day. 'What good do you think it does?'

I unpinned my hat and laid the hat pins on the

hall table. 'I'm not torturing myself. I just need to know that Lucy is all right, Lily,' I said.

'But there's nothing you can do if she isn't, dear,' she pointed out.

'I know.' I sighed. 'I know you're right. I am being silly but I just can't seem to help myself.'

'I reckon the best thing you could do would be to move away from Norwich, Alice. Then you wouldn't be able to go to that park every day.'

I nodded. 'Maybe. When the war's over...' In other words, not yet.

At last the war ended, restrictions eased and things began gradually to return to normal, although normal after the war wasn't the same as normal before it. How could it be? As Lily and I agreed, women who had been earning good money doing men's jobs during the war were hardly going to be content to stay at home and be the unpaid family drudge now it was over.

Lucy started school. I saw her in her red and white checked school dress and maroon blazer, her panama hat with its maroon and blue striped hatband plonked squarely on her fair curls and her little school satchel over her shoulder. Was it my imagination or was she beginning to look a little like Giles? It was possible, after all, he would have been her uncle. But perhaps it was just wishful thinking on my part because I wasn't close enough to take a proper look.

I saw her taking a short cut through the park with – of all people – Margaret, on her first day at school. Her mother was tugging impatiently at her hand. Oh, how like Margaret! I wanted to shout out to her, 'Don't you realize the child is nervous? It's her first day at school, for goodness sake. She needs your loving understanding.'

But of course, I didn't. Instead, I turned away with tears in my eyes and went home. I was no longer a part of Lucy's life, she had moved on and so must I.

It was not many days later that Lily announced that she was going to retire.

'I've made a good living over the years, renting out these flats, so I think I shall retire, sell up and buy myself a bungalow on the coast. I've always fancied living at the seaside,' she said.

'Oh,' I said, quite taken aback. 'I shall miss you, Lily.'

'Well, why don't you come with me, Alice?' she asked. 'After all, we've been friends for a long time now and we get on well together.'

I was doubtful. I didn't think I could live with Lily, not in a small bungalow.

She must have read my thoughts. 'Of course, I'm not suggesting that we should live together,' she said quickly. 'But it might be nice if we could find a couple of small bungalows not too far apart.'

'On which coast?' I asked guardedly.

She shrugged. 'Norfolk? Suffolk? I haven't really thought, but I wouldn't want to move too far away from these parts, would you?'

I shook my head. 'I hadn't really thought of moving anywhere at all, to tell you the truth,' I said.

Nevertheless, I turned her suggestion over in my mind for several days. Money wasn't a problem, I was not at all badly off because over the years I'd managed to save quite a lot of money. Before Margaret turned me out (there was no other way of putting it because that was exactly what she had done) she had always been very generous, never letting me pay for anything, and even without that I had managed to earn quite a bit with my sewing and dressmaking. And I had nobody to consider but myself.

I took a deep breath and went down to Lily's room. 'Yes. All right. Why not? This might be a good time to make a fresh start, Lily. I think I'd very much like a bungalow on the coast.' It was quite gratifying to see how her face lit up at my words.

We took our time, visiting various places on both the Norfolk and Suffolk coast before we settled on this new estate in Crawfordness. It was only a small estate and the bungalows being built were just the right size for us. We earmarked two, at the end of the road but on opposite sides. We each wanted to have our own home but we were anxious to be near enough to be company and to help each other out.

It worked very well. We went walking on the beach together and we joined the local church, which helped us to get to know people. Lily took up painting, something she had always wanted to do, and I joined a quilting class.

Then two years ago, Lily became ill and died. I still miss her and her wise words.

But there was one thing I did that was against Lily's advice. As soon as I moved in I couldn't resist writing to Margaret, just to let her know where I was. Not that she would care, of course, I realized that.

I'm so glad I did. If I hadn't I wouldn't be sitting here writing my story down for you, Lucy...

Thirty

'Oh, dear!' was all Lucy could say when she had finished Alice's story. 'So that's what the quarrel was about! I didn't expect anything like that!'

Ben finished reading the last page, took a final swig of coffee and put his mug down. 'No, neither did I,' he said thoughtfully. 'And of course, now we know that Alice isn't your grandmother, after all.'

'I'm surprised Mummy never told me that. Although, perhaps it's not so surprising because to be honest, she never really spoke about

Granny at all, except to complain what a poverty-stricken childhood she'd had.'

'Perhaps she was ashamed at the way she'd treated her.'

'And well she might have been! It was a shameful thing to do.'

'Do you think she might have regretted it later?'

'Maybe. I don't know. Like I said, she never spoke about her much.' Lucy ran her hands through her hair. 'Oh, it's all so complicated,' she said miserably.

He came and sat beside her. 'No, it isn't, Lucy. It's just that Margaret's mother was Lizzie and not Alice, which makes Lizzie and not Alice your real grandmother.' He grinned. 'And, for what it's worth, it makes the chauffeur chappie and not Giles your grandfather.' He paused and put his hand up to brush a stray strand of hair away from her face, changed his mind and lowered his hand again. 'But it's still in the family, so you don't have to worry,' he added quietly.

She wasn't listening; her mind was still on what she had been reading. 'And that's all the quarrel was about, the fact that Granny – Alice – hadn't told Mummy she wasn't her proper mother. Yet she was a real and loving mother to her in every sense except the fact that she hadn't actually given birth to her. Oh, poor Alice.' Lucy's eyes filled with tears. 'After all the sacrifices she'd made to care for Margaret and give her the best she could in life, to have been rejected like that and virtually thrown out of the house.' She shook her head sadly. 'It's an awful thing to say, but it was typical of Mummy to have behaved like that. She's always been terribly selfish and self-centred. A bit like her real mother, I guess. Lizzie seems to have wanted everything her own way.' She was quiet for a few moments, then she dashed away her tears and a smile spread across her face. 'Those memories I have of being cuddled and loved, it must have been Granny – Alice, who used to take me on her lap and sing to me. She says in her story that she looked after me till I was three and it's quite obvious from what she's written that she loved me very much.' She frowned. 'She said she used to come to the park and watch me with the various nursemaids Mummy employed to look after me, but it's funny, I never saw her. At least, I don't think I did. Of course, there were people there regularly that I got to recognize ... I wonder if she could have been one of them...'

'Do you want to go back and see her again?' Ben asked. 'She thought you might not want to once you'd read her story.'

'You think she was afraid I might reject her like my mother did?'

He nodded. 'Something like that.'

'Of course I want to see her again,' Lucy said firmly. 'She was so brave and courageous in the way she brought up my ungrateful mother. I think it's terrible, the way Mummy treated her in the end. And I want to tell her so.'

Ben reached in his pocket for his diary and began leafing through it. 'I've got to go to the fair tomorrow and Saturday, but that'll be it. Then it's just a case of getting stuff dispatched and the unsold stuff back here.' He looked up at her. 'I could manage Sunday, if that's OK with you.'

'What? This Sunday? Oh, thank you, Ben, that would be lovely,' she said eagerly, then, more formally, in case he thought she was being too familiar, 'I'd be very grateful, if you're sure you can spare the time.'

He looked at his watch. 'Talking of time, I must go. I've got another early start tomorrow.' He got to his feet, stifling a yawn. 'This story of Alice's is ruining my beauty sleep,' he said ruefully.

She accompanied him to the door. 'Thank you for today, Ben, it was quite an experience,' she said.

He nodded. 'I'm glad you enjoyed it.'

'Oh, and were you right? Did you guess the end of Alice's story?'

He shook his head and gave a little grin. 'No, I must admit I was way out. I've been quite wrong, so far.'

'What do you mean, so far?'

He gave her a quizzical look. 'Well, the story isn't finished yet, is it? Cinderella hasn't tried on the glass slipper.' He dropped a fleeting kiss on her forehead and left.

She put her hand up to where his lips had touched, frowning. 'I wonder what he meant by that,' she murmured, puzzled.

When she pulled back the curtains on Sunday morning Lucy saw that it had dawned disappointingly chilly, with an autumn mist hanging in the air and wisping through the buildings across the square. But by early afternoon when they started off for Crawfordness the sun had burned through and the day was bright and warm, although as they drove through the countryside huge cobwebs sparkled with jewels of dew among the blackberries in shaded hedgerows.

Lucy was glad she had put on a long-sleeved blouse – white with a narrow dark blue stripe – and a navy wool skirt and had thrown a navy cardigan over her shoulders, because she found she was shivering in the car. But whether from cold or nerves she wasn't sure.

Ben glanced at her. 'Are you cold? I can turn the heating on.'

'No, I'm not cold.' She rubbed her arms nervously.

'I don't know what you've got to be nervous about,' he said, a little puzzled. 'Alice is the one who should be nervous. You know how you feel about her but she's got no idea what to expect from you. When I rang the vicar yesterday I didn't give anything away, I simply asked him to let her know we'd be coming.' He glanced at her again. 'It must be quite something to bare your life story to someone who's a virtual stranger, especially a story as traumatic as hers. She's probably in pieces wondering what you've made of it.'

She nodded, fingering the cameo brooch at her neck. 'Yes, you're quite right, Ben.' She gave him an apologetic little smile. 'I know I'm only being stupid. But it's quite a big thing for me, too.'

He nodded and uncharacteristically crashed the gears. 'Damn,' he said. Then, 'Yes, of course, I realize it's a big thing for you, too, Lucy.'

They reached Crawfordness and pulled up outside Alice's bungalow.

'That one, opposite, must have been where Alice's friend, Lily Muir, lived,' Lucy said, pointing. 'I'm glad they had a few happy years here before Lily died.' She sat looking at the bungalow until Ben gave her a little nudge.

'It's no good just sitting there. You can't put off going in to see Alice much longer. I'm sure she saw the car draw up,' he said. 'She's probably standing behind the curtain right now, wringing her hands and wondering what on earth you're going to say to her.'

'Come on. Let's go, then.' Quickly, before she had time to change her mind, Lucy got out of the car and without waiting for him, hurried up the path and rang the doorbell.

Alice opened the door; she had a guarded, uncertain look on her face despite her welcoming smile. She held out her hand but Lucy ignored it and put her arms round her.

'Oh, thank you, Granny,' she said. 'Thank you for sharing your life story with me, well, with

Ben and me, because he read it, too.' She stood back a little and asked anxiously, 'You don't mind, do you? That Ben read it, I mean?'

Alice shook her head, her eyes shining with unshed tears. 'No, of course I don't mind. I've a lot to be grateful to Ben for. If it hadn't been for his detective work in seeking me out, well...' She looked past Lucy to him. 'If it hadn't been for you, Ben, I guess I would never have got it all down on paper.'

They went into Alice's comfortable lounge. Today the electric fire had been removed and a coal fire was blazing in the hearth. In the corner a tailor's dummy was draped with a white sheet. Alice came in behind them with tea things on a tray.

'You'll have to excuse Agatha,' she said, nodding towards the dummy. 'The wedding dress I'm making for the vicar's daughter is nearly finished so it's easier to keep it there. My little sewing room isn't really big enough to accommodate me, the sewing machine and the dress so Agatha has to live out here.'

'You're still involved with dressmaking, then, Alice,' Ben said, sitting down beside Lucy on the settee.

'Oh, yes. Of course, I don't do as much as I used to, I don't need to.' She nodded towards the tailor's dummy. 'That's a labour of love. The vicar and his wife have been so good to me over these past years, particularly since Lily died, that I offered to make Rebecca's wedding dress for her as a little thank you. I'm really enjoying doing it, too.'

'Can I see it, Granny?' Lucy asked.

'Yes, of course. I've modelled it roughly on the one Princess Margaret wore but I've modified it a bit because Rebecca wanted a sweetheart neckline.' Alice went over to the corner and carefully removed the sheet that was draped over Agatha. The dress was in white slipper satin, the neckline bordered in a double row of tiny seed pearls, and the fitted bodice had more seed pearls at the waistline. The skirt flared out at the back into a sweeping train. 'I've still got the sleeves to set and the skirt is only pinned on at the moment,' Alice explained.

'It's quite beautiful,' Lucy breathed. She smiled at Alice. 'You're very clever, Granny.'

Alice shrugged. 'I've had plenty of practice, over the years. My Aunt Maud taught me well, although I didn't realize it at the time.' She turned to Lucy. 'Of course, you wouldn't remember, but I used to make all your clothes when you were tiny,' she said. 'In fact, right up until the time I ... the time I left.'

Lucy smiled. 'I realize now, it was you who used to cuddle me, wasn't it?'

Alice nodded, her eyes shining. 'That's right.'

'You see,' Lucy went on, the words tumbling over each other as she explained, 'I've always had this wonderful memory of somebody taking me on their lap and singing to me, but I knew it couldn't have been Mummy because she wasn't at all the cuddling type. And I knew it was no use asking her about it, she'd no time for what she called fanciful imaginings. But if I was unhappy – and I was often unhappy when I was young – I used to curl up on my bed and conjure up this wonderful warm feeling of someone's arms round me, loving me.' She looked up at Alice, her eyes brimming with tears. 'I know now, it wasn't just wishful thinking on my part, it was real; it was you who used to hold me, Granny.'

Alice nodded, smiling at the memory although her eyes were brimming, too. 'Yes, I used to teach you all the nursery rhymes and I read you bedtime stories every night.' She made a deprecating gesture. 'Well, I had plenty of time, you see, whereas Margaret was always busy...'

'You don't need to make excuses for her, Granny. I know exactly what my mother was like,' Lucy said with a trace of bitterness.

'Quite like her own mother, from what I read,' Ben remarked, joining in the conversation for the first time.

Alice nodded. 'Yes, Margaret was very like her mother. Lizzie liked her own way all the time and was headstrong enough to get it.' She became serious. 'But it was Lizzie's determination that helped us through when we left the Hall, there's no doubt about that. We were both in the same boat so we were able to help each other.' She shook her head. 'I know I could never have managed without her.'

'And I'm sure she couldn't have managed

without you, Granny,' Lucy said warmly. 'And neither could Margaret, my mother. Did she ever stop to think, I wonder, what would have happened to her if you hadn't kept her and brought her up as your own daughter? She could have ended up in one of those awful orphanages, like the one in *Jane Eyre*.'

Alice's eyes misted over. '*Jane Eyre*. That used to be my favourite book. I wonder what happened to it. I suppose Margaret threw it away. It was a bit dog-eared.'

'No, she didn't. I've got it. It's in my bookcase. That's how we knew we'd got the right Alice. It's got "Alice Clayton" on the flyleaf,' Lucy said eagerly.

'That's good. I'm glad you've got it.' She put her hand up and touched the cameo brooch on Lucy's blouse. 'I'm glad Margaret gave you the cameo, too.'

'Yes, so am I, although I didn't realize its significance until I read what you'd written about it,' Lucy said, shaking her head. 'But I'd always liked it and she just said to me one day, "Well, you might as well have it. I don't want it." I thought she didn't like it much; it wasn't the kind of thing she ever wore.'

Alice shook her head. 'It was the one piece of Lizzie's jewellery that I wouldn't sell, however hard up we were, because Lizzie told me it had belonged to *her* grandmother. Naturally, I handed it on to Margaret. I'm surprised she didn't tell you it was something of a family heirloom when she gave it to you.'

Lucy fingered the cameo at her throat. 'Knowing Mummy she probably didn't think it was that important, Granny.'

Alice watching her, sighed. 'Oh, I wish I was, Lucy,' she said sadly. 'I only wish I was.'

Lucy glanced at her, frowning. 'What do you mean? Wish you were what?'

'I wish I was your granny.'

'Of course you're my granny, silly. Now I've found you, you'll always be my granny,' Lucy said happily, helping herself to another scone.

'That's a lovely thing to say, but don't forget you have another grandmother, or rather a great-grandmother, who has a more rightful claim to the title, Lucy,' Alice said seriously.

Lucy looked at her and then at Ben. 'What are you talking about?'

'Surely, you must have realized that Lady Bucknell is your great-grandmother, Lucy,' Ben said. 'It's quite possible that one day Rookhurst Hall could be yours.'

Thirty-One

Lucy bit her lip, frowning. 'Lady Bucknell is my great-grandmother. Yes, I suppose that must be right,' she said reluctantly, after a long pause. 'I hadn't really thought that far back, to tell you the truth. But, of course, Lady Bucknell's daughter, Lizzie, was Margaret's mother, wasn't she?' She laid a hand on Alice's arm. 'What a pity Margaret wasn't your real daughter, Granny.'

Alice smiled and shook her head. 'That wouldn't have made any difference to your possible inheritance, would it? If I had been your real grandmother, then it follows that Giles would have been your grandfather. Either way it leads back to Lady Bucknell.' Her eyes misted. 'If my little Alfie had lived he would have been just as entitled to Rookhurst Hall as you are now, my dear.'

Lucy waved her hand impatiently. 'Oh, it's all nonsense. You're both forgetting Peregrine. He still lives in one wing of the Hall and looks after the estate. You told me that yourself, Ben.'

'Yes, that's right,' Ben said, nodding. 'I did.'

'Well then.' She spread her hands eloquently.

'Has he got no family?' Alice asked.

'No, he's got no children,' Ben said. 'So if Lucy can prove she's entitled to inherit...'

Lucy burst out laughing. 'Oh, dear. I should have to practise the "gracious lady" bit.' She put on a credible imitation of Lady Bucknell's imperious tone. 'Mr Manton, I want you to look at my grandfather clock. It struck thirteen at ten o'clock last night.'

Now it was Alice's turn to laugh. 'Oh, Lucy. That's just the tone I remember her using. But she was very kind, really. I remember that I got on very well with her.'

'Would you like to go and see her, Alice?' Ben asked suddenly.

Alice thought for a minute, then she said, 'I'd certainly like to go and see if the Hall has changed much. But I don't see how I could simply turn up to see M'Lady. It wouldn't be right. Not after all this time.'

He leaned forward and put his elbows on his knees. 'I could take you, Alice. Right now. Lady Bucknell has asked me to call on her. She's got something she wants me to buy – if she hasn't changed her mind, that is.' He nodded towards Lucy. 'She knows Lucy is my assistant so all we have to say is that we were taking Lucy's grandmother out for an afternoon drive and as we were passing...' He spread his hands.

Alice still looked doubtful.

'Bessie is still there. I remember you wrote about Bessie,' Lucy said, by way of encourage-

327

ment. She could see that Ben was clearly anxious to get the whole business of her and her grandmother over and finished with as soon as possible.

'Oh, I'd very much like to see Bessie again,' Alice said, weakening.

Ben got to his feet. 'Let's go, then.'

Alice fussed a little and insisted on changing her flowered dress, which Lucy had thought looked very nice, for a perfectly tailored green dress and jacket, which she had made herself and looked even nicer.

'Ah, just a moment,' she said, as they were about to get into the car. 'I'd like to take a few flowers from my garden with me.'

'I'm sure Lady Bucknell has plenty of flowers, Granny,' Lucy said with a glance at Ben in case he was getting impatient.

'Oh, they're not for Lady Bucknell,' Alice said enigmatically.

Five minutes later she climbed into the car carrying a small bouquet of late summer rosebuds.

'Who are they for, if not for Lady Bucknell?' Lucy asked.

'You'll see,' Alice said with a smile.

They drove along several miles of country roads before they arrived at the village of Rookhurst.

'If you don't tell them, nobody would ever suspect you had once been a servant at the Hall, Granny,' Lucy remarked as they drove through the village. 'You look much too prosperous and elegant.'

'Nice of you to say so, dear, but I can assure you I'm not that prosperous and I don't feel at all elegant inside. I'm not sure—' She broke off and pointed excitedly. 'Oh, look, that's the cottage where I used to live with Aunt Maud. It looks dreadfully run down, doesn't it.' She shook her head sadly. 'I don't suppose it's been lived in for years.'

'It doesn't look like it,' Lucy said.

'Would you like to stop?' Ben asked, putting on the brake.

'No. I couldn't bear to look in at the windows and see it all empty and neglected,' Alice said sadly. 'Aunt Maud's home was always cosy and welcoming and that's the way I want to remember it.'

Lucy put her hand over Alice's. 'I think you're very wise.'

They drove on through the village, Alice craning her neck and remarking on the changes, marvelling at the new housing estates that had sprung up and were still being built.

'Goodness, Rookhurst Hall used to be right outside the village, now there are houses nearly up as far as the Lodge,' she said as they turned into the drive. 'Oh, yes. I remember all this. I remember walking up this drive with Aunt Maud, it was such a long way for my little legs.' She leaned forward and looked round. 'My word, it wasn't overgrown then like it is now. But in those days there was an army of gardeners to look after it.' She leaned back, smiling to herself. 'I remember the day she brought me to start work here, how I clung to her hand because I was so nervous.' She sighed. 'Of course, I didn't know then how ill she was.' She sighed again. 'It was all such a long time ago. Sometimes I wonder where all the years have gone.'

Ben parked the car and helped her out.

'Your flowers, Granny,' Lucy reminded her.

'No, leave them there, I'll collect them later.' She turned anxiously to Ben. 'Shouldn't we be going to the tradesmen's entrance?' she whispered, as he led the way up the steps to the front door.

He waited and took her arm. 'Indeed, no. You're Lucy's grandmother and you're with me and I always use the front door,' he said, ringing the bell, his tone brooking no argument.

Bessie answered the door and Ben explained how he came to be dropping in on Lady Bucknell at four o'clock on a Sunday afternoon. Lucy stayed with a rather nervous Alice in the background while he was speaking.

Bessie gave them both no more than a cursory glance. 'I'm sure M'Lady won't mind. She don't get that many visitors,' she said with a shrug. 'I'll go and tell her you're here.'

'It's no use, I can't pretend. If she doesn't recognize me I shall have to tell her who I am,' Alice said nervously when Bessie had gone, leaving them standing in the huge open space of the hall. She nodded towards the staircase. 'I'd like a pound for every time I've dusted down those stairs,' she remarked. 'But the carpet wasn't as worn in my day and those banisters were all highly polished. I used up a lot of elbow grease in this house,' she added drily.

Bessie came back. 'M'Lady says she'll be pleased to receive all of you,' she said.

Alice stepped forward and held out her hands. 'Bessie. Don't you remember me? I'm Alice. Alice Clayton.'

'Alice? Alice Clayton?' Bessie repeated as she stared at her. Then her face broke into smiles and she took the hands Alice offered and pumped them up and down. 'Oh, *Alice*! Yes, of course I remember you.' She stood back. 'My word, you look as if you've come up in the world. But there, you always was a bit of a lady, wasn't you? And you went off very sudden, too, as I remember.' She gave Alice's hands another little shake and dropped them. 'But you'd better go in to M'Lady. Mustn't keep her waiting.' She lowered her voice. 'P'raps we'll be able to talk later.'

'Yes, I'm sure we shall,' Alice said warmly.

Bessie nodded towards the big drawing room. 'She's in there. I reckon you can remember the way, can't you?'

'Yes, I reckon I can,' Alice said with a smile.

She led the way to the drawing room, then stood aside for Ben and Lucy to go in.

Lady Bucknell was sitting in her usual place by the long French doors, which today were closed against any autumn chill. Through the windows the last of the dahlias could be seen,

331

still colourful though looking a little tired and windswept. The trees too were beginning to dapple with yellow as the leaves turned. It was obvious that the gardens lacked the attention of a gardener, because the lawns badly needed trimming under the leaves that had fallen and there were weeds in the borders.

Today, Lady Bucknell was dressed in a dark blue dress, rather outdated, with long sleeves and a high neck. She had a lavender-coloured cashmere shawl round her shoulders. Once again, Lucy was conscious of a great deal of gold: a thick gold chain attached to her spectacles, a double strand round her neck, a gold wristwatch on one wrist and a gold bangle hanging loosely on the other. Her gnarled fingers were again heavy with rings.

'You remember Lucy, my assistant, Lady Bucknell?' Ben said, by way of introduction. 'And this is her grandmother.'

'How do you do?' Lady Bucknell bowed her head graciously. 'You will forgive me if I don't get up to greet you but I suffer quite badly from arthritis, which makes movement rather difficult. Please sit down, all of you.'

Lucy and Alice sat quietly together on the settee Lady Bucknell indicated. It was a little distance from the chair where Ben was told to sit in order to discuss antiques with the old lady. Alice glanced covertly round the room while they were talking.

'Nothing's changed,' she whispered to Lucy. 'Not a single thing. Everything just looks a bit more shabby and some things could do with a good polish.' She gave Lucy an impish grin. 'Makes my fingers itch to get at it.'

'Well, you can't. Remember you're a guest here,' Lucy whispered back.

Alice shook her head, suddenly serious. 'It's not right. I don't feel comfortable sitting here like this,' she said.

'There, that's our business finished.' Lady Bucknell turned to them with a gracious smile. 'Thank you both for being so patient. Now, we'll all have tea. Mr Manton, perhaps you would be good enough to ring the bell for Bessie to bring it in.'

This was too much for Alice. She got to her feet. 'Just a moment. Before you do that, Ben, I think I should introduce myself properly to M'Lady.'

Lady Bucknell looked up at her, quite put out at what she perceived as a breach of etiquette. 'That really won't be necessary, Mrs Whatever-your-name-is, since it's hardly likely that we shall meet again. Mr Manton has already told me that you are his assistant's grandmother and that's quite enough for me, even if it is a little irregular. One doesn't normally bring a troop of relatives on a business visit.'

Ben blushed at that and opened his mouth to reply but Alice forestalled him.

'I don't think you quite understand the situation, M'Lady,' she said. 'It's quite obvious that you don't recognize me, although I must say you haven't changed much over the years.

You see, I'm Alice Clayton. I worked here for over six years. I was here all through the Great War and the dreadful 'flu epidemic that came after it. I started here as kitchen maid but I was housemaid by the time I left. Don't you remember me? My aunt Maud used to make dresses for your daughters.'

'I have no daughters. They're all dead,' Lady Bucknell said flatly. She sat up straight in her chair and felt for the spectacles hanging round her neck. She put them on and leaned forward. 'But you say you're Alice, who used to be housemaid here? Come closer, so I can see you better.'

Alice smoothed her skirt and took a step nearer to the old lady, who looked her up and down somewhat disdainfully.

'Ah, yes, I can see you are now. You look much the same. You always did think you were a cut above the usual run of servant.' She sniffed and turned her gaze on Lucy. 'And this is your granddaughter.' She stared at her, still seated on the settee. 'Were you aware that your grandmother was once a servant here?' she asked.

'Not until recently,' Lucy answered. She had detected a sudden but definite cooling in the atmosphere at Alice's revelation and she was beginning to doubt her grandmother's wisdom in confessing her identity. 'Not that it's important.'

'Of course it's important,' Lady Bucknell snapped. 'It's always important to know one's roots. It's what makes up one's identity and establishes one's place in society.'

'Well, put it like this, then. It's not important to me,' Lucy repeated with a hint of defiance.

'Shall I ring for tea now, Lady Bucknell?' Ben said, to defuse what he could see becoming a potentially tricky situation. He was still standing with his hand on the bell pull.

Lady Bucknell hesitated almost imperceptibly. Then she said, 'No, that won't be necessary, Mr Manton, thank you. Come and sit down. Alice can go and ask Bessie to bring it in. I'm sure she won't have forgotten the way to the kitchen. No doubt she and Bessie will have much to talk about.' Lucy was almost certain there had been a slight emphasis on the word 'kitchen'.

'Certainly, M'Lady,' Alice said cheerfully. 'I'll tell Bessie it will be tea for three.'

'Tea for two,' Lucy said, her fury barely concealed. 'I'll take my tea with Granny. In the *kitchen*.'

Thirty-Two

Lucy followed Alice, seething with rage.

'How dare that old woman treat you like that, Granny,' she hissed as they walked.

Alice paused so that she was walking beside her. 'Think nothing of it, dear. That's how the gentry treated their servants fifty years ago.' She gave a little laugh. 'Haven't you heard the old rhyme, "God bless the squire and his relations, and keep us in our proper stations"? M'Lady simply doesn't realize how times have changed. I don't hold it against her and neither must you, dear.' She caught Lucy's arm and squeezed it. 'Anyway, it will be much more comfortable chatting to Bessie in the kitchen than drinking Earl Grey tea in the drawing room.' She made a face as she pushed open the baize door to the kitchen corridor. 'Ugh. I don't like Earl Grey tea.'

'No, neither do I,' Lucy agreed. She stopped suddenly. 'Look at that!' she said in disgust. 'Thick carpet on one side of that door and brown lino on the other.'

'Well, what do you expect? You're in the servants' quarters now, dear.' Alice appeared quite amused at Lucy's appalled reaction.

They reached the kitchen, where a delicious smell of baking filled the air. Bessie looked up from laying a tray with delicate tea things and pushed her heavy black-rimmed spectacles back up to the bridge of her nose.

'Only lay up for two, Bessie,' Alice said with a grin.

'Whoops, been turned out, have you?' Bessie grinned back at her, wiping her hands down her pink nylon overall.

'Yes. I was out on my ear as soon as I told her who I was.'

'That was daft. You shouldn't have told her, then you could have had gentrified tea and shortbread for once.'

'I'd rather have kitchen tea with you, Bessie, and catch up on all the gossip.' She turned to Lucy. 'This is Lucy.'

'Your granddaughter?'

'Yes, that's right,' Lucy answered.

Bessie stared at her for a minute. 'Pardon me for staring, dearie, but you remind me of somebody, can't think who.' She turned to Alice. 'She's a lovely girl. A real credit to you, Alice.' She picked up the tray. 'Just hang on a minute while I take this through to them in there.' She jerked her head in the direction of the drawing room.

'I'll put the kettle on for ours while you're gone,' Alice said.

Lucy reached down cups and saucers from the dresser. 'I wouldn't have believed this class thing still existed if I hadn't just seen it with my

337

own eyes,' she remarked, still smarting with the injustice of it.

'Oh, I'm sure it's dying out. There used to be an army of servants and gardeners here, now it looks as if Bessie has to manage very much on her own.'

'A couple of women come in from the village to do the cleaning and the laundry's sent out,' Bessie said, coming back through the door. 'I just do the cooking and look after M'Lady.' She jerked her head in the direction of the west wing as she sat down to the tea Alice had poured. 'Mr Perry and Mrs Rosemary have their own housekeeper. They live quite separate from M'Lady.'

'Mr Perry must be getting on a bit now,' Alice said. 'Nearly ready to retire?'

'Oh, no, he's not sixty yet. And he'll never retire, he can't afford to.' Bessie stirred her tea, added another spoonful of sugar and stirred it again. 'Not with the way his wife tips his money down her neck.'

'What do you mean by that, Bessie?' Alice asked with a frown.

Bessie leaned across, so that her ample bosom rested on the table. 'She drinks like a fish,' she said in hushed tones. She gave a shrug. 'Well, I 'spect she's bored, bein' there on her own all the time, because he's always out on business or playing golf.' She shook her head. 'To tell you the truth, it wasn't exactly a marriage made in heaven in the first place. I think it was his mother's fault. M'Lady insisted he got married in order to provide an heir to the Hall although anyone could see he was never the marrying kind.' She looked up. 'Oh, don't misunderstand me, there was nothing ... well, you know.' She gave a sage nod.

Alice nodded back. 'I know, Bessie. You mean he was a typical bachelor.'

'That's it exactly.'

'And did he?' Lucy asked. 'Did he provide an heir?' She helped herself to an iced fairy cake.

'Did he heck! They've neither chick nor child in nearly thirty years of marriage. Of course, it's too late now.' She put her head on one side. 'Perhaps that's what her trouble is, disappointment that she couldn't have children.' She shrugged. 'I dunno. Anyway, they keep to their part of the house and we keep to ours so I don't know much about what goes on there.'

'If they haven't got children what will happen to all this when they've gone?' Lucy asked. She couldn't help thinking that for someone who didn't know what went on, Bessie seemed to be a mine of information.

Bessie shrugged. 'A lot of the land's already been sold. He's had to sell it to keep the house in good repair. Even now the roof in the east wing leaks like a tap. There's a housing estate already going up on part of what used to be farmland, out towards Atterwood way.' She shook her head. 'Mind you, it's like eating your own tail, if you ask me. As he sells the land he gets money to spend and when that's gone there's less to farm so less money coming in to keep things going, so he has to sell more land. Soon there won't be any left to sell.'

'Then what will happen?' Alice asked.

'He's talking of handing the hall over to the National Trust when M'Lady dies.' Bessie leaned back and bit into a third iced fairy cake. 'Mind you, it's only talk, so I don't suppose anything'll ever come of it. But with nobody to leave it to he could do worse, couldn't he? After all, it's a lovely old place and they'd look after it and probably let him stay on in the west wing. Well, it'd be a pity to pull it down, wouldn't it?'

'Yes,' Alice agreed, staring hard at Lucy. 'It would certainly be a pity if it was demolished.'

Bessie didn't notice. She was leaning forward again, this time with her elbows on the table. 'But what about you, Alice? You left a bit sudden, didn't you, all them years ago? And Miss Lizzie, too.' She jerked her thumb in the direction of the drawing room. 'M'Lady's got herself a bit muddled over the years. She thinks Lizzie died in the 'flu epidemic like the twins but I know different.' She paused and frowned. 'It might have been after you'd gone, so you wouldn't remember, but what really happened was that Miss Lizzie took off early one morning in the Bentley – nobody heard it go – and that was the last we ever saw of her. Goodness knows where she went or what happened to her. Disappeared into thin air, she did.'

'Well, I never,' Alice said, acting suitably impressed.

'They traced the Bentley to a little back-street

garage in Ipswich. She must have sold it to get money.' Bessie leaned back in her chair. 'I reckon she went abroad to live because she was upset over that chauffeur chappie who died; I always reckoned she was a bit sweet on him. But of course, I don't know.' She drained her tea. 'Now it's your turn, Alice. What have you been doing all these years?' She winked. 'My guess is that you ran off 'cause you was in the fam'ly way. I know that young gardener was sweet on you and he left about the same time. Marry him, did you?'

'No, I—' One of the bells high up on the wall tinkled.

'Oh, blow. That means they've finished their tea,' Bessie said, heaving herself to her feet. 'M'Lady wants the tray removed. I'd better go and fetch it.'

Alice and Lucy got up from the table. 'Yes, it's obviously time for us to go,' Lucy said. 'Ben will be waiting.'

'Well, it's ever so nice to have seen you again and chatted over old times,' Bessie said, heading for the door. 'You'll have to come back and see us again, sometime.'

'Oh, no doubt we will,' Alice told her, shooting a glance at Lucy. 'Saved by the bell,' she murmured as Bessie left. 'She'd have a field day with the truth, wouldn't she?'

They left without seeing Lady Bucknell again, for which Lucy was profoundly grateful. When they reached the car Ben was already waiting. Alice reached in and took out the

341

bunch of rosebuds. 'There's something I'd like to do before we leave, if you don't mind waiting, Ben. I promise it won't take long.'

'May we come too, Granny?' Lucy said, guessing where she was going.

Alice smiled. 'Oh, yes, of course. I'd like you both to come with me.'

She led the way past the front of the house and along by the east wing, through the kitchen garden, where rows of cabbages, leeks and parsnips fought for existence among the weeds, and out on to the meadow beyond. Here, the ground was soft and springy and sloped gently up towards a small wood. Not far from the top of the slope, hidden from the house by a stand of specially planted trees, there was an area, about forty feet square, fenced off by iron railings. Inside were rows of crosses, most of them made of oak, but three, a little larger and set to one side, in stone. They all had names carved on them, two or three in some cases, where a grave was marked containing more than one member of a family.

'So this is where the 'flu victims were all buried,' Lucy breathed.

'Yes, it was all done very properly and reverently,' Alice said. She tried the iron gate and it opened to her touch. Inside, she went straight to one of the stone crosses and laid her flowers on it. Then she stood for a moment, looking down at it, quite still.

Lucy and Ben, standing a little distance away, could see the inscription: GILES ALFRED

342

BUCKNELL, ELDEST SON OF SIR GEORGE AND LADY ADELAIDE BUCKNELL. 1895–1918.

'I guessed this was where she was coming. Look, he was only twenty-three when he died,' Lucy whispered to Ben.

He nodded, pointing to another memorial. 'They've made a memorial to the twins, even though they couldn't have been buried here,' he said. 'And there's the one to Sir George.'

She turned away. 'It's all so sad.' At that moment, more than anything she would have liked to put her head on Ben's shoulder and feel his comforting arms round her, but the warm relationship they had once shared had gone, to be replaced by nothing more than a cool friendship. She moved away from him, lest the temptation should prove too great.

Alice came back to them, her eyes moist although she was smiling. 'Thank you,' she said simply as they went back to the car.

'Well, Lucy, now you've been back and seen your inheritance,' she said, when she had finished blowing her nose and composing herself. 'Since Peregrine has no children you'll only have to say the word and it will come to you, eventually.'

'She'll have to prove she has a rightful claim to it, of course,' Ben said. 'But that shouldn't be difficult.'

'I'm sure we can get Margaret to send us her birth certificate. And you've got yours, haven't you, Lucy?'

'Yes, of course I have,' Lucy said briefly.

'And, of course, you've got the cameo. M'Lady would recognize that, I'm sure. It's something of a family heirloom.' She glanced at Lucy. 'Where is it? You had it on earlier. You haven't lost it, have you?'

'No, it came off. It's in my pocket,' Lucy said.

'Pity we didn't think to show it to M'Lady,' Alice said thoughtfully.

'Why, do you think we might not have been relegated to the kitchen for tea if she'd seen it?' Lucy asked, her voice edging towards sarcasm.

'No, but...'

'Well, I would have thought that, with the birth certificates and the definite family likeness, would be more than enough to convince the authorities,' Ben said, swerving to avoid a dead rabbit. He glanced swiftly at Lucy through the rear view mirror. 'I'm not sure you'll inherit the title with the stately pile, though. I'm not sure you'll be able to call yourself Lady Armitage.'

'Oh, what a pity. I was really looking forward to that.'

For the rest of the journey she stared out of the window and said nothing.

They arrived back at Crawfordness. As they got out of the car Alice said, 'I think we've drunk enough tea for one day, don't you? In any case, perhaps something a little stronger might be appropriate to celebrate Lucy's potential inheritance. I think I can find some sherry, or even some whisky, if that's more to your taste, Ben.'

'You can leave me out. I'm going for a walk on the dunes.' Lucy slammed the car door and stalked off towards the sea.

'What's got into her?' Ben asked, looking at Alice and then at the figure striding over the beach.

Alice watched for a moment. 'Perhaps you'd better go and find out, Ben,' she said thoughtfully. 'I'll go in and pour the drinks.'

'You may be a bit premature,' Ben called over his shoulder. 'She doesn't look in much of a mood to celebrate.'

Thirty-Three

Lucy had gone some way before he caught up with her, catching her by the arm and swinging her round to look at him. 'Lucy,' he began sternly. 'What on earth's got—?' His voice dropped and he said more gently, 'Hey, hey, what's the matter? What are you crying for?'

She tried to wrench her arm away but he wouldn't let go. 'Leave me alone. And don't start telling me what to do. I'm fed up with everybody thinking they know better than I do myself what I ought to be doing. Fed up with people assuming I'm desperate to turn up and lay claim to an inheritance that I might or might not be entitled to and that might not be worth a bean anyway.'

'I guess events are moving a bit too fast for you, Lucy,' he said quietly. 'What you need is a nice cup of tea.' He began to propel her back up the beach. 'Come on, let's go back to Alice.' He put his arm round her and handed her a large white handkerchief. 'Here, dry your eyes.'

But his action had the reverse effect and she began to cry even harder. He put both arms round her and held her close until at last her sobs subsided a little.

'Goodness me, you're making pretty heavy weather of it, for someone in the running to inherit a sizeable estate,' he said, in an attempt at humour.

'I'm sorry,' she said with a sniff, trying to pull herself together. 'I know I'm just being stupid, but it's all so...'

'I understand. It must be quite overwhelming, trying to come to terms with it all. Never mind, we're here now.' He pushed open the door. 'I think a cup of tea rather than anything stronger, Alice,' he said as Alice came forward and saw Lucy's tear-stained face.

'Oh, dear, whatever's gone wrong?' Alice said, full of concern. 'Have you two...?'

Ben shook his head warningly. 'No. Nothing like that, Alice. Lucy will tell us what's troubling her when she's ready.'

They waited with as much patience as they could muster until Lucy had drunk two cups of tea and washed her face.

'Now,' Alice said. 'Are you ready to tell us what's upsetting you so?'

Lucy nodded, licking her lips. 'Yes. I'm sorry for that outburst.' She turned to Ben and gave him a still slightly watery smile. 'And I'm sorry for weeping all over you, Ben.'

'A shoulder to cry on is all part of the service, M'Lady,' he answered with a grin.

She shook her head. 'Don't call me that,' she said irritably. She licked her lips again. 'Now, ever since I read your story, Granny, I've been thinking about the fact that when Peregrine dies it's possible that I could be the only legitimate heir to Rookhurst Hall.'

'That's right, dear. And I'm quite sure it won't be difficult to prove your claim in a court of law,' Alice said, nodding.

'Well, I've thought about this a lot and I daresay you'll call me all sorts of an idiot but I really don't want it. I don't want anything to do with it.'

'Isn't that rather rash, Lucy? You realize you could be throwing away a great deal of money,' Ben pointed out. 'At the very least, if the house was pulled down and the land sold for building it would be worth, oh, I dunno—'

'But you wouldn't pull the house down, would you, dear?' Alice cut in. 'After all—'

'You're not *listening*, either of you,' Lucy said crossly. 'I've told you, I want no part of it. I'd almost made up my mind before we went there today, but when I saw the way Granny

347

was treated by Lady Bucknell I was so disgusted that I knew I didn't want anything to do with the place. I could never treat people the way she treated Granny and I wouldn't want to live with people who acted in that way. I don't know what Peregrine is like but his wife doesn't have much of a life if she's an alcoholic, poor woman. I know I could never be happy living in that mausoleum. It didn't *feel* right. No, I think Peregrine's idea of leaving the place to the National Trust is much the best. That way lots of people would be able to come and enjoy the house and grounds.'

'But what about you, Lucy?' Alice asked. 'Don't you realize you're throwing away the chance of being a potentially rich woman?'

She nodded. 'Oh, yes, I know all that. But what's the use of being rich if you're not happy? And I know I wouldn't be happy living in that great pile. Especially with Lady B.' She smiled for the first time. 'In fact, I could get a perverse satisfaction in going to visit her as Ben's assistant, knowing that all of it could have been mine if I'd chosen to claim it.'

'You mean to tell me you're happy to turn your back on all that in order to stay as you are?' Ben said. He looked quite bemused.

'There must be some ulterior motive,' Alice said under her breath.

'Pardon?' they both said together.

'Nothing. I think I'll go and make more tea.' Alice got up and left the room.

'Are you quite sure you're making the right

decision, Lucy?' Ben said, when she had gone. 'After all...'

Lucy shook her head wearily. 'I've thought about it until my head hurts, Ben. It's kept me awake at night, worrying about it, and I know I don't want anything to do with that kind of life. Apart from anything else I wouldn't want the responsibility of it all. Anyway, I don't want to leave y— Laxhall St Mary's. I'm happy where I am. At least ... what I mean is ... Oh, dear.' She sniffed and dabbed her eyes again with his handkerchief.

He took her hand. 'Are you trying to tell me you'd prefer to remain in a grotty little antique business, not earning all that much, for the rest of your life?' he asked gently.

'Oh, I wouldn't call it a grotty little antique business. But does that mean you're offering me a rise?' she said, with an attempt at a grin.

'No, not really. I had in mind something more in the nature of a partnership.'

She frowned. 'But I don't know enough about antiques for that. And anyway, what about your father?'

'I didn't mean that kind of partnership.' He hesitated, separating the fingers of her hand, linking them with his own, then releasing them and doing the whole process over again. Then he looked up and said quietly, 'Lucy, will you marry me?'

'Marry you? But, Ben, I didn't think you liked me much,' she said, bewildered.

He stared at her, astonished. 'What on earth

gave you that idea?'

'Well, you've been very cool and offhand with me...' She frowned. 'I don't know, ever since we read Alice's story, I suppose.'

He sighed. 'You're absolutely right, of course. The truth was, I got cold feet and backed off as soon as I realized you were in the running to inherit Rookhurst Hall. The antique business is doing very nicely, but it couldn't begin to compare with a stately home – even a third class one – and the last thing I wanted was to be accused of fortune hunting. So I thought the best thing was to see this business with your grandmother through as quickly as I could, to help you claim your share of the inheritance and then quietly fade into the background. I told myself I'd get over you, I needn't ever see you once you were safely ensconced in your family seat ... Easier said than done, since I'd fallen for you in such a big way, but that's what I told myself.'

He stopped speaking as she put her hand over his mouth. 'Yes,' she said, her eyes shining.

'Yes what?' he mumbled behind her hand.

'Yes, oh, yes, I'll marry you, Ben. Please, as soon as you like.' She took her hand away from his mouth. 'And I don't want to hear another word about—' It was she who never finished what she was going to say this time because his mouth stopped her from speaking.

Later, with her head on his shoulder, she said, 'And all the time I thought you'd guessed how I felt about you and decided the best way to deal with a silly little secretary who'd been stupid enough to fall for the boss was to be cool and distant.'

'It wasn't easy, I might tell you,' he said.

'What wasn't?'

'Being cool and distant when all I wanted to do was to take you in my arms and kiss you. Like this.'

'We should go and tell Granny she'll have another wedding dress to make,' she murmured against his cheek.

Hand in hand they went to find Alice.